The Doctor and the Midwife

OTHER BOOKS

BY SARAH ALVA

Everything She Wants

A NOVEL

The Doctor and the Midwife

Sarah Alva

Covenant Communications, Inc.

Cover image: *Heart Stethoscope* © Michael Burrell, istockphoto.com

Cover design by Christina Marcano © 2020 by Covenant Communications, Inc.

Published by Covenant Communications, Inc.
American Fork, Utah

Printed in the United States of America
First Printing: September 2020

10 9 8 7 6 5 4 3 2

ISBN 978-1-52441-299-9

+

Praise for Sarah Alva

"An enemies-to-lovers trope with notes of *You've Got Mail*—what's not to like? Well, the hero (and a bit of the heroine) in the beginning, but he's got an arc, so stick with him and you'll be rooting for him in the end. I've had two children, so all the birth terminology and scenarios were familiar and a bit nostalgic. The differences in viewpoint surrounding birth made for a great butting of heads for the two main characters. I liked it!"
—Sarah Monzon, author of *Molly: A Sweet Romantic Comedy* (Sewing in SoCal, #1)

"Sarah Alva is contemporary romance's rising star. Don't miss this delightful journey of self-discovery that will tug at your heartstrings and keep you turning pages well into the night. *The Doctor and the Midwife* is a heartwarming story with fun, fresh characters you'll laugh and cry with. Did I stay up until midnight to finish it? Why, yes. Yes, I did."
—Traci Hunter Abramson, Seven-time Whitney Award winner, author of *Change of Fortune*

"Sarah Alva delivers punchy lines and barbed insults, along with all the joy, confusion, and twitters of falling in love. *The Doctor and The Midwife* will give you all the feels."
—Chalon Linton, author of *Flying in Love*

"In the vein of beloved classic romantic comedies like *Pillow Talk* and *You've Got Mail* comes *The Doctor and the Midwife* by Sarah Alva. An absolute delight from beginning to end, the story introduces us to charmingly flawed and perfectly suited Audrey Novak, a certified nurse midwife who specializes in home births, and obstetrician Dr. Ammon Parker. Their opposite approaches to childbirth give them a battlefield to confront their differences, gain new perspectives, and ultimately fall in love. Alva's writing is alive with wonderful characters, clever banter, and an engaging plot that brings laughter and tears. I thoroughly enjoyed this story and know you will too!"

—Michele Ashman Bell, author of *Wish Me Love*

"Sweet, quirky, and cute contemporary romance. For those who loved *You've Got Mail*, this is for you."

—Paige Edwards, author of *Deadly by Design*

"Funny, sweet, and romantic, *The Doctor and the Midwife* is everything I love about reading contemporary romance. Ms. Alva's characters pulled me in from the first page, and their love story held me captive until the very end. This is one book I will be recommending to all my friends!"

—Tiffany Odekirk, author of *Love Sidelined* (Jennings Family series)

To the Andersons and the Alvas
Thank you for welcoming me into the family even when I was
"just the girlfriend" crashing your Thanksgiving dinners.

Acknowledgments

This book would not have been possible without the amazing support of the women in my writing group: Miranda Renaé, Stacy Codner, Emily Inouye Huey, Apryl K. B. Lopez, and Julie Whipple. Thank you for being my moral-support team. An extra special thank-you belongs to Julie for answering all of my questions about the University of Utah Hospital Labor and Delivery unit and for sharing her knowledge of all things rock climbing.

Thank you to my beta readers, Emily Daw and Chris Swords. Your enthusiasm and feedback solidified my belief in this project. Tiffany Odekirk, thank you for your amazing and thorough critique, which brought this book to the next level.

Amy Parker's encouraging words at just the right moment helped me push through a difficult revision. Thank you for being an early fan and cheerleader. Many thanks to my incredible editor, Kami, and all the wonderful people at Covenant for continuing to make my publishing dreams come true.

Thank you to the dozens of women who shared their birth stories and answered my questions about home birth. Any errors in its portrayal are my own.

And, of course, a thank-you to my boys, Jonah and Solomon, who made me a mom, and my husband, Brandon, the best battle buddy during bedtime.

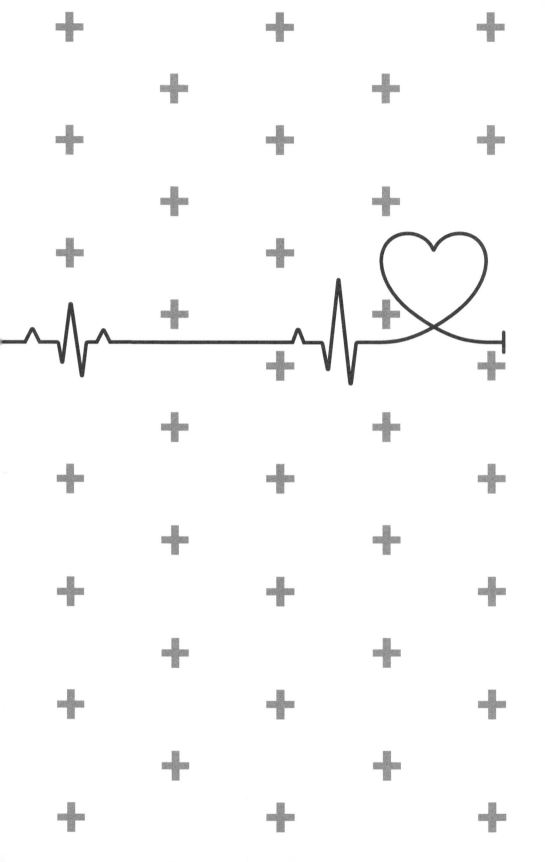

Chapter 1

AUDREY NOVAK STOOD OUTSIDE THE gate to Windy Corner Apartments, her brain feeling like mashed potatoes. She'd been called away yesterday afternoon for a birth, and the adrenaline that had sustained her through the early-morning hours had crashed as she drove home. Now she couldn't remember the code to unlock the gate.

Audrey's thighs were sore from squatting with the birthing mother, her stomach ached because she hadn't eaten a full meal since lunch yesterday, and she desperately needed to wash her hair. The locked gate was the only thing that stood between her and a hot shower and food inside her apartment.

"Rough night?" a voice to her left said. It took her a second, but she turned in the direction of the voice. Her eyes landed on an Adonis. He stood holding his leg in a quad stretch, his other hand gripping the Windy Corner sign for balance. Her gaze fixated for a moment on the short, clean nature of his cuticles. *The fingernails of a surgeon*, her mushy brain thought. He released his leg.

Her eyes then bounced to his face. He smiled at her, his teeth braces-straight and toothpaste white. His strong jaw was covered in cleanly manscaped stubble, the kind that was more than a five-o'clock shadow but not quite a beard. She noted his blond hair and the sporty shades covering his eyes.

"Do you need the code to get in?" he asked. He pushed his sunglasses to rest on top of his head, revealing startling blue eyes.

Audrey just stared at him. She *knew* he had asked her a question. The auditory receptors in her brain seemed to be working just fine. But the part of her brain that could open her mouth and cause speech had stalled.

Audrey blinked a few times, distracted by the way the sun made his hair look like spun gold. She'd been told her auburn hair looked like copper in the sunlight. Was he noticing that about her right now?

The gate began to open from the other side, and Audrey managed to take a step back before it hit her in the face. At least her more primitive reflexes still seemed to be working. Her down-the-hall neighbor Freddy Kappal stepped through the gate. "Oh, hey, Audrey," he said, then pointed a finger at her. "Is that blood on your face?"

Audrey touched her cheek.

Freddy laughed. "Just kidding." He then looked at the guy stretching his legs. "Ammon, you ready to go?"

Ammon nodded. He took a few steps in Audrey's direction and paused. Her heart bounced oddly as he reached across her. He smelled like citrus. His long surgeon's fingers typed in the code on the keypad, and with a quick flick of the wrist, he opened the gate. She caught a glimpse of his smirk as he and Freddy jogged off.

So *that* was Ammon Parker.

✦ ✦ ✦

After a shower, during which she washed her hair twice, Audrey fixed herself a bowl of leftover vegetarian curry and sat at the kitchen table. She felt much more like herself and now had the good sense to be mortified by her recent interaction with her new neighbor. Had she really not said a single word to him?

Her roommate, Ellie Lavish, padded out of her bedroom, yawning. Even though she'd just woken up, Ellie looked photo-ready. Her dark hair was in a messy top bun that only girls with cheekbones like hers could pull off. And she had flawless skin, which Audrey knew Ellie worked hard at, applying at least three different creams on her face each night.

"When did you get home?" Ellie asked.

Audrey glanced at the clock on the stove. It was 8:32 a.m. "About a half hour ago."

Ellie nodded and joined her at the table. "How was the birth?"

"One of the least beautiful I've attended," Audrey replied. "The mother's water broke while she was pushing and doused me in fluids."

Ellie grimaced. "And now you're eating?"

Audrey laughed and took another bite.

She and Ellie were an unusual pair. They had met at a church service project about a year ago. Ellie had just graduated from Utah State and had moved to Salt Lake. Audrey had just returned to the city from working with Doctors Without Borders in Ethiopia. And while Ellie was makeup and designer handbags and Audrey was essential oils and Teva sandals, they'd bonded over their love of old movies and formed a quick friendship. In January, when Ellie's old roommate, Charlotte, got married, Audrey had moved in.

After swallowing her bite of food, Audrey pointed her fork at Ellie. "You never mentioned Freddy's new roommate looks like Captain America."

"I thought it would be a given that he'd be absurdly muscly and hot since he's friends with Freddy." Ellie shrugged.

Sure, Freddy was hot, but he was too goofy for Audrey's taste. That didn't mean his friends were going to be good-looking, too—as evidenced by Audrey and Ellie's friendship. Audrey was nowhere near Ellie's level of beauty.

"So you ran into Ammon, then?" Ellie asked.

"Outside the gate as I was getting home."

Ellie grinned. "So he saw you in all your midwifery glory?"

"If by 'midwifery glory' you mean raccoon-eyed and unable to form a complete sentence, then, yes."

"You probably still sparked his interest," Ellie said.

"I doubt it," Audrey replied.

Ellie persisted. "He's an ob-gyn, you know."

Audrey did know this. All the single women at church had gone spastic two Sundays ago when Freddy had mentioned his doctor friend would be moving in now that his sister, Lucy, had gotten married and moved out. Audrey hadn't been instantly impressed though. She caught babies all the time, and men didn't go gaga over her because of it. Plus, she knew most of those women would lose interest once they found out he was an OB.

"He and Freddy left before we could really talk, anyway."

"You saw Freddy, too?" Ellie asked with a little too much interest.

"Oh, is it *his* turn to ghost you?" Audrey asked with a laugh. Freddy and Ellie had a noncommittal on-again-off-again *thing* going on. It was too complicated for Audrey to keep up with.

Ellie narrowed her eyes. "Anyway. What's your schedule like this week?"

Audrey yawned and took another forkful of food before answering. She'd let the change in topic go. She had no interest in getting in the middle of Ellie and Freddy's not-so-love affair. "My friend is being induced on Thursday," Audrey said. "And she wants me to be her doula. Unless she goes into labor early, my schedule should be pretty predictable."

Ellie scoffed, and Audrey knew why. Her schedule was never predictable. She could be called away at any moment to go catch a baby at a home birth, and she supported women during hospital births as a doula. Being friends with her meant understanding she might have to cancel plans at the last minute or leave in the middle of something, and Audrey was grateful Ellie did understand.

"Do you have any more patients due this month?" Ellie asked.

Audrey took a bite of curry to stifle another yawn. It was only April 9, so of course she still had patients due. "Not until later this month," Audrey said. "Unless someone goes early, I should be free for the next two weeks, except this Thursday. Oh, and Tuesday I have my usual volunteer shift at the free clinic." She liked to keep busy.

"Right," Ellie said.

"Do you have something big planned for this week?" Audrey asked.

"I volunteered us to help set up tables for the church social tomorrow night."

"Okay."

"And we need to finish our movie marathon."

"Agreed."

Ellie said the next thing fast: "AndFreddywantstogorockclimbing."

Audrey laughed. "Oh, Freddy again?"

If Ellie blushed, she'd be blushing now. Instead, she shot Audrey a withering gaze. "He wants us to go as a group next Saturday," she said. "He probably would have asked you himself, but unless it's a pregnant lady messaging you, you're kind of a hard person to get ahold of."

Audrey shrugged and decided not to tease Ellie further about Freddy. "I'll talk to him at church tomorrow," she said. "And we'll figure out a route to climb."

"Thank you," Ellie replied. "I know he'll appreciate it."

Audrey yawned yet again. She'd been up for twenty-six straight hours. As tempting as it would be to sleep the whole day, she knew she had to limit her nap to four hours; otherwise, she'd flip her days and nights. She finished her food, put her dishes in the dishwasher, and retreated to her room.

Her bed felt ridiculously amazing as she lay down. Before she forgot, she plugged in her phone, then opened the calendar app to add rock climbing for next Saturday. She'd better take care of any texts or emails before she passed out, especially if they were from one of her patients. She opened her text messages and saw only one, from her mother, which she would ignore for now. No use opening that bag of crazy. Nothing in her email needed her immediate attention.

Then her phone chirped with a notification from the Mountain Collective app, an online forum for rock climbers, letting her know she'd had some responses to a comment she'd posted. Her stomach gave a little excited flip as she opened the app.

Audrey had learned about a climbing route called Craggletooth Rock two-and-a-half years ago from a friend. It was somewhere up Big Cottonwood Canyon, and her friend Shannon had wanted to climb it but had never been able to find the crag. A handful of times, different people had posted pictures on the Mountain Collective from their climbs. The story was always the same: they'd come upon the route by accident and had never been able to find it again.

Yesterday, another set of pictures had appeared from Craggletooth Rock, posted by screen name BeerBabes&Bouldering. She'd commented on his picture, *Awesome pics! Can you tell me how to get there?*

She read the replies to her comment. BeerBabes&Bouldering had left directions, but the thread continued with other users arguing about the location of Craggletooth Rock. No one seemed to agree on the exact coordinates or how to get there. Audrey didn't have time to try all the different hiking routes suggested to find the crag. A comment on the thread from BelayingonofHands piqued her interest though. *You're all wrong*, he'd written. *I know exactly where it is.* She'd seen posts from this guy over the last few years. She remembered him only because he showed up in both the Washington and Utah networks like she did, although they'd never talked to each other.

How do you know? another user had asked.

Because I set the course was BelayingonofHands's reply.

Audrey sat up in bed, no longer feeling tired. She was finally going to learn how to find Craggletooth Rock.

She tapped on BelayingonofHands's picture to pull up his profile. Like most climbers, his profile picture was of him scaling some impossible slab. She couldn't make out any of his specific features. He was a tiny tableau against a massive rock. She clicked the icon to send him a private message. *Will you tell me how to get to Craggletooth Rock?* she typed with shaky fingers.

His response came instantly, which she didn't expect.

No.

She sat up in bed, taken aback by the reply. *Why not?* she typed back.

BelayingonofHands: *Because Craggletooth is for the pure in heart.*

Audrey: *And BeerBabes&Bouldering is pure in heart?*

BelayingonofHands: *I can't help who finds it by accident.*

Audrey: *Okay. What do I need to do to prove I'm pure in heart?*

Audrey watched the dots blink that indicated BelayingonofHands was typing a reply. Her mouth dried out.

BelayingonofHands: *Await further instructions.*

Audrey groaned aloud. This was the closest she'd ever come to locating the climb. Why did guys always want to play games? Wasn't anyone straightforward and non-manipulative anymore? Audrey tried not to let her cynicism ruin this opportunity. She'd go along with it and see what he wanted. She had to try. She owed at least that much to Shannon.

Chapter 2

IT HAD BEEN SO LONG since Ammon Parker had been to a church singles activity that he'd forgotten how truly awful they could be. Tonight's had been a devotional followed by a dinner. The devotional speakers had been some author and his wife extolling the virtues of marriage and not so subtly suggesting everyone in the room was not trying hard enough to get married. Ammon, a twenty-nine-year-old man who hadn't even gone on a date in the last two years, was guilty as charged.

Bleary-eyed, Ammon stood in the hallway as he waited for the food line to go down. He was hungry and exhausted and knew he couldn't handle the small talk and the "Oh, you're the new guy?" that would happen if he stood in line with people. He had wanted to take a nap before his seven p.m. shift started at the hospital, but Freddy had woken Ammon up at four thirty so they could go to the devotional together.

Ammon wandered over to the announcement bulletin board and pretended to be interested in the job postings and roommate-wanted fliers. If he were looking for an organ-playing workshop or wanted to be a youth camp counselor, boy, would he be in business.

He pulled out his phone and opened the Mountain Collective app. He thought about the woman who had contacted him wanting directions to Craggletooth Rock. He should probably just tell her instead of giving her the runaround, but the spot was almost sacred to him. It was one thing for someone to happen upon it, but to intentionally allow someone to climb the space felt different.

As a boy, Ammon and his grandfather would hike to Craggletooth Rock once a summer and spend the day climbing and talking. He'd told Ammon the reason the climb was so hard to find was because it was only for the pure in heart.

On those summer days, his grandfather would tell him stories from the ER, leading Ammon to want to become a doctor himself. During Ammon's third year of medical school, his grandfather had died. He was granted four days off school for the funeral and bereavement, and during his time home, Ammon had set the route on Craggletooth Rock, drilling permanent bolts into the rock face to make future climbing safer and easier. Setting the route had been Ammon's tribute, a way of making a part of his deceased grandfather permanent.

Ammon tapped on Bellinghamster's profile picture. It was a view of a stunning vista from a climb in Southern Utah's red-rock country. He swiped through her other pictures, looking for one of her face. Instead what he found was photo after photo of the climb or the view, none of the typical view-from-the-top selfies that tended to litter the forum. It might not seem like a big thing, but Bellinghamster seemed to be more into the climb than showing off. She was the kind of person Ammon would want to find Craggletooth Rock. She'd probably appreciate it in the same way his grandfather had.

Ammon clicked back to her profile to see what else he could learn about her. She belonged to both the Washington and Utah networks of the Collective. Considering the screen name, she was likely from Bellingham, Washington, a small town near the U.S.-Canada border. Why did a woman from Washington want to climb a random crag in Utah? He tapped the message icon and typed, *Tell me about yourself. What makes you pure in heart?*

He sent the message, closed the app, and went to get dinner. He got into the now-much-shorter line and scanned the room for Freddy. Ammon spied him sitting at a table to the left, Eleanor Lavish beside him.

Ammon heard someone get in line behind him. He turned to see the woman he'd run into the previous morning. Today her reddish-brown hair was tamed into soft-looking curls. She wore a green dress Ammon couldn't help think suited her athletic figure just fine.

"Hey," he said to her. "We were never properly introduced yesterday morning."

She looked up at him with a guarded expression. Her cheeks and nose were sprinkled with freckles, something he hadn't noticed yesterday. Her hazel eyes were rimmed in long eyelashes. Ammon liked the shape of her mouth, her lower lip slightly fuller than her upper.

"I'm Ammon Parker," he said, holding out a hand.

"Audrey Novak," she replied, taking his hand. Her knuckles felt rough and chapped like his were from ample handwashing. She pulled her hand away first.

They stepped forward in line, reaching the paper plates at the edge of the table. Ammon motioned for Audrey to go first. "Thank you," she said, taking a plate. He watched her slender hand scoop rice onto her plate. Of course dinner was Hawaiian Haystacks.

"You were wearing scrubs yesterday morning," he said. "Are you a nurse?"

"Because I'm a woman, I must be a nurse?" she asked. She then pointed to the gravy and asked the girl refilling the chow mein noodles, "Is this vegetarian?"

Vegetarian? Oh man, was she one of those people?

The refill girl frowned. "Um, it's Campbell's Cream of Mushroom."

"Okay, thanks," Audrey said and ladled some over her rice.

"Sorry, my comment was sexist," Ammon said. "So you're a doctor."

He detected an amused smirk below her lips. "I'm not a doctor," she said.

Ammon loaded his plate with rice, chicken, and gravy. "So you *are* a nurse?" he asked.

"I'm not really a nurse either," she replied. Ammon eyed Audrey's haystack: cheese, green onions, and almond slivers. "I'm a midwife," she said and left the line. His stomach flipped a little. She probably wouldn't balk at his chosen profession like a lot of women from church did.

Ammon quickly finished making his haystack and followed her. "What hospital do you work at?" he asked as he caught up to her. "I'm up in L&D at the U."

"I don't work in a hospital." She stopped at the table where Freddy and Ellie sat, set her plate down, and took a seat. Ammon took the chair next to hers, a cold dread replacing the butterflies.

"You don't work in a hospital," he repeated.

Her hazel eyes assessed him for a moment. "I'm a home birth midwife."

And here Ammon had thought he'd met the perfect girl: someone pretty who understood the same medical stuff he did. Instead . . .

"Do you have any idea how dangerous home birth is?" he asked.

Her pretty mouth moved into a frown. "Of course you'd say that," she replied. "You're an obstetrician. You're trained to think that way."

"It's not my training," Ammon said. He put his fork down. "There's medical proof that certain events in childbirth can be deadly and are best handled in a hospital setting."

Her gaze on him turned cool and steady. "Yes, but a lot of life-threatening situations occur because of unnecessary hospital interventions. And since I don't practice in a hospital, I don't have to worry about them happening."

"That's just willful ignorance," Ammon replied. "Women hemorrhage after birth with or without hospital intervention."

"But it happens a lot less often."

"But it happens."

"Yes."

"So what do you do when your patient hemorrhages?"

"I can do fundal massage, administer a Shepherd's Purse tincture, or give—"

"That's ridiculous," Ammon interrupted. "A massage and some herbs aren't going to make a difference if the patient is bleeding out."

"And there's no guarantee you'd be able to save her either," Audrey replied, her cheeks growing pink with anger.

"But it's a lot more likely," Ammon said. "At least in a hospital I have an OR and a blood bank. All you have is your magic crystals and Reiki."

Ellie placed a hand on Audrey's arm, but she brushed it away. Freddy watched the two of them with a huge, amused grin.

"I think you have a fundamental misunderstanding of what happens at a home birth," Audrey said.

"I've seen the results of one gone wrong," Ammon replied, leveling his gaze to hers. "I don't need to understand 'what happens at a home birth' to know midwives provide inadequate medical care."

Audrey narrowed her eyes, and Ammon felt a searing crackle of energy between them. He found himself pulled in by both her passion and anger. Why did she have to be attractive?

"I'm a safe provider," she said firmly.

"I have no doubt you believe that," Ammon said. "But I'm never going to agree with you." She gave him a glacial scowl before turning her attention to Ellie, effectively ending their argument. He picked up his fork again and shoved some food into his mouth.

Freddy glowed with delight. He loved conflict in all forms. "I thought you and Audrey would hit it off," he whispered. "But you two fighting is way more entertaining."

"Yeah, well, I don't plan to talk to her again."

Ammon ate another forkful of food, trying to keep his eyes from wandering over to her. That was the shortest crush he'd ever had.

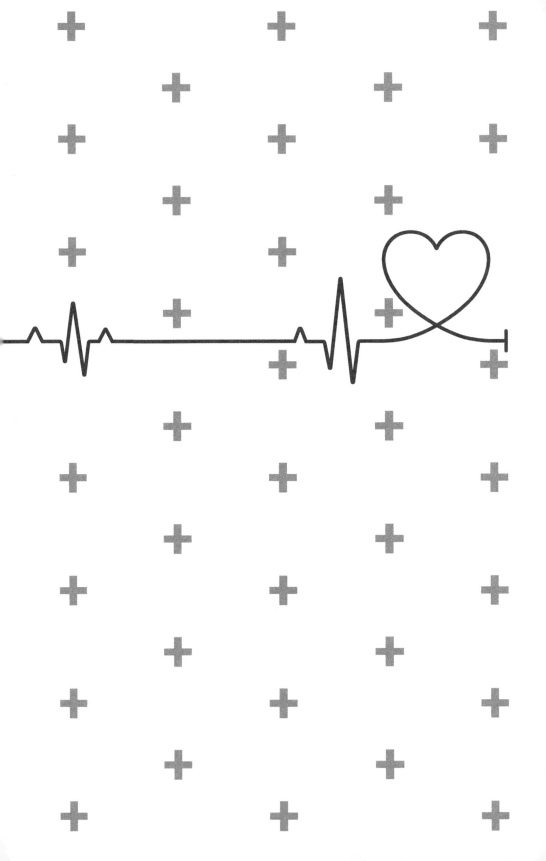

Chapter 3

AFTER HELPING STACK THE CHAIRS and put the tables away, Audrey and Ellie left the church and started their walk back to Windy Corner. The sun was a tiny sliver behind the mountains to the west, and the clouds in the sky were painted peach. Audrey walked around a puddle in the parking lot, still grinding her teeth in irritation. She really needed to learn how not to let arrogant men like Ammon get to her.

"Just to be clear," she said to Ellie, "Ammon started it, right?"

"Um . . ."

Audrey leveled Ellie with a sharp look, and Ellie laughed. "I was trying to be nice," Audrey continued. "Although ob-gyns are usually not my favorite people, especially male ones, I was willing to get to know him before making assumptions."

"Uh-huh," Ellie said.

"He's the one who stereotyped me."

"He did," Ellie agreed. "And don't forget his mansplaining."

"Exactly. Thank you." Audrey felt absolved and decided she didn't need to talk or think about Ammon Parker again.

A block later, they reached the gate to Windy Corner. Audrey typed in the code, and they went into the complex. Once inside their apartment, Audrey went to her room to change out of her dress and into pajamas. Then she needed to check if any of her patients had tried to contact her during the social. She was tied to her phone more firmly than a teenaged Instagrammer was.

Good. No missed calls or text messages. But she did have a message waiting for her in the Mountain Collective app. *Tell me about yourself. What makes you pure in heart?* BelayingonofHands had written.

That was a broad question, and Audrey wasn't sure what kind of answer he was looking for. What did he consider pure-in-heartedness? And what a weird phrase to use. She went to his profile to see what she could figure out about him. Aside from the profile picture of him as a tiny climber, all of his pictures were distance shots of climbs. That didn't give her the type of information she was hoping for, except it did reveal he was more into the actual climb than what he looked like while climbing.

Some people climbed for the journey or the challenge of the route, others for the view from the top. And some climbed and snapped endless selfies along the way to show off how cool they were. The climb was about themselves and not the thing they were trying to conquer. Audrey climbed for the view. BelayingonofHands, if his pictures were any indication, climbed for the challenge. She could respect that. This guy probably didn't have an Ammon Parker–sized ego.

She clicked back over to his profile picture. While he might not be a self-absorbed climber, he could still be a creeper. The internet wasn't necessarily the safest place to meet people. Until she had a better sense of who this guy was and what he was all about, Audrey knew she needed to be careful about what she revealed to him so he couldn't become a stalker.

She tapped the message icon to reply. *I'm not sure what I should tell you. Can I really trust someone I randomly met online?*

His reply came immediately. *Who's to say* you're *not a predator?*

Exactly, she typed back. *And since this is all so dicey, I think you should just give me the coordinates to Craggletooth Rock so we can both go on our merry way.*

BelayingonofHands: *Nice try.*

Audrey: *Then, I want to keep this anonymous. I don't want you to know my name, where I live, or what I do for work. Basically anything that could lead you to me in real life.*

BelayingonofHands: *That's fair. Anonymous, then. For both of us.*

Audrey: *So how do you plan to figure out if I'm worthy enough to climb Craggletooth Rock?*

BelayingonofHands: *I'll think of something.*

Weirdo, Audrey thought. She clicked her phone's screen off and wandered out to the living room. Ellie sat on the couch scrolling through options on Netflix.

Audrey settled onto the couch beside her. "Should we finish our movie marathon?"

"You queue it up and I'll make the popcorn." Ellie handed her the remote.

✛ ✛ ✛

Audrey shuffled to bed at one in the morning, the last words of *Casablanca* ringing in her ears. Ellie had fallen asleep halfway through the movie, the third in their classic movie marathon. But Audrey had forced herself to stay awake. Every time she saw the movie, she ached for the star-crossed lovers. She wanted something that real in her life, even though it would probably hurt her in the end. A girl could be a strong, independent woman *and* a hopeless romantic at the same time, right? She didn't *need* a man in her life—she had a satisfying career and good friends—but she wanted someone to share her life with.

Audrey brushed her teeth—her makeup would have to be a disaster she'd deal with later—then stumbled to her room. In her hand, her phone chirped. She couldn't stop the groan from coming out. If it was a patient going into labor, Audrey would probably cry. She knew better than to stay up late given her on-call lifestyle, but sometimes she just needed to veg.

She saw it was a notification from BelayingonofHands. What was this guy doing messaging her in the middle of the night?

I need to know you're the type of person who won't post the coordinates to the route all over the internet if I tell them to you. The best way to do that is to test your character. Over the next few weeks, I'm going to ask you some questions about the type of person you are and maybe even give you a few character-determining tasks to perform. Once it's clear you're a good person who can keep a secret, I'll give you the coordinates. Does this sound reasonable?

Audrey reread the words. She couldn't decide if she was being manipulated or if he was earnest in his request. She leaned back on her headboard. It was possible she'd one day stumble upon the route like other climbers had. Was she willing to wait for luck to lead her there? She plugged her phone in to charge. She would play his game, but there was no need for him to know how eager she was. She'd get back to him after she slept.

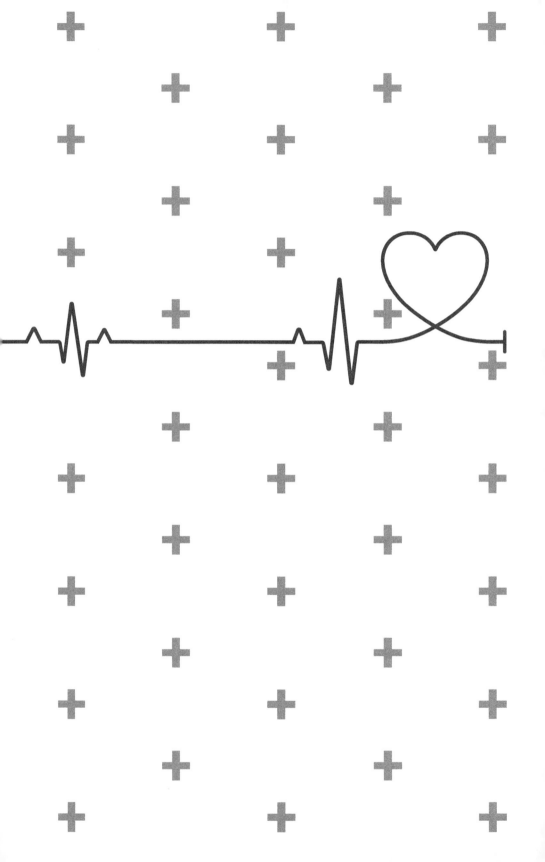

Chapter 4

ONLY AFTER AMMON HIT SEND did he realize he probably shouldn't have messaged Bellinghamster at one o'clock in the morning. Only creepy guys messaged women in the middle of the night. Hopefully the message didn't wake her up and she'd find it at a reasonable hour and not notice the time stamp.

"The patient in room 5 needs her progress checked," his attending, Kathleen Ferguson, said as she walked by him in the hall. Ammon pocketed his phone, feeling a little chastised. He removed his glasses, which he wore during long shifts at the hospital instead of his contacts, and rubbed his tired eyes. With a deep breath, he replaced his glasses and headed to room 5, occupied by a patient he hadn't met yet.

As someone for whom most things came easily, Ammon was finding his residency challenging in every single way. He might come off as a confident doctor, especially when arguing with a home birth midwife, but a large part of him wasn't sure he'd picked the right field of medicine. He viewed every new patient he met as an opportunity to recapture the excitement he'd felt years ago in med school when he'd done his labor and delivery rotation. If he could feel that absolute awe again of bringing a baby into the world, maybe he'd feel like he made the right choice. That he belonged here.

"Get out of my room," the patient yelled as soon as he entered. "I said no medical students."

Ammon stepped forward and put on a charming smile that usually put patients at ease. "Good thing I'm not a medical student," he said as he opened a package of sterile gloves. "I'm working with Dr. Ferguson tonight. I'm Dr. Parker."

The patient sat up in bed, her round belly smooth and bulbous beneath the white sheet. "I told you to get out."

Ammon snapped the gloves onto his hands. "I'm just here to check your dilation."

"I don't want a pretty-boy medical student touching me."

Ammon felt a flush moving up his neck. "I understand, ma'am, but I am not a medical student." He took a deep breath. "I am a colleague of your doctor, and I am here to assess your progress."

She pointed a finger at him, her teeth clenched. "I said get. Out."

Confusion and shame heating his face, Ammon offered a polite nod and then left the room, his eyes landing on a bewildered nurse before he disappeared into the hall. He ripped off his gloves as he moved, his face hot and burning bright red. The darkness of an open room caught his attention, and he retreated into it. The motion-activated lights clicked on, and he shut the door behind him.

Ammon took deep breaths. He removed his glasses and scrubbed a hand over his face, willing the embarrassment to leave. He felt like such an impostor. He leaned against the edge of the bed and stayed very still, waiting to see how long it would take for the lights to turn off. He willed his mind to go blank, to not think of this last interaction or the hundreds of small missteps he'd made since his residency started two years ago. Being a doctor was hard. He had known theoretically that it would be, but living it day-to-day was something different.

Just as the lights clicked off, he heard a knock at the door. Shoot. He'd been found.

Dr. Ferguson poked her head into the room. "You in here, Ammon?"

He pushed himself off the edge of the bed and put his glasses back on. "Yeah."

She was the only attending who called residents by their first names, like they were her real colleagues. Usually he was Dr. Parker or, more often, just a clipped Parker.

She stepped into the room, the lights flickering on.

"Sorry about that patient," she said. "I knew she didn't want any medical students. I didn't know that also meant residents."

"It's fine." Ammon raised his head, his face cooling. "Most people don't know the difference."

She leaned against the bed near him. "I shouldn't have sent you in there without introducing you first. This one is my bad."

"Okay."

Dr. Ferguson was a rare doctor, he was discovering. Most of his attendings had egos, even the nice ones, and wouldn't admit fault or apologize. Even Ammon had to pretend he was confident and competent, even if internally he questioned himself. Part of the show of ego was to instill confidence in his patients. No one wanted a doctor who clearly had no idea what they were doing. But another part of it was culture.

Dr. Ferguson pushed a handful of her black-and-purple braids over her shoulder. "Everyone gets fired by a patient at least once," she said. "You know Dr. Callister?"

Ammon nodded. Callister was Ammon's least-favorite attending. Talk about ego and posturing. "He's been fired *multiple* times, even while the patient was crowning."

An amused smile pulled at Ammon's lips. He could believe it.

"You're not at that level," she said. "But I've been fired before. And Sandoval's been fired before, too, if you can believe that one." She smiled and Ammon did too.

"I can't," Ammon replied, the last of his embarrassment gone. "Sandoval is the best doctor on the floor."

"Hey," she said, crossing her arms over her chest. Ammon laughed.

"You're going to be fine," she continued. "This work is hard. As obstetricians, we are taking care of women at their most vulnerable time. It takes practice and time to figure out how to navigate it all."

Ammon had studied how his various attendings interacted with their patients. Dr. Ferguson was unflappable, the stress or exhaustion never seeming to get to her. And because she was a woman, her patients seemed to naturally trust her. It reminded him that, as a male, he had to do more to earn his patients' trust, and he was still trying to figure out the best way to do that. Dr. Sandoval had a cheerful and endearing father-like bedside manner, and Callister was confident and more than a little boorish. Neither of those felt right to Ammon. He didn't know what type of doctor he was yet.

"Why don't you take your lunch break now," Dr. Ferguson said, pushing herself off the edge of the bed. "And then we'll see if Dr. Sandoval has a patient you can help with."

"Okay." Ammon nodded.

She gave one last small smile before exiting. Ammon stayed very still until the room went dark again.

+ + +

Monday morning, as he unlocked his car door, his phone beeped. He got in the car and checked his phone, expecting to see a new message on the family group Marco Polo, but it was a notification from the Mountain Collective. At some point during the night, he'd forgotten he'd sent Bellinghamster a message. *I'll play your game,* she had written. *But I will tell you up front you are wasting my time and yours with this. I'm 100% trustworthy.*

Ammon smiled and started his car. What could he have this woman do to prove she deserved the coordinates? This could be a nice distraction. Usually he left the hospital trying to remember why he'd wanted to be a doctor in the first place.

When he got back to his apartment, instead of heading straight to bed, he changed into workout clothes and exchanged his glasses for contact lenses. He hadn't worked out much in the last week because he'd been too tired, but today he decided to push through his exhaustion. He'd hit the apartment complex's gym for a half hour, then eat and head to bed. He'd become a bit of a gym rat in the last few years. He used to hike, mountain bike, or climb to get exercise, but he didn't have hours of free time to do those activities anymore. Instead, he'd put in a hard thirty minutes to an hour at the gym—lifting and running, mostly—to help burn off his stress. He preferred being outdoors, but at this phase of his life, he had to take what he could get.

He walked into the gym and did a quick survey of the space. It was well outfitted, especially for an apartment complex gym—two each of ellipticals, treadmills, and stationary bikes, and a number of different weight benches and free weights. In some open space in front of the mirrors, he spotted Ellie and Audrey. They tossed a medicine ball back and forth between sit-ups. He had no interest in talking to Audrey again, so he mounted a treadmill in the back by the door and hoped neither of the women noticed him.

Before starting his run, Ammon put his earbuds in and queued up his phone to catch up on the family Marco Polos. His sisters usually posted cute videos of his nieces or nephews. Ammon and one of his brothers-in-law were in the midst of a bad pun contest, but he hadn't thought of one yet to send on.

In the middle of a rant from his youngest sister, Eve, about the rising price of the "good" wheat bread at Costco, he heard, "Hey, Ammon."

He considered for a split second pretending he hadn't heard his name. It was probably Ellie, because why would Audrey want to talk to him? But he wasn't entirely sure. He hadn't spent enough time with either of them to recognize their voices.

He paused the video message on his phone and glanced up. Ellie gave him a cat's smile. He felt a little like prey. Audrey examined the medicine ball in her hands with fake interest. He waved and turned the treadmill up to a brisk jog.

"Can you help us?" Ellie said louder.

Ammon motioned to his earbuds and shrugged a universal *I can't hear you*. He most certainly did not want to help them. He'd just spent the last fourteen hours of his life interacting with people, and he was an introvert to a fault—another reason he maybe should not have picked an area of medicine that required interacting with people. He should have gone into research so he could hide in a lab all day. Now he just wanted to exercise in peace. He should probably get his own set of weights so he could lift in his apartment.

Ellie rolled her eyes. "I know you can hear me."

Ammon stopped the treadmill and pulled out his earbuds. "What?" he said a little too loudly. He hoped he was selling this *I couldn't hear you* thing, but he made the mistake of glancing at Audrey, who scowled. His acting obviously needed work.

"We want to do a pull-up contest but need an unbiased third party to count," Ellie said. "Audrey likes to cheat."

"I do not," Audrey replied, glancing at Ammon out of the corner of her eye.

"Will you help us?" Ellie asked.

Ammon was proud of himself for not rolling his eyes. "Yeah, sure." He got off the treadmill and joined the two women.

"Audrey will go first," Ellie said to him.

"I don't think Ammon is an unbiased third party," Audrey quipped.

Ammon grinned; he couldn't help himself. "For this, I will be," he said.

Audrey shook her head but didn't say anything.

They moved over to the pull-up bar along the wall. Audrey stood in front of the bar and took a few deep breaths before grabbing hold. Ammon tried not to notice her feminine curves in her fitted gym clothes as she hung on the bar, but he was only human. And Audrey was without a doubt a beautiful woman.

He didn't want to be caught checking her out, so he focused on the back of her head and her mess of red curls as he counted her pull-ups. Her first three seemed pretty effortless, which was impressive, but he wasn't about to let her know that. The next three seemed to take some concerted effort, her arm muscles quaking. On her seventh pull-up, she let out a very unladylike grunt as she pulled her head above the bar. This woman was hard-core.

Once she cleared the bar, she dropped off and let out a large whoop of satisfaction. "A new personal best!" She exchanged high fives with Ellie. Her gaze didn't even travel in Ammon's direction, and he wondered why Ellie had *really* called him over.

Audrey took long sips from her metal water bottle. "Your turn," she said to Ellie, still ignoring Ammon.

"You know what? My wrist is bothering me," Ellie said. "I probably shouldn't."

"Oh, come on," Audrey said, recapping her bottle. "You know it's really just a competition with yourself."

Ellie gave a noncommittal shrug before turning to him. "Ammon, why don't you go instead."

Oh. That's why Ellie wanted him here. To cause trouble. Freddy had warned him about her. Ammon studied Ellie for a second. It was basic physiology that he would be able do more pull-ups because he was a man and in great shape. Beating Audrey didn't seem like a good idea since she already didn't like him. And it would be too obvious if he purposely lost to her. Ammon had five older sisters and knew the last thing a girl wanted was to have a guy let her win. He really had no good options here.

"I'll pass," he said.

Audrey quirked a brow. "Are you afraid to win or lose?"

"I wouldn't lose," he said, a smirk he couldn't stop forming on his mouth.

"And you think I'm so insecure I'd be upset if I lost a pull-up contest?"

Why'd she have to goad him? Ammon pressed his lips together. "Fine." He moved to the bar and climbed on. He hung for a moment, adjusted his grip, and did his first pull-up. "One," he said unnecessarily loudly. "Two."

He took a quick peek at Audrey, who folded her arms over her chest and appeared unimpressed. He did the next five quickly and easily. "Seven," he said. Should he stop or really push himself? He probably had ten more left in him. Ugh. He never knew what he should do to please women like

Audrey. He stole another glance at her. She raised her eyebrows in challenge. Fine.

He dropped his left arm and pulled himself up with just his right. "Eight." He kept his attention trained on Audrey and switched arms. "Nine." Then switched arms again. "Ten." He gave her a cheeky grin. "Eleven."

She scoffed and turned away. "Show-off," she muttered as she headed for the door.

Ammon hopped off the bar, feeling a mixture of pleasure and annoyance. He'd gotten to her. Again.

Ellie watched her friend leave. "I think I miscalculated," she whispered under her breath. She turned to Ammon and gave him a false bright smile. "See you Saturday? Maybe?"

"What's Saturday?"

She gave another noncommittal shrug and followed after Audrey.

Ammon let out a deep breath. He truly didn't get women. Another reason he'd probably picked the wrong field of medicine.

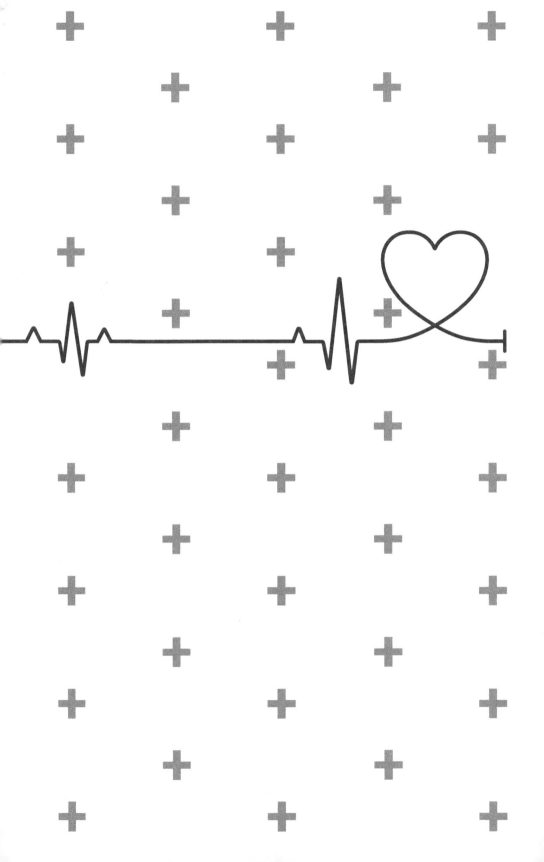

Chapter 5

TUESDAY MORNING, AUDREY WALKED INTO the clinic at five minutes to eight, the familiar scent of cheap coffee, musty carpets, and disinfectant greeting her. The waiting room was already full, women and a few men flipping through magazines or scrolling through their phones.

Audrey volunteered as a women's health nurse practitioner once a week at the free clinic in downtown Salt Lake. Her patients were mostly low-income women without insurance or women experiencing homelessness. Audrey performed routine exams, administered a lot of pregnancy tests, and wrote prescriptions for common infections. The work was tedious and most of the time downright uninteresting, but after her time in Ethiopia, she couldn't sit back knowing there were women in need in her own community. She had to share her skills where she could.

Audrey checked in with the office coordinator, Nancy, to get the information for her first patient of the day.

"I'm glad you're here," Nancy said, handing Audrey a patient file. "That sweet teenage patient of yours has been here since seven thirty waiting for you. She didn't want to be seen by anyone else."

Audrey glanced around the waiting room and spotted the familiar young woman. Her blonde hair spilled over her growing belly, where she rested a hand. "Claire," Audrey called.

The teen looked up, and tension melted out of her shoulders. Claire hefted herself out of the hard-plastic chair and waddled toward Audrey.

Audrey smiled but noted the crease between the girl's eyebrows. "Everything okay?" she asked as they walked down the narrow hallway back to a small exam room.

"I don't know," Claire answered. She climbed onto the exam table, and Audrey sat on a black rolling stool. She moved the stool so she'd be right in front of Claire.

"You seem worried. What's going on?"

The girl swallowed, and her eyes turned red. Audrey could tell Claire wanted to cry but knew she wouldn't. Audrey had been meeting with Claire since she was six weeks along—it was in this very exam room that she'd confirmed Claire's pregnancy. She had been there to talk to Claire about her options a few weeks later when her boyfriend had dumped her and Claire was contemplating an abortion. Two weeks after that, Audrey had been there when Claire had decided to keep the baby. Soon after, the girl's mom had cut her off because she'd wanted Claire to put the baby up for adoption. Having been raised by a teen mom herself, Audrey had misgivings about Claire's decision, but having an opinion wasn't Audrey's job. Her job was to educate and support her patients. So Audrey had helped Claire find housing, a full-time job, and a GED course. She'd helped Claire sign up for Medicaid to cover the expense of the birth. And Audrey had every intention of being at the birth as Claire's doula. Through all that, she'd never seen Claire cry.

Audrey waited patiently for the young woman to compose herself. When she finally spoke, her voice sounded thick. "I don't think she's moved since last night," Claire said, her hand rubbing her stomach.

Audrey's chest clenched with anxiety. "Okay. Sometimes babies have extended sleep cycles, and their movements change as they get bigger. Let's check for a heartbeat."

Claire shook her head. "I don't think I'll be able to stand it if you don't find one."

Audrey nodded, her brow creased. "Let's try something else first. When was the last time you ate?"

Claire glanced away. "Lunch yesterday."

Audrey wasn't going to scold the teen for not eating. She knew Claire did her best. "Let's feed you, then," she said. "Once your blood sugar is up, baby will probably go crazy."

She went to the supply room. It was not uncommon to have patients who needed food along with their checkups, so the room was well stocked with snacks. She grabbed a package of peanut-butter crackers and, from the fridge, a Pepsi. The sugar would get the baby moving.

Audrey returned to the exam room to find Claire had moved to a chair. Audrey handed her the snacks, and Claire popped the tab on the Pepsi first. She took a slow sip. "Do you think it's because I haven't eaten?" she asked. "She's not dead, is she?"

Without the confirmation of a heartbeat, Audrey couldn't say for sure. "Let's give her a few minutes." She gestured toward the snack. "Eat up." Claire's mouth curled into an unsuccessful smile, and she took another sip of soda. Audrey returned to the black stool and flipped through Claire's chart, reviewing her blood pressure and weight from her last visit two weeks before.

She usually saw pregnant patients only once or twice because most transferred care to an ob-gyn or hospital nurse midwife. Claire had kept coming back, requesting Audrey every time. Audrey didn't mind but knew that soon Claire would need to start seeing the doctor who would ultimately deliver her baby at the hospital. Medicaid didn't cover home birth.

"Oh, thank goodness," Claire suddenly said. "She moved!"

A tiny rush of relief washed through Audrey. "Thank goodness," she echoed. She put Claire's file back on the countertop. "Let's have you hop back up on the exam table."

Claire smiled big, her teeth showing, and left her chair. Once on the table, she lay back and lifted her shirt. Audrey applied lubricant to the wand of the fetal heart Doppler and pressed it to Claire's stomach. The quick, reassuring whoosh of the baby's heartbeat sounded through the room. Audrey listened longer than she usually would, making sure the beat was fast and consistent. "She sounds great," she said. "Her heartbeat is between 130 and 140 beats per minute, which is perfect." She took the Doppler off Claire's stomach and handed her some tissues to wipe off the lubricant. Audrey found the tape measure and measured Claire's belly. "Thirty-three centimeters for thirty-three weeks—right on track." She motioned for Claire to sit up. Claire pulled her shirt back down and sat on the edge of the table, her face slack with relief. Audrey took her blood pressure next and scribbled down the numbers in Claire's chart. "Everything looks good. Why don't you finish your snacks." Audrey smiled and motioned for her to hop off the exam table. Claire settled back into the chair and took another sip of the Pepsi. "If this happens again," Audrey said, "drink something cold and sugary and do some kick counts. If you're still worried, call me, okay? Don't wait."

Claire nodded but kept her head down.

"And can we talk about why you haven't eaten since lunch yesterday?" Audrey asked.

Claire sighed and plucked the pop tab a few times. "I got busy, I guess. Then none of the food I had at home sounded good, so I went to bed hungry. When I woke up this morning, I realized I couldn't remember the last time I felt her move and came straight here."

Audrey nodded and touched Claire's arm. Her eyes grew red-rimmed again, and Audrey's heart contracted. She always got emotionally invested in her patients, even when a little more distance would probably be the best thing. But she couldn't help it. She was a rescuer. She squeezed Claire's arm before letting go. "If you didn't have any food, you would tell me, right?"

"Yes," Claire replied, sighing again. "I signed up for WIC a few months ago like you said. But it's so restrictive on what I can buy—only healthy stuff, you know? Sometimes I just want a cheeseburger."

Audrey laughed. "I understand. But you need to eat, okay? Even if it's just toast and peanut butter and you have to choke it down."

"Okay," Claire said, setting her soda down and grabbing for the crackers.

"Have you been able to make an appointment with Dr. Ferguson?"

"Yeah, I saw her last Thursday. She seems nice."

"She's a good friend of mine. She'll be your doctor when you go to the hospital to have the baby, so I'm glad you've been able to meet her."

"She wants me to start seeing her for my prenatal visits . . ." Claire trailed off and took a bite of a cracker.

"Her office accepts Medicaid, so you wouldn't have to pay, if that's what you're worried about."

Claire narrowed her eyes. "Are you trying to pawn me off onto her?"

"No, that's not what I meant at all."

"Because you said you'd be with me until the end. That you'd be there with me as my doula, or whatever it's called, when the baby came."

"And I will," Audrey promised. "You are welcome to keep seeing me on Tuesday here at the clinic. But it might be nice to get to know Dr. Ferguson better. That's all I was suggesting." Audrey leaned closer to Claire and caught her eye. "I'm here for you. I will be there when you have your baby. You have my cell-phone number. I don't give that to just any patient."

Claire assessed her. Audrey tried not to feel hurt by the girl's suspicion. Everyone who had meant something to Claire had abandoned her, so it shouldn't have surprised Audrey that she'd think Audrey would eventually abandon her too. Audrey knew all too well about abandonment; her biological father had written the book. She sympathized, and she wouldn't hurt Claire that way. "I've got you," Audrey said.

"Okay," Claire eventually said.

Audrey tried not to smile too big. "Everything's going to be okay."

"Sure," Claire replied with a half shrug. "Whatever."

+ + +

As Audrey unlocked her bike from the rack outside the clinic, her phone chirped. She pulled her phone from her backpack and read the text message: *My blood pressure is climbing. I'll probably be induced tonight. Call me.*

It was from her friend Jessica, whom Audrey was planning to be a doula for. Her induction wasn't supposed to be until Thursday night. Moving it up signaled a serious change. She dialed her friend immediately and asked for an update.

"My platelet count is low, and my liver enzymes are high," Jessica said. "It's HELLP syndrome." A lump grew in Audrey's throat, and she placed a hand over her chest to keep the anxiety at bay. HELLP syndrome could be deadly. The only cure was to deliver the baby. "I've been checked into the hospital and they have me on fetal monitors and some sort of medication, and I'm supposed to get a blood transfusion soon."

"Have they said anything about doing an emergency C-section?" Audrey asked.

"The baby is fine, and I'm responding well to treatment. They're willing to give me a trial of labor."

Audrey nodded, her mind spinning. "How are you feeling about this?" she asked.

"A little scared," her friend replied. "But Dr. Sandoval assured me we've caught it early, and since I'm at almost thirty-seven weeks, the baby should be fine."

"That's all true," Audrey said. "This is a best-case scenario when it comes to HELLP." She pushed from her mind what happened in the worst-case scenario. "What time do you want me at the hospital?"

"They said I'll be taken down to Labor and Delivery between ten p.m. and midnight. It depends on when a bed becomes available."

"I'll be there at ten."

The call ended, and Audrey checked the time: four forty-five. She had about five hours to eat, call her home birth patients to make sure no one was going into labor, and take a nap. Audrey mounted her bike and rode the five miles to her apartment.

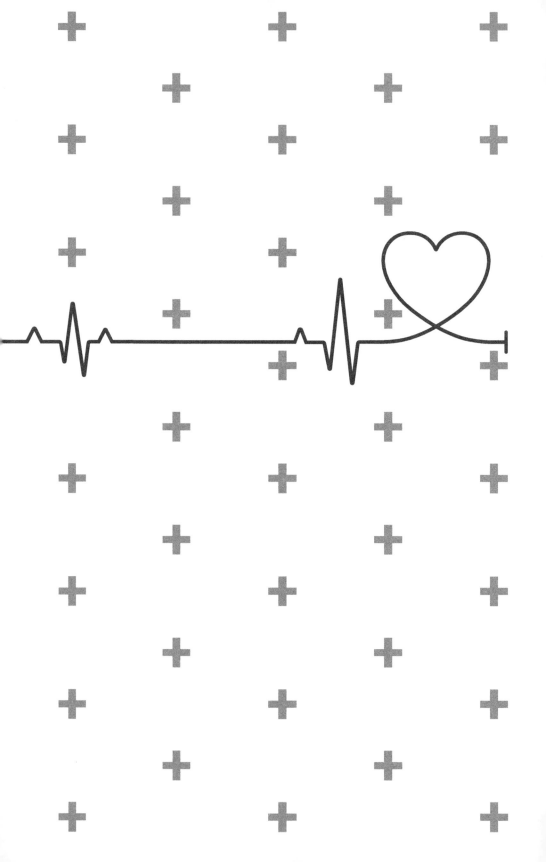

Chapter 6

I<small>F</small> A<small>MMON</small> <small>WERE</small> <small>HONEST</small>, <small>HE</small> preferred patients who didn't have birth plans. If a patient had no preferences, providing medical care was much easier for him. He didn't have to argue or explain anything. He'd say, "It's time to check your dilation" or "We are going to break your water to move things along," and she'd say, "Sure, whatever you think, Doctor." But this patient, despite the fact that she had a life-threatening condition, had a lot of opinions about what was going to happen to her.

"My doula will be here soon," the patient said.

Ammon looked up from the birth plan she'd handed him and nodded. Great. A doula. Just another obstacle to him doing his job. He returned his attention to the plan to review her list of demands—four pages' worth. But Sandoval loved birth plans and doulas. He encouraged all of his patients to have both.

Ammon took off his glasses and rubbed his eyes. He was only three hours into his fifteen-hour shift, and already he needed a Red Bull. He returned his glasses. "Thanks for making your wishes so clear," Ammon said evenly. "We will of course do our best to follow your requests and discuss all procedures and interventions with you."

Dr. Sandoval entered the room. He smiled at his patient. "Jessica, how are you feeling?" He went to her bedside. "This must be a bit of a shock."

Ammon's pager went off. One of his other patients was probably ready to deliver. Ammon touched Dr. Sandoval's arm. "I've got another patient," he said.

"Yes, of course. But come back as soon as you can. This is your first HELLP patient, yes?"

Ammon nodded.

"Good. I'll have you take the lead on the induction. I'll start the Foley bulb, and once you return, we'll see if Jessica is ready for Pitocin."

Ammon nodded, wondering how Dr. Sandoval knew without seeing her birth plan that the patient wanted a Foley bulb. Or maybe he'd just assumed and was right. The hospital midwives referred their high-risk patients to Dr. Sandoval because he was so naturally minded and patient-centered. He was a doctor of maternal-fetal medicine, a specialty of obstetrics, who cared for high-risk patients: pregnant women who were sick or had developed significant prenatal complications, women whose pre-born babies were going to be born with known health problems, and women pregnant with twins or triplets. Dr. Sandoval even delivered breech babies naturally. Ammon could learn a lot from him, and maybe he would be eager to learn if he didn't already feel so burned out.

Only eleven more weeks on the night rotation, but he had two more years left in his residency. Sometimes he wondered if he had the temperament to be a good doctor. He knew he didn't want to be like Dr. Callister. Callister was arrogant and misogynistic. But Ammon didn't think he had it in him to be like Dr. Sandoval, endlessly patient and cheerful. And he could never be like Dr. Ferguson, because he wasn't a woman.

Two hours later, Ammon stopped by the nurses station to get an update on the HELLP patient. Dr. Sandoval had left detailed notes for him since he'd been called away. The Foley bulb had been inserted into the patient's cervix. Ammon needed to check for cervical readiness and decide if a ripening agent would be necessary after all. He prayed it wouldn't. He did not want to have that conversation with a patient who had already decided, per her birth plan, that ripening agents were bad. If the cervix was ready, Dr. Sandoval had instructed Ammon to start Pitocin at the lowest dose. *Please refer to Jessica's birth plan often*, Dr. Sandoval had written. *And work with the doula and patient, not against them.*

Ammon felt a tiny sting at the implied accusation. He always tried to follow birth plans, even if they made him grumpy. He wanted to crumple up the note but instead folded it in half and walked to the patient's room. Upon entering the room, he found himself locking eyes with an attractive redhead, a woman he hadn't thought about once since Monday, the home birth midwife with the pretty, sharp mouth. Her jaw fell slack with surprise, and his heart did a funny little skip. "What are you doing here?" he asked, not even trying to keep the annoyance out of his voice.

The patient sat up in bed and glanced from Ammon to Audrey.

"I'm here for Jessica," Audrey said coolly.

Ammon shook his head. "Jessica is one of Dr. Sandoval's patients, and her chart said nothing about her being a home birth transfer, so I'm a little confused."

"Audrey delivered my first baby two-and-a-half years ago," Jessica chimed in. "But because of complications with this pregnancy, I've been seeing Dr. Sandoval. Audrey is acting as my doula instead of my midwife this time."

Ammon pasted on a smile. "Great," he said, then turned to Audrey. "You willing to stay within your limited scope of practice as a doula?"

Audrey folded her arms over her chest. "Are you willing to not slice my friend open?"

Ammon chuckled. This girl was something. He turned his attention back to the patient. "Jessica, I'd like to check on the Foley bulb."

Jessica looked from Audrey to Ammon again.

"Where's Ric?" Audrey asked.

Ammon raised his eyebrows. There was no way Audrey was referring to Dr. Sandoval. For all his warmth and friendliness, he still didn't let patients call him by his first name. Only colleagues called him Ric, and Ammon wasn't even colleague enough to get that honor.

"I'm sorry, who?" Ammon asked.

"Ric," Audrey repeated slowly. "Dr. Sandoval."

Ammon narrowed his eyes. Should he warn her about her faux pas or let her learn the hard way? "He's in a C-section and should be back soon," Ammon replied. "I'll be taking care of Jessica and working with him tonight."

Audrey's pretty mouth remained in a neutral line.

"He'd like me to check on the Foley bulb and start Pitocin if Jessica's cervix is ready," Ammon continued.

"Jessica," Audrey said, turning to her. "If you aren't comfortable with Dr. Parker, we can request someone else." She glanced at Ammon out of the corner of her eye. Her glare was sharp, and Ammon returned it with a pleasant smile instead of the insult on the tip of his tongue. He'd maintain professionalism, even if she couldn't.

Jessica shook her head. "No, it's fine."

Ammon checked on the bulb. She'd hardly progressed, and with her condition, there wasn't time to wait to see if another hour or two would change that. He checked the blood pressure monitor and the fetal heart rate. Things appeared to be stable now, but the sooner the baby could be delivered, the better.

"I need to start you on Cytotec," Ammon told Jessica, purposely not looking at Audrey. "I know your birth plan stated you'd prefer to avoid that drug, but your cervix hasn't progressed, and for the safety of you and the baby, it's really best if we get things moving."

Jessica glanced at Audrey, who wore a polite smile, before looking back at Ammon. She nodded. "Okay. I understand."

Ammon moved out of the dominant hands-on-hip pose he'd subconsciously taken. He'd been expecting a fight. He stole a peek at Audrey, who raised her eyebrows only slightly at him but didn't say anything. "Okay, then," he said. "I'll let the nurse know." He made a graceless exit, wondering why he felt so flabbergasted.

+ + +

Audrey watched Ammon go, irritated by the little flutters in her stomach whenever he looked at her. It was just physical attraction. Everything other than his appearance was terrible.

"Is he, like, absurdly hot for a doctor?" Jessica asked. "Or are those my pregnancy hormones talking?"

Audrey smoothed a hand through her hair. She'd always had a weakness for men in scrubs, and they suited Ammon just fine. She tried not to think of the way they hung low on his hips or how they showed off his arm muscles. "I guess he's kind of good-looking."

Jessica laughed. "How do you know him?"

"What?"

"Come on, I saw the daggers you two were shooting at each other."

"I met him at church, and he disparaged my profession." Audrey shrugged.

The nurse entered the room, and Audrey stepped back. She needed to get into the right headspace for this birth and not let Ammon derail her. So what if he was "absurdly hot for a doctor"? And happened to hate her because she helped women birth babies at home? Audrey could be professional. Plus, Jessica needed her for what looked like was going to be a long night.

The nurse administered the Cytotec and left the room. "We should get some sleep," Audrey said to Jessica.

Her friend nodded as she reached for her phone on the bedside table. "Let me text Doug and let him know what's going on." Doug was her husband and was staying with their toddler until Jessica was in active labor.

Audrey went to the chair and unfolded it into a bed. She'd ask the nurse for a pillow and blanket the next time she came back. Part of Audrey was exhausted, but the other part of her was wide-awake. Jessica should be terrified. HELLP could turn deadly fast, sending Jessica into multiple-organ failure. For all of Audrey's natural-mindedness, she'd have a C-section if she were in Jessica's position. But Audrey wasn't Jessica's midwife right now, so it would be inappropriate for her to voice any medical opinions. Plus, she needed to put her nerves away. This wasn't her baby's birth, and she had to trust Ric was pursuing the right treatment. Trusting Ammon, however, was another story.

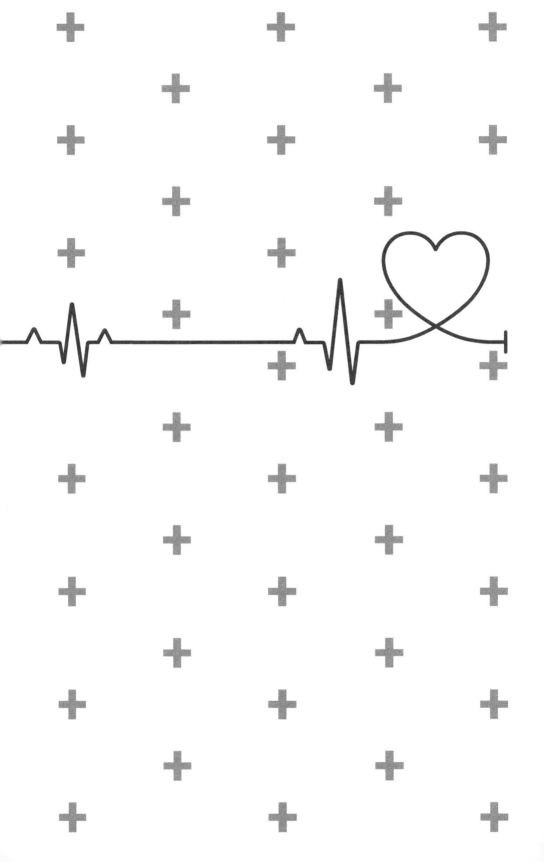

Chapter 7

AMMON AND DR. SANDOVAL STARED at the monitors. The patient, Jessica, was between contractions. Her blood pressure was as good as it could be, given the situation. Her latest blood work proved her liver enzymes had not reached dangerous levels yet. The baby's heart rate was strong, but the baby appeared to be stuck. The patient had been pushing for an hour and a half, and the baby wouldn't budge.

"What are our options?" Dr. Sandoval asked Ammon.

He knew Sandoval was testing him. "C-section," Ammon said.

A contraction started, and Ammon and Dr. Sandoval watched the wave-like line grow on the monitor. Audrey talked in a quiet voice by the patient's ear and encouraged her to "breathe the baby down." Ammon held back a sigh. What they needed was for Jessica to push this baby out with all her might. "Breathing down" was not enough.

The contraction ended, and the baby had made no progress. Ammon continued. "A vacuum or forceps delivery."

Ammon glanced in Audrey's direction. She watched him carefully while applying a wet washcloth to Jessica's forehead.

"What else?" Dr. Sandoval prodded.

"An episiotomy," Ammon offered. Audrey cleared her throat, but he ignored her.

"What else?" Sandoval pressed.

Ammon thought for a moment and came up blank. But the fact that Sandoval was still asking for something meant Ammon hadn't given the complete answer yet.

Out of the corner of his eye, he saw Audrey step away from Jessica. "Ric, how's the baby's heart rate?" she asked.

Ammon gave her a scathing glare. Throughout the whole birth she'd been "Ric this" and "Ric that" and Dr. Sandoval hadn't corrected her. Ammon shouldn't let her get to him, but the woman was annoying. "You know very well the baby's heart rate is fine," Ammon said before *Ric* could answer.

She leveled her gaze at him. "As a midwife, I do know that. As a doula, I don't. Right now I'm a doula." Her mouth turned into a pretty smile. "So how is the baby's heart rate?"

"The baby is fine," Dr. Sandoval answered. "And Jessica's vitals are stable. There is no hurry, other than Jessica appears to be getting tired."

Another contraction started, and Audrey returned to Jessica's side. Jessica lay in the bed on her back and pushed while Audrey took hold of her hand.

"Would it be okay if I move her into another position?" Audrey asked when the contraction ended. "She's only on her back because that's where she feels most comfortable, but it's not an ideal position for pushing. If we get her on all fours, Baby might reposition enough for him to engage."

"That's a perfect idea, Audrey," Dr. Sandoval said. Ammon felt himself bristle. Sandoval turned to him. "*If labor stalls or baby is stuck, changing positions might improve our luck,*" he sang. "Doulas and midwives do know a thing or two." Ammon clenched his jaw as his face heated with embarrassment. He nodded, and when Sandoval went to the patient's bedside to assist Audrey with the reposition, Ammon clung to his last sliver of maturity and didn't stick his tongue out at her. Luckily, he probably wouldn't have to work with her ever again. He'd been working out of this L&D unit and its clinics for the last two years and hadn't run into her until tonight. He would have remembered her red hair and intensity. He just needed to keep it together a little while longer, and then she'd be out of his professional life forever.

+ + +

Audrey left Jessica's side only when she was wheeled to the postpartum wing. Relief made Audrey feel buoyant as she walked down the hall of the Labor and Delivery ward. Jessica was going to be okay. As expected, her HELLP symptoms began to improve once the baby was born. And the birth had gone without complication. She offered a silent prayer of gratitude.

She saw Ric at the nurses station as she rounded the corner toward the exit. He smiled and stopped her. "It was wonderful working with you again," he said. She saw Ric and his family about once a month for Sunday dinner, but working with him was different.

"A part of me misses this place," Audrey replied.

"Well, we certainly miss you," he said.

She doubted that was true. After finishing her midwifery degree at the U of U, she'd worked at the hospital for about a year. She'd been a bullheaded midwife who'd made the medical students cry.

But Ric had become a good friend to her, a sort of father figure. Eventually, he'd invited her to attend church with his family. For most of her life, Audrey had been the opposite of a churchgoer, but soon she'd found herself desiring to know more about God. Now she attended church every week with Ellie.

"How's your home birth practice going? You're about to hit the year mark, aren't you?" Ric asked.

"Good. I have about two births a month, which is all I want," she said. "So I have more time to do volunteer work."

"You know," Ric said, "the doula program is always looking for volunteers. You did such an excellent job with the birth of Jessica's baby. And I'd be lying if I wasn't being a little selfish in asking you to sign up just so I could see you more."

"To be a volunteer doula?" Audrey asked.

"Why don't you talk to Mel. She's coordinating the volunteers. She can give you all the details, and then you can decide."

Audrey nodded. "I think I can carve out the time," Audrey told Ric. "I'll be sure to talk to Mel."

It would be nice to work in the hospital again. The hardest part about deciding to become a home birth midwife had been giving up her rights to the hospital. Audrey had enjoyed working there. She liked having a set schedule (two clinic shifts and two L&D shifts a week). And she loved the other nurse midwives and some of the doctors she had worked with. But she'd hated the bureaucracy and seeing women's birth preferences derailed because of unsupportive providers. She'd ultimately left because she wanted a smaller workload so she could get to know her patients better and provide more personalized care.

She loved helping women who seemed to need it most. Her home birth patients were mostly prepared for the experience of childbirth. They read books and took classes and approached birth with confidence. But she'd seen so many women show up to the hospital woefully undereducated or ill-prepared for birth. If she volunteered at the hospital, she could support these women. And maybe birth would be a better experience for them.

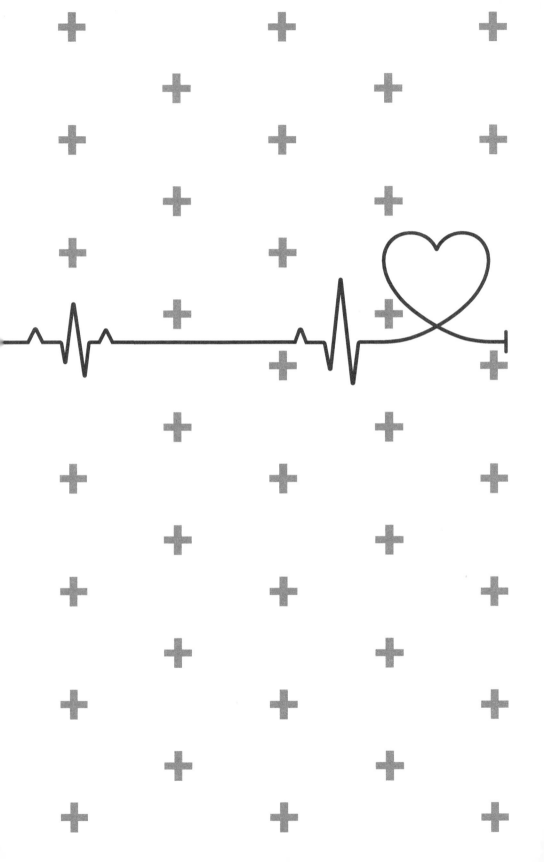

Chapter 8

AMMON SAT AGAINST A WALL outside the hospital, nursing a Red Bull and thinking terrible things about Audrey Novak. She'd just swept right into the room and taken over the birth, embarrassing him in the process. He went over every moment, trying to find an instance when she'd left her scope of practice as a doula so he could file a complaint against her, but he was coming up blank. She'd walked the line between doula and midwife with irritating professionalism. He took another sip of his drink. If he kept his focus on Audrey, he wouldn't have to look inward at his own failings and insecurities as a doctor. Because that was far too difficult. It was much easier to blame the pretty midwife. His therapist roommate, Freddy, would say this was all very unhealthy.

It was that time between night and dawn when the air was chilly and the sky purple, the sun still hidden behind Mount Olympus. Ammon pulled out his phone and logged into the Mountain Collective. He scrolled through his notifications, then opened his messages. He tapped on Bellinghamster's icon and typed, *How do you treat people you don't like?* Maybe he could learn something from her. It seemed the list of people Ammon didn't like was growing by the day, which was too bad because before medical school and his residency, Ammon had been a really fun guy.

Out of the corner of his eye, he caught a flash of familiar red hair. It was Audrey. He quickly stood, his heart racing. "Hey," he called. She stopped and turned around. She rolled her eyes as soon as she saw him. *Well, the feeling is mutual, babe.*

He closed the distance between them in two steps, ending up much closer to her than he'd intended. "I don't appreciate what you did back there," he said.

Audrey scoffed. "You mean offer a helpful suggestion that led to the safe arrival of a baby?"

"The next time you act as doula, let the doctors do their jobs."

Audrey looked up at him, her hazel eyes drilling into his. Something in the air changed between them. Her gaze remained intense, but the rest of her features softened as the sun peeked out from the mountains behind them. Her skin looked flawless in the early dawn. Ammon smelled rose petals in the breeze. *She'd be the perfect height to kiss.* The random thought irritated him further. If only she weren't so beautiful.

"You should have known the answer, Ammon," she said softly. The truth of her words cut more than any insult could have. And that was the problem. Ammon should have known. Dr. Sandoval was always trying to get him to see the less-invasive way.

Ammon took a step away from her, his pride taking a direct hit. All the shame and self-doubt he masked with arrogance threatened to bubble to the surface. He clenched his fists, trying to muster the anger to cover it all back up. It seemed like lately he was having more and more moments like this, when his carefully constructed facade of overconfidence could be destroyed with the tiniest insinuation of a weakness. He knew this wasn't sustainable. But he couldn't keep appearing to not have a clue what he was doing.

"Just don't step on my toes like that again," Ammon bit back. He walked away from her and went back to his place at the wall, letting off a string of Freddy Kappal curse words as he finished his energy drink. *Only two more years of residency*, he told himself. *Two more years.*

But then what? Would he really leave obstetrics and do family practice? He felt too far in to change specialties, and he'd have to start his residency all over if he switched to something new. If only he could feel as confident about his decision as he had when he'd first made it and when he learned he'd gotten his first choice residency in Utah. But nothing had felt right in the last year. When the rest of the residents seemed to finally be hitting their stride, he was floundering.

✦ ✦ ✦

Ammon found Dr. Sandoval at the nurses station. "Ah, Ammon, there you are," he said. "We need to prep for a C-section in OR B."

Ammon followed him down the hall as Dr. Sandoval gave him the patient details: scheduled C-section followed by a tubal ligation. Ammon would do both.

They stopped outside the OR and put on their masks, glasses, paper hats, and booties, then went to the sinks to begin the scrub-in procedure. Sandoval watched Ammon over his mask. "I understand you know Audrey socially," he said as he lathered his hands.

"Not really," he answered, puzzled about when Sandoval would have obtained this information. "I met her at church on Sunday, and she lives down the hall from me." Ammon scrubbed under his fingernails with the nailbrush. "Did you know she's not even a doula but one of those insane home birth midwives?"

Sandoval chuckled. "Yes, she's a home birth midwife, but I would never describe Audrey as 'insane.'"

Ammon raised his eyebrows.

"I've known her for about five years."

"She's had enough transfers that you've become buddies?" Ammon scoffed. That would explain why she was on a first-name basis with him.

Sandoval chuckled again. "I think I assumed wrong when I said you know Audrey."

Ammon gave a noncommittal bob of his head.

"I met Audrey when she was a midwifery student."

Ammon stopped scrubbing his hands and looked up at Sandoval. A midwifery student? That would mean . . . "Audrey's a CNM?"

Ammon could tell by the crinkle of his eyes that Sandoval was smiling behind his mask.

"She worked in our L&D department for about a year after graduating and then went on to build her own home birth practice. If anyone should assist women wanting to birth at home, it should be Audrey," Dr. Sandoval continued. "She's very good at what she does."

Ammon didn't know how to take this revelation. When he'd found out Audrey midwived babies at home, he'd assumed she had the minimum training necessary to do so and was therefore an unsafe provider. Utah had extremely lax home birth laws; anyone could be a midwife if they declared themselves one. And Ammon's time as a resident had shown him how dangerous an undertrained midwife could be: mothers showed up near death from blood loss, babies were born a shocking shade of blue, infection ravaged what should have been an otherwise healthy infant.

That Audrey was a certified nurse midwife with a master's degree in women's health, effectively the equivalent of a nurse practitioner, with all the prescribing power of a doctor . . . well, that changed his perception of her entirely. Why hadn't she mentioned this when they met on Sunday? Why did she say, "I'm a home birth midwife" and proceed to let Ammon dress her down? She had fought back, albeit not in the way he would have expected her to, given her schooling.

Audrey was an enigma, and Ammon couldn't decide if he should try to figure her out or let her be.

Chapter 9

AUDREY ARRIVED HOME FROM THE hospital at five thirty a.m. After being up all night, her limbs felt heavy, every step like trudging through quicksand. She walked past the couch, resisting the magnetic pull to lie down and sleep for two years.

Too tired to cook anything, she grabbed a protein shake from the fridge and settled into one of the hard wooden chairs at the table. If she sat on the couch or went to her room, she'd never get up. She had learned while on call as a midwifery student how to arrange her life so she could go at a moment's notice. If she got a call two hours from now from one of her patients that it was time, she needed to be able to leave right away. So right now, she needed food, a shower, and then rest.

To keep herself awake, she pulled out her phone and checked for messages. A text from Claire sent around midnight let Audrey know her patient had eaten well that day and the baby was kicking like crazy. There was a voicemail from her mom, which Audrey didn't bother listening to. She'd have to call her mom back at some point, but after she'd had a good night's sleep and a huge meal of comfort food. Then she'd be ready to deal maturely with whatever crazy her mom was going to dish. And there was a notification from the Mountain Collective. She opened the app and saw a message waiting for her from BelayingonofHands. *How do you treat people you don't like?* he asked.

Audrey took a sip of her protein shake. What an appropriate question. The image of Ammon's face, angry in the predawn light as he accosted her after the birth of Jessica's baby, popped into her head. Obviously, she hadn't been very nice. And she'd ignored her own mother, whom she actually loved. If she wanted the coordinates to Craggletooth Rock, she couldn't admit to this guy she was awful to people she disliked and liked. She needed him to think she was pure in heart, because now that she was thinking about it, maybe she wasn't.

If she told this guy she was always nice to people, he'd know she was lying. No one was always nice. But being honest about her shortcomings came with its own set of risks. He could decide she wasn't worthy of Craggletooth and put an end to this game. And then she'd be back to square one.

Audrey turned off her phone's screen. Maybe after she'd slept, she'd find the right words to be honest. She finished her shake, then dragged herself down the hall to shower.

✚ ✚ ✚

Ammon silenced his alarm for the fourth time, knowing that for every extra minute he slept, the harder the upcoming shift would feel. Extreme sleep deprivation felt so much better than slight sleep deprivation. It was the difference between waking up at four a.m. to catch a flight for vacation, the excitement ahead negating the lack of sleep, and waking up at eight a.m. for nine o'clock church. If Ammon could get up two hours before his seven p.m. shift started and get a run or some weight room time in along with a big meal, the night would go better. But the clock was quickly approaching six p.m. and Ammon kept hitting snooze. At this rate, he'd only have time for a quick shower and a McDonald's drive-through run, which then made the exercise that much more important. He didn't want to put on twenty pounds during his residency.

The door of his bedroom was outlined in light. Ammon had put tinfoil over his windows to block out the sunlight and shoved a rolled-up blanket against the bottom of the door, making his room dark enough for middle-of-the-day sleep. Ammon often found himself disoriented. Was the light outside from a sunrise or a sunset? Clocks had become a sort of lifeline for him. Whenever he entered a room for the first time, he searched the walls until he found one. They grounded him when, most of the time, he felt like he was floating in a semireality. There were few windows in Labor and Delivery, and when he was home, he was asleep in his self-created cave. It could be day or night. It could be Monday or Saturday. And because he caught random bits of sleep in so many different places, he could be anywhere.

Ammon could hear Freddy clanking around in the kitchen. Maybe he had cooked enough for both of them. A guy could dream. Ammon sat up and yawned. He gave himself a pep talk before getting out of bed. *You just got to walk a few steps to the bathroom. Once you shower, you'll feel better.*

His phone chimed with a notification. He put his glasses on and read the screen. It was a message from Bellinghamster. He suddenly felt wide-awake.

Here's the honest answer, she wrote. *I don't treat people I dislike as generously as I should.*

Blatant honesty. Huh.

However, it's a weakness I'm aware of. I can be hotheaded and judgmental, and sometimes my expectations for people are too high.

Whoa—that was exactly how Ammon would describe himself, if he ever chose to be introspective.

I think I can try harder to be nice, to give people the benefit of the doubt, to let things slide and not say whatever horrible thing pops into my head. I don't have to always be right or the smartest. But I can strive to be the kindest.

That's my honest answer. I am horrible to people I don't like. But I'm willing to improve.

Ammon tapped the phone against his chin. That was a little unexpected. Then again, he wasn't really sure what he'd been expecting.

He typed back a reply: *Your honesty definitely works in your favor. Any specific ideas how to be nicer to people? Asking for a friend.*

Ammon left his room, the light from the hall scorching his eyes. He blinked rapidly and made his way to the kitchen. Freddy stood at the counter, assembling a turkey sandwich. The guy had even sliced a tomato. Ammon's mouth began to water, his submandibular glands aching. "I'll give you a million dollars if you make me one," Ammon said.

Freddy wielded a mayo-covered knife. "Nope," he said. "All I want is your firstborn."

"Done."

Freddy got out two pieces of wheat bread. "You like yours with lots of ketchup, right?"

"And don't forget the grape jelly."

Freddy nodded thoughtfully but slathered the bread with mayo. "Ellie said you worked with Audrey last night. How was that?"

"When did you talk to Ellie?" Ammon asked, deflecting.

"She texted me about rock climbing this weekend and mentioned Audrey doula'd one of your patients."

"Can I come climbing with you?" He really wasn't interested in talking about Audrey. Plus, he'd only been climbing a handful of times since moving back to Utah two years ago, and he was dying to climb more.

"Of course." Freddy held the sandwich out. Ammon reached for it, but Freddy pulled it back. "If your firstborn is a boy, you must name him Freddy. If she is a girl, she will also be named Freddy. Got it?"

"Got it," Ammon replied, taking the sandwich. He took a bite. "You can have my secondborn, too."

Chapter 10

As Audrey pushed open the doors to Labor and Delivery, she recited to herself the reasons she was coming by so late. She'd taken a longer nap than she planned. She'd gone to the grocery store and then Target, and well, going to Target was never a quick thing. She'd wanted to give Jessica plenty of time to bond with her new baby before checking on them. Mel, the volunteer doula coordinator, told Audrey she'd be working overnight and to stop by after seven p.m.—they'd been good friends when Audrey had worked at the hospital before. Coming to the hospital at nine p.m. had nothing to do with the fact that Ammon might be around. But Audrey's pesky, traitorous eyes still searched for him as she walked to the nurses station.

She'd spent most of the day thinking about him. Not in *that* way. But thinking about how they'd once again argued. The message from BelayingonofHands had forced some introspection, and this time she was determined to have a conversation with Ammon that didn't end in hostility. She'd hold her tongue, no matter what he did or said. She needed to be a better person so she'd actually be worthy of Craggletooth Rock.

Audrey found Mel at the nurses station, and Mel handed her a clipboard of paperwork. Audrey started filling in the blanks, which took a long time because every five seconds she kept popping her head up to check for Ammon.

She finished the paperwork and handed the clipboard back.

"I won't make you go through the mandatory orientation," Mel said. "When would you like to start?"

"How does next Thursday sound?"

"Great. We'll see you then."

Audrey headed to the bank of elevators to go up a floor to Jessica's room. Jessica had texted and assured Audrey she'd still be up, as her new baby wasn't letting her get any sleep. The door to the elevator slid open just as she arrived. Ammon stood inside, flipping through a chart. Audrey sucked in a breath, failing to calm the butterflies in her stomach. Okay, here was her chance. She stepped in and saw the floor she needed was already selected.

"Hi," she said, her voice coming out much quieter than she expected.

Ammon glanced up from the chart and returned his gaze to the papers. She waited for his obligatory return greeting, but it never came. She took a slow breath. *Do not engage, do not engage*, she repeated to herself. Pointing out his rudeness was not kind. He knew he was being rude. He had obviously seen her and was choosing not to talk to her. So Audrey could choose to not be rude back. It was simple. So simple. So, so simple. She felt a pressure growing between them, like she was swimming to the very bottom of the deep end of a pool.

The elevator chimed and the door opened. Ammon ducked his head and swiftly exited. Audrey let go of the breath she'd been holding. Her kindness campaign might be a little harder than she'd anticipated.

When she got home later that night, Audrey wrote back to BelayingonofHands.

Here are the steps I'm following for my kindness campaign. You may share them with your "friend."

1. *Avoidance. Don't seek him out. Don't go where he will be.*
2. *Do not engage. If you end up in the same room as him, do not play into his rudeness. Be polite and professional. Be above it.*
3. *Keep your mouth shut. See above.*
4. *Think before you speak, or more specifically, don't say the horrible thing that pops into your head, because sometimes you will have to talk to him.*
5. *Apologize. In the likely event you do end up saying something horrible, be quick to say sorry, because you know he never will.*

A response came back within a few minutes, which surprised her. It was eleven p.m. *I couldn't help but notice your use of the pronoun* he. *Is it possible you're thinking of a specific person? Or is* he *a universal placeholder? I think in the current political climate the gender-neutral* they *is the more appropriate pronoun.*

Audrey couldn't help but smile. BelayingonofHands had some wit to him. She kind of liked it. She typed back, *I am thinking of a specific person. Just a guy I sometimes work with. He's just your typical insecure egomaniac.*

Audrey grimaced after sending the message. That was a decidedly ungenerous assessment of Ammon. Ugh, even when he wasn't around, she couldn't be nice to him.

BelayingonofHands wrote back. *First, I think your kindness campaign is already a failure. And second, I sometimes work with a woman who could be described as "your typical insecure egomaniac," but I would never use those words. I'm a nice guy. ;)*

Audrey smiled again. *So nice you'll tell me where Craggletooth Rock is?*

TBD, he replied.

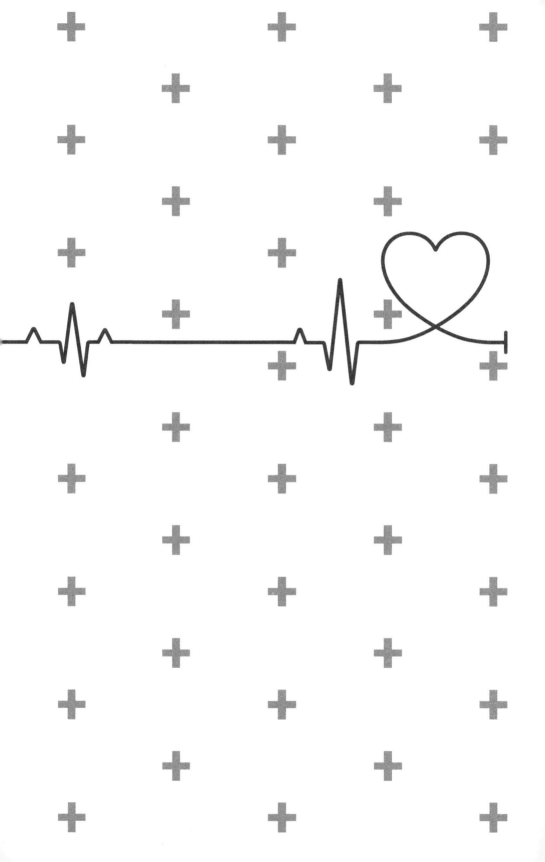

Chapter 11

THE DAYS WERE LONG, AND the rest of Ammon's week went by in a sleepless blur. The only good thing about working the night shift was getting Friday and Saturday nights off. He could have some semblance of a social life.

He had been up for hours Saturday morning when Freddy finally left his room and shuffled down the hall at seven. If Ammon wasn't careful, he'd mess up his carefully devised sleep schedule to keep him nocturnal. So even on his two days off, he stayed up until midnight and slept for four hours. He'd take another nap from four p.m. to eight p.m.

Freddy ran a hand through his dark hair, making it stand on end. "Ellie wants to leave in the next ten minutes."

Ammon shrugged. He was ready. "You can tell Ellie it was my fault when we're late."

"Aw, you're such a good friend."

Ammon cooked eggs while Freddy "freshened up"—his words. They ate, then headed to the parking lot where Ellie waited, leaning against her car, scrolling through something on her phone. She didn't look up for a whole thirty seconds. And when she did, her gaze was bored. "So I *didn't* imagine the conversation where we agreed to go rock climbing this morning," she said sarcastically.

Ammon frowned. He'd had only a few interactions with Ellie over the last two years he'd been back in Utah, and each one left him wondering why Freddy liked her. Maybe the fact that she looked like Gal Gadot had something to do with it: dark hair, smoldering brown eyes, lips with just the right amount of pout. Ellie was gorgeous but too intense and moody for Ammon—much like her roommate, Audrey. Those two were peas in the proverbial hot-but-mean-girl pod.

"Ammon had some bathroom troubles this morning," Freddy said.

Ammon held in a groan. *Way to throw a guy under the bus.*

"Bad burrito," Freddy continued.

Ellie rolled her eyes and mumbled, "Gross." She pushed herself off the car and opened the driver's side door.

"Was that necessary?" Ammon asked through his teeth.

Freddy flashed him a smile. "Less likely to get a lecture or questions this way."

Freddy took the passenger seat, and Ammon sat in the back. Freddy did most of the talking as they wound their way up Little Cottonwood Canyon. They pulled off at Coalpit Gulch. Ammon knew the climbing area well.

They left the car and walked down the trail toward the rock face. Ammon took in a deep breath, the green smell of the early, cold April air cleansing his lungs. The sunshine felt like a long-lost friend. Working indoors was counter to his nature. Before med school, Ammon had been an avid climber, hiker, and mountain biker—a stereotypical outdoor junkie. His hair had been long, and he'd sported an unkempt beard. He had a bandanna in every color. But he didn't feel like that person anymore.

When they cut out of the trees at the rock face, Ammon noticed a woman standing with her back to them. Her hair was tied up in a pink bandanna, and there was something familiar about the way she stood.

"We're finally here," Ellie called.

The woman turned around, and Ammon's heart *womp-womped*. It was Audrey. Of course. It was only natural a crunchy midwife would also be outdoorsy. Her Michelle Obama arms were proof enough that she climbed.

She smiled at Freddy and Ellie but didn't even glance at Ammon. Since she'd already set up the top ropes, the route was ready to climb.

"Ammon knows how to belay," Freddy volunteered. "Me and Ellie want to go first." Great. Ammon would have to stand next to Audrey for the next half hour.

The two climbers cinched on their harnesses, and Ammon avoided looking at Audrey. She still hadn't said anything to him yet either.

Once Freddy and Ellie were scaling the rock face, Ammon decided it was time to break the silence. He thought about Bellinghamster's kindness campaign. He could be nice to Audrey.

"Dr. Sandoval said you used to work at the hospital," he said. A friendly, neutral topic. They both liked Dr. Sandoval.

"Yeah."

Ammon waited, but she didn't say anything else. He glanced at her. She kept her attention trained on Ellie. Ammon returned his gaze to Freddy and let out some rope for him.

"You're a CNM," he said. "Any reason you didn't mention that when we first met?"

"I didn't think it mattered," she replied, still not looking at him, which was fine because she *should* be paying attention to Ellie, but he couldn't help but feel like she was being rude. "You already seemed to have your mind made up about me," she continued and turned to him briefly. Man, she was pretty. She had the perfect amount of freckles. He noticed a tiny hole in the side of her nose where she might have once had a nose ring. Interesting.

"Of course it matters," Ammon replied, returning his attention to Freddy and the ropes. "You're a highly qualified birth professional. I can respect that."

She scoffed. "Because you know I've done a lot of schooling and hold an advanced degree, I'm suddenly worthy of your esteem?"

"Yes—no. What I mean . . ." He thought of what Sandoval had said about Audrey and thought again of the kindness campaign. "What I meant is if someone is going to help women give birth at home, I'm glad it's someone with your qualifications."

She narrowed her eyes at him. "Do you even hear yourself?"

What had he said wrong this time? "Yes. You're a highly—"

"Qualified birth professional," she finished with him. "Birth doesn't have to be a complicated medical event, Ammon. You don't need an advanced degree to catch a baby. I know plenty of women who didn't undergo the same training as I did who are competent and safe midwives. Don't be so elitist."

Kindness campaign, kindness campaign, Ammon chanted to himself. *Do not say the horrible thing that has popped into your head.*

He shook his head. "Maybe we should talk about something else."

Audrey blinked and opened and shut her mouth a few times before speaking. "Okay. Yeah." She let out a small growl. "Sorry for the ad hominem attack."

Ammon turned his head up to Freddy and Ellie. "Apology accepted." A silence grew between him and Audrey. It wasn't a nice silence, though, since he worried she was still seething over something he'd said. Why were things so explosive—and not in a good way—between them?

+ + +

Audrey felt like she was diving too deep, the silence building an uncomfortable pressure between them. Clearly, she had no self-control when it came to Ammon. The guy grated on every wrong nerve. He seemed to bring out the worst in her. She stole a peek at him. It was too bad his inside didn't match his beautiful outside.

"So you like to climb?" Ammon asked, glancing in her direction. She averted her eyes, color rising to her cheeks. Had he noticed her ogling him again?

"Yes," she answered too quickly. It sounded like she was snapping at him. She bit the inside of her cheek and cringed inwardly.

More awkward silence. They watched their climbers scale the rock face. "What's your favorite climb?" he asked.

"I like Maple Canyon," she said, trying to soften the edge around her voice. He seemed to be making an effort, so she would too. She needed to get back on her kindness campaign to make up for her earlier rudeness. "What's your favorite climb?"

"Actually, Maple Canyon."

Audrey let out the rope for Ellie. She and Freddy were getting close to the top.

"You know what I haven't been able to figure out?" Ammon said.

She eyed him warily for a moment. "What?"

"Why I never saw you at the hospital before. Sandoval said you started your home birth practice only a year ago, and I've been at the hospital for two. Our paths should have crossed before now."

She felt the line pull in her hands and looked up to Ellie. "I spent a year volunteering before starting my practice," she answered, letting out more rope.

"Really? What did you do?"

Audrey didn't love talking about her volunteer work. She worried about coming off as pretentious. "I worked in Ethiopia with Doctors without Borders."

She felt his eyes on her and stole a glance. He didn't wear sunglasses today, and she couldn't decide if she'd describe his eyes as sapphire or cerulean. His scrutiny made her skin feel prickly.

"That's really cool," he finally said. "I want to do something like that as soon as I finish my residency. If I can manage to stay single."

Audrey scoffed before she could stop herself. "If you can manage to stay single? Are women throwing themselves at your feet in droves?"

He shrugged and turned his attention back to Freddy. "Actually, girls at church tend to get weird when they find out what kind of doctor I am. So it's likely I'll stay single."

She bristled at his use of the word *girls* when he really should have said *women* but decided to let it go. Kindness campaign and all. "Yeah," she said. "I can see that. Why did you choose obstetrics, anyway?"

"Miracle of childbirth," he said.

Audrey laughed. Actually, she snorted. "No, really. Why choose obstetrics? You don't even seem to like women."

"I more than *like* women," he said.

Freddy and Ellie reached the top. "Hey," Freddy shouted down. "We're going to take some pictures."

"I didn't mean it *that* way," she replied, letting go of Ellie's rope. "I meant you don't seem to *respect* women. And it is a little questionable why you'd want to be caring for a woman's lower half." As soon as the words left her mouth, Audrey tensed. She was awful. Why couldn't she be nice to him?

Ammon crossed his arms across his very fine chest. "You know, you're just as bad as every other woman I've met since starting residency. Because I'm an attractive, straight, unmarried male, I must be some sort of pervert for going into women's health?"

"So you think you're attractive?" Audrey asked. Kindness Campaign: out the window.

"I've had it confirmed a time or two," Ammon replied smugly.

"Does your arrogance know no bounds?"

The corner of Ammon's lip quirked up. "I've seen you checking me out."

Audrey rolled her eyes. "I haven't been checking you out," she said. It was, of course, a bold-faced lie. She had been checking him out. A lot. More than was decent.

"Audrey." The sound of his voice saying her name did something weird to her stomach.

"Ammon."

"You're not even the tiniest bit attracted to me?"

"No," she said.

He took a step closer to her and bent his head to lock eyes with her. "Really?" He took another step. His blue eyes smoldered. She would have been annoyed if it weren't so hot. "Are you sure?"

She steeled her gaze; meanwhile, goosebumps broke out over her arms. He was close enough now that she knew he used Tide laundry detergent and had a small scar on his left cheekbone. He had just the right amount of scruff on his face. Her eyes drifted to his lips and lingered.

"Because," he said, closing more of the space between them. Her eyes met his again, and his pupils dilated. "I can admit that when you're not talking, you're kind of pretty." He angled his face and inched his body closer, closer. "I like your freckles." His breath smelled like cinnamon. He reached out and trailed his fingers down to her neck, resting on her pulse point. An extraordinary shiver moved down her spine. Even if Audrey's face appeared as unaffected as she hoped, her rapid pulse under his fingers gave her away. "And there it is." She felt his breath in small puffs on her lips, the sensation shocking and delicious. "I win," he said, a whisper of space between them.

"Belay!" Freddy yelled from above. Ammon pulled away from Audrey, a triumphant grin on his face.

Audrey blinked, and heat rushed to her cheeks. That little . . .

"Belay!" Ellie called, and Audrey grabbed the rope. "You play dirty, Ammon Parker," she said, not risking a glance at him.

"It's the only way to play," he replied.

Chapter 12

His phone's beep startled Ammon from sleep. Was it time to get up already? In the dark, he slapped his hand around on the top of his nightstand until it landed on his phone. He brought the screen to life and squinted at the time: 3:36 a.m. The beep hadn't been his alarm. It was a message from Bellinghamster. Who was this woman who kept strange hours like he did? He found his glasses and read her message.

Yesterday was a kindness campaign failure, she wrote. *That guy I sometimes work with has infiltrated my circle of friends. I tried my best to follow all my guidelines, but I was horrible to him anyway. He seems to bring out the worst in me. And the worst of me is shockingly bad. I make Darth Vader seem like a nice guy. But I can't seem to help myself. He represents everything I detest and work against. I have no idea what I'm going to do. Avoiding him altogether is not an option anymore, and if we end up working together, I'll have to talk to him. I'd love to say he's the one who starts it, but I know it's me. I'm the problem. Maybe a kindness campaign is too ambitious. Or my guidelines need to be revisited. Given how unpure my heart is, should I give up on your ever telling me how to find Craggletooth Rock?*

Ammon sat up and replied. *Your guidelines worked pretty well for me, so don't give up on them just yet. Maybe you need to change your approach. I ended up kind of flirting with the woman I don't like, and it played to my favor. I *might* have laid it on a little thick, but it disarmed her long enough for us to stop fighting. But now she's probably in love with me, and that'll create its own set of problems.*

Bellinghamster's response came back instantly. *Flirt with him? Also, I doubt she's in love with you. No one has that kind of charm.*

Ammon smiled. *I can be very charming. You're an impeccable speller, by the way. I really admire that in a person.*

Bellinghamster: *Is this you trying to flirt with me?*

Ammon: *Maybe.* He repositioned himself, settling back against his pillow. *Flirting is my default language when I talk to women socially.*

Bellinghamster: *I see.*

Ammon: *What are you doing up so early?*

Bellinghamster: *Working. Oh, gosh! Did I wake you?*

Ammon: *It was almost time for me to get up anyway.*

Bellinghamster: *Do you really think flirting with him will work? What if it backfires and I end up making a fool of myself?*

Ammon: *You don't have to flirt with him. Just offer him some compliments. Egomaniacs love praise.*

Bellinghamster: *There's absolutely nothing I could compliment him about. Unless I were to say, "My life is so much better when you're not around."*

Ammon chuckled out loud. This woman was pretty entertaining. He typed back, *I want you to compliment this guy the next time you see him and report back how it went. It will be your first task.*

Bellinghamster: *And this proves I'm pure in heart how?*

Ammon: *It demonstrates you're humble enough to take my awesome advice. I followed your kindness campaign and had a positive outcome (i.e., former enemy is now in love with me), so I'm sure compliments will work for you.*

Bellinghamster: *Fine. I'll try it. P.S. She's not in love with you.*

+ + +

"You're not looking forward to seeing her," Ammon said to his reflection. He turned on his electric razor and moved it along his cheek, manscaping his scruff. With the long hours he worked, being cleanly shaven was impossible. If he kept a purposeful five-o'clock shadow, he could go a few days without having to shave.

"She doesn't actually like you. She was angry, not attracted," he continued, thinking about Audrey's rapid pulse under his fingertips. "Plus, you're too busy for a romance with a prickly midwife."

Freddy pounded on the bathroom door. "Are you done with your affirmations?"

Ammon flung the door open to find Freddy standing in the hall. Had he been listening?

"I can't believe you still do that," Freddy said.

"Yeah, well, they work," Ammon replied. "Don't you tell your clients to do positive self-talk?"

Freddy shrugged. "So you've got a crush on a certain prickly midwife?"

Drat. He *had* been listening through the door. "More like she has a crush on me," Ammon said.

He found her physically attractive, but he'd rather not spend time with a woman who thought so little of him, hence the pep talk in the mirror. Whatever misguided signals his hormones were sending him needed to be squelched. Flirting with her had probably been a mistake, but like he'd told Bellinghamster during their early-morning chat, it was the easiest way he'd found to communicate with women. Plus, Audrey was fun to tease. Another reason he needed to stay away from her. If he wasn't careful, he'd end up in something toxic.

"I'm pretty sure Audrey hates you," Freddy said.

Ammon crossed his arms over his chest. "Hate's a little strong, don't you think?"

"Detests, then."

"Semantics," Ammon mumbled.

Freddy slapped him on the shoulder. "Now, get out of the bathroom."

✛ ✛ ✛

Ellie sidled up to Ammon in Sunday School and took the empty chair next to him. "Freddy's teaching the other Sunday School class," Ammon said.

"Which is why I'm here," she replied, revealing her teeth in what he thought was supposed to be a smile but couldn't quite tell. Ellie scared him. Audrey wasn't afraid to tell Ammon exactly what she thought of him. Ellie played nice, which in many ways, was worse. Kind of like a stalking cat: sleek and beautiful in the grass until the moment she pounced. "But I'm surprised you're here too."

"I get enough of Freddy's pontification by living with him," Ammon replied.

Ellie nodded. "I bet."

Ammon surveyed the room for familiar faces. Ellie really was the only person he knew in their church other than Audrey and Freddy, so he should probably be grateful he wasn't sitting alone or, worse, with a marriage-minded female. He couldn't help but notice he'd not seen Audrey at church.

"She's at a birth," Ellie said.

"I wasn't—"

Ellie's expression killed whatever lame thing he was going to say.

"She got called away at two a.m. or something," Ellie said. "She texted at nine to say not to expect her anytime soon."

Ammon knew long births were hard on both the laboring woman and her birth attendants. He was lucky he got to leave at the end of his shift even if the baby hadn't been born yet. Audrey, he imagined, had to be there the whole time.

Instead of paying attention to the lesson, he wondered what, if anything, Audrey did to move labor along. At the hospital, he'd suggest Pitocin and would break the patient's water. But how would he manage a home birth?

He thought about the different tricks the doulas and nurse midwives at the hospital used. He'd probably start with motion: walking, rocking, dancing, sitting on a yoga ball, squats—whatever she felt most comfortable doing. They could also try hydrotherapy, massage, or visualizations. Eventually he could break the patient's water, but that increased the risk of infection, so it would have to be a last resort.

Ammon stopped himself. *Well, look at that.* He did know how to manage a labor without hospital intervention. Dr. Sandoval would be so proud of him.

Chapter 13

AFTER TWENTY-FOUR HOURS OF LABOR and still no baby, Audrey knew it was time for a transfer to the hospital. Her patient Kelly hadn't progressed beyond five centimeters in the last five hours. Audrey had even broken Kelly's water two hours ago, and still nothing had changed.

Audrey held the fetal heart Doppler to Kelly's stomach and listened. The fast whoosh of the baby's heartbeat sounded through the dim room. Baby was fine, but Kelly was getting tired. Continuing at home wouldn't be dangerous, but Audrey wasn't sure it was in her patient's best interest. At this rate, Kelly would have nothing left in her when it came time to push.

Another contraction started, and Audrey listened carefully to the baby's heart rate. Kelly's birth team surrounded her: husband fanning her face, doula providing counterpressure at her hips. Kelly let out a low guttural moan as the contraction peaked. "Baby sounds great," Audrey said when the contraction ended. She looked from Kelly to her husband, Mike, to her doula, Jen, nodding her head in what she hoped appeared reassuring, but she knew everyone was exhausted. Kelly had gone into labor Saturday night around nine p.m. and hadn't called for Audrey to come until two a.m. Sunday. Now it was late Sunday night.

Another contraction came, and Audrey stepped back, letting Kelly's support team take care of her. Audrey went to her apprentice, Charlotte, who dozed on the couch. She nudged the young woman's shoulder and her eyes fluttered open. "What? Oh, Audrey. Sorry! Did I sleep too long?"

She rubbed Charlotte's arm. They'd been taking catnaps in shifts. "It's okay. It's been a long labor."

"Is the baby almost here?" Charlotte sat up quickly, her tired blue eyes suddenly bright.

"No," Audrey said, keeping her voice quiet. "I'm going to suggest a hospital transfer since she's stopped progressing. We've tried everything, and I think she needs Pitocin. I want you to observe how I suggest this, as many home birthing mothers find this upsetting."

Charlotte nodded and yawned. She and Audrey moved back to the other side of the room. Kelly was breathing through another contraction, and Audrey waited for it to end. Then she crouched down in front of her, offering her a water bottle.

"How are you feeling?" Audrey asked.

Kelly panted between sips of water, her face sweaty from exertion. Her doula massaged her shoulders. "I'm really tired," Kelly said.

Audrey grabbed her hand and squeezed it. "I bet. You've been doing such amazing work. I'm so proud of you."

"Do you think she'll be here soon?" Kelly asked. "I don't know how much longer I can do this." Tears appeared at the corners of her eyes.

"You and Baby are both healthy," Audrey said. "But you haven't progressed in the last five hours. We can continue to wait to see if things change on their own, but transferring to the hospital to get some extra help might not be a bad idea."

Kelly's eyes were wide as she looked from her husband to her doula.

"It's up to you," Audrey continued. She glanced at Charlotte, who observed the conversation with her usual intense curiosity.

Another contraction started. Audrey pulled back again since Kelly's birth team had a system that was working for them. Audrey was as involved as the patient wanted her to be. At some births, she sat in the corner the whole time until the mom caught the baby herself, and then Audrey would step in for immediate postpartum care. At other births, she provided comfort measures and was an integral part of each moment.

She handed the water bottle over again once the contraction ended. Kelly took desperate sips.

"What would a transfer look like?" Mike asked. "What would happen when we got to the hospital?"

They had discussed this scenario weeks ago during a prenatal checkup, but Audrey didn't mind going over it again.

"Since this isn't emergent, there's no reason to call 911. We'll take separate cars to the hospital and present Kelly at Labor and Delivery as a home birth transfer. I'll give a brief rundown of the labor and hand over care. At that point, I'll act as additional labor support. I suspect they'll want to start you on Pitocin and will offer you pain management."

More tears leaked from Kelly's eyes, and Audrey's stomach clenched. She could imagine what Kelly was feeling. Women who birthed at home did so for a reason. Suddenly having to change plans, to decide to birth in a place she had been wanting to avoid, had to be disappointing and maybe even scary.

Audrey took Kelly's hand again. "Think about it. Talk through it. Either way, I'm here."

+ + +

An hour later, Audrey was driving to the university hospital. It was about eleven p.m. when she pulled into the parking garage. She offered a silent prayer for her patient and birth team. Mike had taken Kelly to the front of the hospital and dropped her off with Jen. Charlotte pulled up in her car and parked next to Audrey.

Charlotte slugged along beside Audrey as they made their way up to the hospital. This was only Charlotte's second birth and a bit of a rough introduction. She was Ellie's friend, Freddy's cousin, and a student at Midwives College of Utah. Charlotte was shadowing Audrey a semester earlier than her program required. She'd just gotten married a few months before, and her husband, Charles, wanted to start a family. Charlotte was determined to finish her program before that happened.

Kelly and Jen waited at the elevators for Audrey and Charlotte to join them. "Mike's parking the car," Jen said. "He'll meet us upstairs."

Kelly sat slumped in the wheelchair. Her face was pale, her blonde hair stuck to her sweaty forehead, and her eyes were bloodshot from crying or lack of sleep, maybe both. Audrey crouched down in front of her. "Talk to me about what you're feeling."

A contraction started, and Kelly scrunched up her face.

"Breathe down and relax," Jen said, brushing a hand over Kelly's tensed forehead. "Picture the contraction as a wave and ride it out."

Kelly let out a shriek as the contraction peaked and a low groan as it ebbed. "You did so great," Audrey said. Charlotte held the water bottle as Kelly took a few sips. Mike joined them.

"Are you ready?" Audrey asked Kelly.

"I'm scared," she said, her eyes welling up with tears.

"I know," Audrey said. "This isn't what you planned for, but we just need a little extra help. I trust the doctors here. You'll see your baby soon."

Mike put his hand on Kelly's shoulder and squeezed it, then wheeled her into the elevator, the others following. They all got off at the second floor. Audrey led the way to OB emergency, where Mel greeted them.

"Hi, Mel," Audrey said. "We have a non-emergent home birth transfer. Is Kathleen or Ric working tonight?"

Mel gave Audrey a hug. "Kathleen's here."

Audrey nodded. When she had to transfer care, she wanted an OB who wouldn't vilify or passive-aggressively punish her patients for attempting to birth at home like many doctors and nurses did. Kathleen and Ric were her go-to doctors.

Mel took over pushing Kelly's wheelchair as they moved down the hall. She introduced herself to the birth team and made reassuring statements as she set Kelly up in a triage room. Two contractions happened in that time, and Audrey could sense Kelly was becoming more and more defeated.

Once the monitors were hooked up, Mel turned to Audrey. "Give me all the details."

Audrey handed her Kelly's chart and summarized the important information, and then Mel went to Kelly and spoke to her softly. Kelly replied through tears. Her husband held one hand, and her doula held the other.

"What happens now?" Charlotte asked Audrey as they watched the scene.

"The doctors take over," Audrey said. "We'll provide Kelly with whatever she needs, be it physical or emotional support or advocacy. And we'll celebrate when the baby arrives."

Chapter 14

AMMON WALKED DOWN THE HALLS of Labor and Delivery, a slight bounce in his step. It was his favorite part of the day: quittin' time. He couldn't wait to get home, scrub the hospital smell out of his skin, and settle in for bed. He headed for the nurses station to sign out and skittered to a stop. Audrey leaned against the counter, talking to Mel, one of the hospital's nurse midwives. It took less than a second for him to regain his stride, but he almost tripped as he made his way to the computer. As he logged into the system to clock out, his fingers hit all the wrong keys. Geez, this was ridiculous. He didn't even like her. At. All. Why was his body behaving like this?

Mel glanced at him, and Audrey turned around. Her eyes widened just a little, and her cheeks started to pink. Was she thinking of their almost-kiss from Saturday? Because suddenly, all he could think about was her racing pulse under his fingers. He approached the two women.

"Hey, Mel," he said, trying to appear cool.

"Hey, Ammon," she replied, then gestured to Audrey. "This is my friend Audrey."

Ammon tried to keep his face expression-free. "We've met. What are you doing here?"

"I had a transfer." Audrey stood straighter.

He couldn't stop the self-satisfied smirk that appeared on his face. "Did you, now?"

Fire lit Audrey's hazel eyes, and Ammon's heart vaulted against his rib cage. Mel muttered something about a patient and slinked off.

"I don't have to explain anything to you," Audrey spat. Ammon flinched at her vitriol. She closed her eyes and took a deep breath. "Sorry. I've been up for almost thirty hours. I'm not my best self."

"I understand," he said instead of the horrible thing he wanted to. Kindness campaign for the win! "What we do is hard work." He had the impulse to reach out and pat her on the back but didn't move.

She rubbed a hand over her face and let out a quiet growl. His skin prickled. What was she thinking? He should probably walk away now before she blew up again. When she removed her hand and looked over at him, her smile was almost pleasant. Yeah, he needed to leave, but his feet were not getting the signal.

"You're right. We do hard work," she agreed. "My patient would have stayed in labor for days without the help of doctors like you." She reached out and grabbed his arm. Her eyelashes fluttered a little. *What was happening?* "I value what you do."

Ammon glanced at her hand on his arm. "Are you trying to flirt with me?"

She removed her hand like she had touched something hot. "No! Gah, I was trying to be nice."

Ammon chuckled. "You *were* flirting with me."

Audrey stood there, cheeks flaming, her jaw clenched. A smile stretched painfully across Ammon's face. "Were you trying to play by my rules?" He fluttered his eyelashes in a poor impression of her.

"I'm tired, and my eyes went all twitchy."

His grin grew even bigger, if that was possible. "You don't have to lie, Audrey. It's okay. I have that effect on women."

"Arrogant jerk," Audrey muttered and stomped away.

Ammon laughed, and a few of the nurses who had seen the exchange gave him side-eye. Yeah, he was a total jerk. But right now, he was a smiling jerk.

+ + +

Ammon woke up at five p.m. He dressed in a pair of basketball shorts and an old T-shirt from his long-term mission to Peru that had a cartoon llama saying, "*¿Cómo se llama?*" Freddy came through the front door of their apartment just as Ammon entered the kitchen. "You wanna go to the gym?" Ammon asked as he went to the pantry to gather ingredients for a protein shake.

Freddy put his keys in the dish on the counter and removed the lanyard with his ID badge from around his neck. "Yeah. Let's get swole," he said, flexing his biceps. He gestured to the protein powder. "Make mine a double," he said and headed down the hall.

Ammon put two bananas, peanut butter, whole milk, and protein powder in the blender and pulsed until everything was smooth. His mouth watered as he poured it into a cup: a testament to how abysmal his diet was as of late. If a protein shake was the most delicious thing he ate in a day, there was a problem.

Freddy joined him in the kitchen. He pointed from his shirt to Ammon's. "Twinsies!" and gave him a high five. They had volunteered in the same mission in Lima, Peru, and had been roommates for six straight months at the end of Ammon's service. Freddy had gotten home a year later, and they'd stayed friends. When Freddy's sister, Lucy, got married in March and he'd needed a roommate, Ammon had jumped at the chance.

After they finished their protein shakes, they headed to Windy Corner's gym. Ellie was on an elliptical. "I think I'll warm up over there," Freddy said and took the treadmill next to her. Ammon picked a stationary bike and took his phone and keys from his pocket, setting them in the cupholder. He watched Freddy and Ellie across the room as he began to pedal. He didn't know Ellie well, but he had noticed the only times he'd ever seen her laugh or genuinely smile were with Freddy.

He checked around the room for Audrey but didn't see her. He couldn't tell if what he felt was relief or disappointment. She'd looked absolutely adorable fluttering her eyelashes in her poor attempt to flirt. He pumped his legs harder and tried to get her out of his head. She was beautiful, but that was it.

His phone buzzed, and he slowed his pace as he took it from the cupholder. He had a message from Bellinghamster in the Mountain Collective. His stomach did a little flip. He opened the app.

You give terrible advice, she wrote. *I complimented him. He thought I was hitting on him. It was humiliating, and now I must go into Witness Protection so I never have to see him again.*

Ammon couldn't stop a huge grin from appearing on his face. *I'm sure it wasn't that bad*, he wrote back.

I'm never going to live this down, she replied.

Maybe he was just caught off guard.

She sent back a thumbs-down emoji. *I don't care anymore. He's impossible. And now I'd like the coordinates to Craggletooth Rock.*

Not yet, Bell, he wrote. *I sense you're a real go-getter, and that plays to your favor. And it's admirable you were humble enough to take my so-called "terrible advice." I'm almost persuaded you're pure in heart.*

She sent another thumbs-down emoji, and Ammon laughed.

"What's so funny?" Freddy had appeared at his side.

Ammon turned off the screen of his phone so Freddy wouldn't be able to read the exchange. "Just talking to some girl online."

"You playing the field?" Freddy wiggled his eyebrows.

Ammon gave him a look. "Does anyone actually say that?"

"Me. I just did." Freddy's grin brightened. "Let's pump some iron so this conversation can feel manly."

They went over to the lat pulldown machine.

"Did you meet her on a dating app or something?" Freddy asked, adjusting the weights.

"No. Some forum for people who climb. She wants the coordinates to Craggletooth."

Freddy sat down and started his reps. "You're telling a complete stranger the coordinates, but you won't tell me, your very best friend?"

"You helped me set the course," Ammon said. "It's not my fault you forgot how to find it."

Freddy rolled his eyes and did another rep.

"Anyway, I haven't told her," Ammon continued. "I'm trying to suss her out, see if she's the type who will keep it a secret."

"I'd keep it a secret."

"You've never kept a secret a day in your life."

Freddy seemed to think for a moment, then shrugged. "I would keep this a secret. I know it's important to you."

"I'm not going to tell you."

"But you're going to tell her."

"I don't know."

"It's because she's pretty, isn't it?"

Ammon shook his head. "I actually don't know what she looks like."

Freddy stood from the machine, and Ammon got on. "But you were smiling all goofy, so you must like her."

"I don't know. She lives in Washington, so it doesn't matter anyway." Ammon did a few reps. Did he like her? He found her funny, and he enjoyed their back-and-forth. But he hadn't been thinking about her romantically.

Freddy glanced across the room to Ellie before turning back at Ammon. "Maybe I should get an internet girlfriend. Because women in real life are way too complicated."

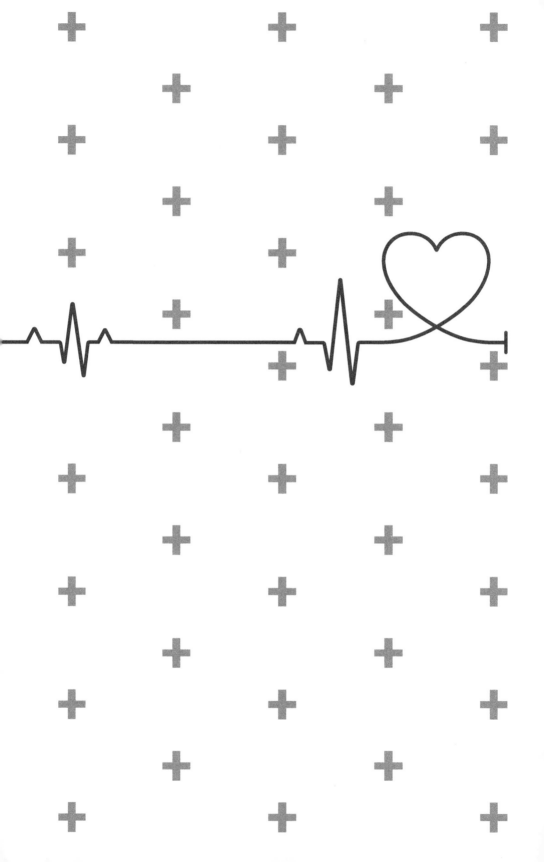

Chapter 15

CLAIRE MET AUDREY OUTSIDE THE free clinic Tuesday morning. Her round belly pressed against the buttons on her shirt. "Dr. Ferguson said the baby is breech."

It took Audrey a minute to register what Claire said; her brain was still foggy from lack of sleep. After she'd come home from the hospital Monday morning, she'd slept most of the day and then had slept poorly that night. She couldn't stop thinking about Ammon and his arrogant grin. Her cheeks burned whenever she thought about that moment at the nurses station. Of course the egotistical jerk would think she'd been trying to flirt with him when she'd just tried to compliment him like Belay had suggested.

Audrey clicked her bike lock closed. "When did you see Dr. Ferguson?" she asked as they stepped through the clinic's door.

"On Friday." Claire followed Audrey to the check-in counter. "I was so worried about the baby's heartbeat that I didn't want to wait a whole week to hear it again."

Had it only been a week since Audrey had last seen Claire? It felt like a month. So much had happened. Audrey signed in at the computer behind the front counter of the clinic. "And she told you the baby's breech?"

Claire nodded.

"Let me take you back to an exam room, and we can talk more." Audrey found Claire's chart and led her back, and Claire settled onto the edge of the exam table. Audrey found the Doppler. "Let's listen to her heartbeat first."

Claire pulled up her shirt, and Audrey applied lubricant to the Doppler's wand. She pressed it against Claire's stomach. Baby's heartbeat whooshed. "A hundred and forty beats per minute. Perfect." Audrey then felt around

Claire's stomach. "There's baby's head," she said pressing on the area below Claire's ribs. Last, Audrey measured fundal height. "Thirty-four inches for thirty-four weeks. Right on track."

Her patient smiled. Audrey handed her a tissue to wipe the lubricant off her stomach, and Claire pulled her shirt back down and sat up.

"So Baby is breech," Audrey said. "But you're only thirty-four weeks along, so there's plenty of time for her to flip on her own."

"What if she doesn't?"

"Dr. Ferguson can try to flip her externally; the procedure is called an external cephalic version. There are exercises you can do. I can try some of my midwife tricks." Audrey smiled and winked. "If she won't flip, though, you might need a C-section, or you can ask Dr. Ferguson if you're a good candidate to attempt a breech delivery. If she's still breech closer to your due date, we'll have a more in-depth conversation about your options."

Claire's forehead remained creased with worry. Audrey found a notepad and wrote down *spinningbabies.com*. "Why don't you visit this website and try some of the exercises to get her to flip."

"Okay." Claire nodded and took the slip of paper Audrey handed her.

Audrey sat down on the stool and pulled herself in front of Claire. "How are you feeling?"

"Scared."

Audrey nodded. "It's normal to feel that way."

"I just want her to be healthy, you know?" Claire replied. She shook her head and looked away. "And I kind of want my mom, too."

Audrey ached at her words. She could only imagine how much it hurt Claire to have her mom disown her. Audrey understood how disappointed Claire's mom must be in her, but to kick her out on her eighteenth birthday when she'd been sixteen weeks pregnant seemed more than a little harsh. Claire wasn't even able to finish her senior year of high school because she'd had to start working full-time to support herself.

Audrey took Claire's hand, thinking of the vital role her own grandmother had played in her upbringing. Audrey's teen mom had been much less mature than Claire, but Claire still needed support.

"I'll be at the birth, no matter what," Audrey said. "And you can call me anytime. I'm serious."

Claire nodded. Audrey could only hope the girl's mom came around in the next six weeks.

Chapter 16

AUDREY BIKED HOME AFTER HER shift at the clinic, her legs feeling like sandbags. It took her at least forty-eight hours to recover from a long birth, which would put her at Thursday. And Thursday was her first overnight shift as a volunteer doula at the hospital, so her sleep would get messed up again. The good news was she had only one more patient due this month and then two patients due at the end of May. Things would settle down for her soon.

She locked up her bike and headed inside. Ellie sat working at her usual place on the living room couch. She appeared to be in the zone, so Audrey didn't bother greeting her. She went down the hall to her room with every intention of lying down, when her phone chirped. Her heart did a little flutter. *Is it Belay?* The reaction surprised her. She hadn't really thought too much about him, but she did enjoy chatting with him. It was nice to talk to someone who could keep up with her.

She tapped in her phone's password and saw it was a text from her mom. Audrey had been avoiding her mom for over a week now and was never going to be well-rested enough to talk to her. She might as well call before her mom sent the cops over to check on her. Audrey settled on her bed, taking a few deep breaths before hitting the call button. The phone rang twice, and when her mom picked up, she didn't say anything, apparently waiting for Audrey to speak first.

"Hey, Mom."

"Well, well, well. I was starting to think you had died."

"That's a little dramatic," Audrey replied.

"Is it? I don't hear from my daughter for a week and I'm supposed to assume you're okay?"

"Yes." Audrey said the words through her teeth. Her mom's immaturity bugged her almost as much as Ammon's ego did, which was probably why Audrey had moved to another state and only returned her mom's calls once in a blue moon.

"So how are you?" her mom asked.

"Busy."

Silence on the other line.

"Good. I'm good," Audrey continued. "I've had two patients deliver in the last week. I went rock climbing over the weekend. I'm remembering to take a multivitamin. Anything else you want to know?"

"Are you still doing all that Jesus stuff?"

It took supreme effort for Audrey to hold back a groan. Her mother asked her this every time they spoke. Audrey's converting three years ago was an affront to her mother's Matriarchy Now brand of feminism.

"Yes, I am," Audrey replied.

"Humph."

Audrey waited for her to continue or change the subject. They'd been through the rounds on this one too many times. When her mom didn't say anything, Audrey spoke. "Is there a reason you wanted to talk?"

"In fact, yes," her mother said. "Two reasons. I've been cleaning around the house, and I came across a shoebox full of birthday cards your father sent you."

Audrey felt an uncomfortable pinch in her chest. That he could still make her ache after all these years caused a rush of anger to quickly replace the hurt. "Toss them," she said. "I thought I'd gotten rid of all that stuff years ago."

"All right," her mom replied. "The other reason I'm calling is because I'm actually a little low on cash at the moment."

Audrey wanted to bang her head against the wall. Her mom was *always* low on cash. "And I've learned of a new business opportunity," she continued.

"A business opportunity?" Audrey stifled a laugh. Her mom was always learning of new business opportunities. Trying to sound interested, she said, "Tell me about it."

"It's lipstick that never comes off."

"Uh-huh."

"Really, Audrey. It's amazing stuff. You can eat and kiss and brush your teeth, and the stuff doesn't budge."

"Interesting." Audrey didn't wear much makeup—just mascara and sometimes lip gloss.

"And I was thinking I could start a little beauty-supply business. I already sell those nail-polish strips, and that business is booming."

Audrey didn't know what her mom's definition of "booming" was, because most of the time, her "booming businesses" were actually collapsing. And if things were so good, why was she low on cash?

Audrey's childhood had been strange. Her mom had had her at nineteen, and Audrey had only seen her biological father a handful of times in her life. Her mom could never keep a conventional job and frequently "invested" most of her money on the latest get-rich-quick scheme. Audrey's grandmother had been the stabilizing factor in her life. They'd lived with her for most of Audrey's childhood and adolescence, except for a few short time periods when her mom would declare it was time they make it on their own. Inevitably, they would have to move back home with less money than they'd left with.

When Audrey was growing up, her mom did Amway, Mary Kay, Avon, Tupperware, Pampered Chef, Melaleuca, and USANA, and she didn't get rich from any of them like she was supposed to. In the last decade, it seemed like a new multilevel marketing company sprang up monthly, so her "business opportunities" were constantly changing.

"I also sell those weight-loss wraps," she continued. "And you know I love my oils. So with me selling from all four of those companies, I've got the whole body covered."

"That's actually not a bad idea," Audrey said, surprised with how much thought her mom had put into this.

"I just need a hundred bucks to become a lipstick distributor."

Audrey shook her head. "Can you write up a business plan first and email it to me?" She'd found over the years that if she made the money contingent on her mom doing something for it first, her mom would never follow up.

"I just told you my plan. You said it was a good idea."

"It is. So just type up a few paragraphs to help solidify your ideas, and I'll send you the money."

"Audrey, why do you do this to me?"

And here came the hysterics and guilt trips.

"It hurts that my own daughter doesn't believe in me."

"Mom, what I'm asking for isn't unreasonable. If you were to ask the bank for a loan, you'd have to write a business plan. It will take you fifteen minutes, tops."

"I let my mother have too much influence over you."

Audrey rolled her eyes. Her grandmother was the reason Audrey had turned out as functional as she did.

"Mom, I've got to go, okay?"

"What about—?"

"Email me a business plan and the money is yours."

Audrey hung up. She closed her eyes and took a deep breath. *Okay. That really wasn't so bad.* The call had ended with her frustrated but not hurt or in tears. That was a nice change. But the frustration sat like a bowling ball on her chest. She wanted someone to vent to. Ellie was home, but her upbringing was even sadder than Audrey's. Ellie would pretend to listen and be sympathetic, but the whole time, Audrey knew she'd be thinking, *At least you have a mom.* Freddy Kappal was a good listener, but he was a therapist by profession, so he'd probably want to psychoanalyze her. And Audrey had been so busy lately she'd neglected her other friendships. She couldn't call someone she hadn't spoken to in months just to complain about her mother.

The only other person she'd been communicating with regularly was BelayingonofHands. She tapped open the Mountain Collective app but hesitated. Was it totally pathetic that she wanted to count this stranger as a friend? Were they friends? She liked talking to him. She enjoyed his quick wit. And he seemed genuinely interested in getting to know her.

What's your family like? she asked him.

Little dots appeared almost instantly, indicating he was writing back.

Big and close-knit, he replied. *Mom and Dad have been married for forty-five years. I have five siblings. We all get along great. It's kind of disgusting, really.*

Audrey laughed.

BelayingonofHands: *Why do you ask?*

Audrey: *Just curious, I guess. My family is pretty unconventional: I had a teen mom, was raised by my grandma, Dad wasn't around, had no siblings (that I know of). It could be kind of lonely.*

She stared at the last sentence. Wow. She'd never really admitted that before, not even to herself. She debated deleting it but left it and sent the message. Part of being lonely was wanting to connect, and maybe this would allow her to connect with him.

BelayingonofHands: *I'm sorry you were lonely.*

Audrey: *I've always been envious of people like you, with big, close families. Growing up, I wanted a brother or sister so bad; they'd have been another vulnerable person who understood what it was like to grow up with my mom's instability. I think that's what attracted me to the teachings of Christ and finding a church community. I love how family-centric everything is.*

BelayingonofHands: *I guess I don't know what that kind of loneliness feels like. I'm the opposite: I get lost because there are so many people and personalities to compete with. By the way, nice use of the semicolon. You're kind of making me swoon.*

Audrey smiled. *There you go, flirting again.*

BelayingonofHands: *So you go to church?*

Audrey: *Every Sunday.*

BelayingonofHands: *Me too. Do you have a family of your own now?*

Audrey chewed on her lip as she considered her reply. Was this line of questioning violating their agreement on anonymity? She wasn't really revealing telling details that would make it possible for him to look her up on Instagram or discover her address. It was probably okay if she answered.

No, she typed back. *It's just me.*

BelayingonofHands: *Oh good. I was worried for a minute there that I was trying to flirt with a married woman.*

Audrey: *So can I assume you're not married either?*

BelayingonofHands: *Single. Probably for a reason.*

Audrey laughed again.

BelayingonofHands: *Does your mom get after you for not being married, or is that just something my mom does?*

Audrey: *My mom thinks marriage is an oppressive patriarchal institution. But I think she only says that because she was never able to maintain a serious relationship. When I was young, her quest for "the one" was almost as constant and desperate as her quest for the next easy buck.*

BelayingonofHands: *My mom is the opposite of yours. I need to be married, STAT.*

Audrey laughed again. *You're kind of funny.*

His reply didn't come right away. And instead of staring at her phone, waiting for a reply like an eager high schooler, Audrey checked her email to see if her mom had sent anything yet. She hadn't, which wasn't a surprise. In fact, it was likely her mom wouldn't write up a business plan and would instead borrow the money from her boyfriend of the month.

Audrey tried hard not to think too much about her childhood. She had done a lot of therapy in college to recover from it. In adulthood, she'd established healthy boundaries between her and her mom, and things had been good for her since moving to Utah five years ago to complete her CNM degree. That she had started going to church and stayed in Utah had been a shock to both Audrey and her mom, but Audrey loved her life here.

Her phone chirped. It was Belay. *Hey, Bell, I've got to run, but maybe I could message you sometime tomorrow?*

Sounds good, she wrote back. Her face split into a huge smile. Oh, this was bad. Stupid, too, getting a crush on some internet guy. But she couldn't stop smiling for the rest of the evening and probably fell asleep with the grin still on her face.

+ + +

Ammon was scrubbing into surgery when he realized he'd been humming. *Humming.* He instantly stopped but not before feeling Dr. Ferguson's grin. "You've been in a good mood all evening," she said, her eyes crinkled with amusement above her surgical mask. "Any particular reason?"

Like Ammon was going to share with Dr. Ferguson that he may or may not be getting a crush on a woman he met online. They'd only chatted a handful of times, and while Bell was witty and intelligent, he didn't need to be going around humming.

"I must have slept well or something," Ammon replied.

Dr. Ferguson let it go, and they headed into the operating room where their C-section patient was being prepped.

Ammon loved surgery. He loved the ritual of scrubbing in. He loved the coolness of the operating room. He loved the clicking of the metal tools on their metal tray. He loved the moment when a baby went from unborn to born in an almost instantaneous transition. The OR was where he felt the most confident in his doctoring abilities.

Ammon went to the other side of the surgical drape to say hi to the patient and her husband again. "Are you ready to meet your daughter?"

The couple smiled back at him with nervous nods.

"She'll be here soon," he said.

Ammon joined Dr. Ferguson on the other side of the drape. He began swabbing the patient's stomach with iodine. Classical music floated through the room, Dr. Ferguson's preferred birth music. "After you pull the baby out," she instructed, "we will lower the surgical screen enough to place the baby directly on Mom's chest for immediate skin-to-skin contact."

"I remember," Ammon replied.

"If the cord is long enough, we'll do delayed clamping and cutting."

"Got it."

Dr. Ferguson held the scalpel out to Ammon. "Are you ready, Dr. Parker?"

Ammon nodded. Before he made the first incision, he said a silent prayer. He always did. It took an immense amount of faith to cut someone open, and he needed all the help he could get.

+ + +

BelayingonofHands: *Keanu Reeves: great actor or greatest actor ever?*

Bellinghamster: *You're kidding.*

BelayingonofHands: *Come on. Didn't you see* A Walk in the Clouds*? A truly artistic performance.*

Bellinghamster: *What are you doing watching* A Walk in the Clouds*?*

BelayingonofHands: *I've seen all the chick flicks. I've got a bunch of sisters.*

Bellinghamster: *I thought for sure you'd say* Bill and Ted's *represents his best work.*

BelayingonofHands: *Don't gender stereotype me like that. Keanu Reeves can play any character in any movie because he delivers every line in the same monotone voice. But he's at his best in romance. Don't even get me started on the genius of* The Lake House.

Bellinghamster: *Is this your way of telling me you're actually a ghostlike being from the future/past and we have to wait for our timelines to match before we can meet in person?*

BelayingonofHands: *There you go again, using "your" and "you're" correctly. I'm a puddle.*

Bellinghamster: *UR weird.*

BelayingonofHands: *Please don't.*

Bellinghamster: *Pls dont what*

BelayingonofHands: *A real comedian.*

Bellinghamster: *What's with you and good grammar, anyway?*

BelayingonofHands: *It makes me feel like the person on the other end cares about what they're saying. I mean, you must not use abbreviations and a ton of emojis for a reason.*

Bellinghamster: *I guess I do care about what I'm trying to say. I want to represent myself well.*

BelayingonofHands: *I appreciate that. And you do.*

Bellinghamster: *I wish I could say the same for you. You were scoring pretty high points in my book until you revealed your Keanu Reeves fetish.*

BelayingonofHands: *Not a fetish. Fandom.*

Bellinghamster: *I totally see the difference now. Thanks for clearing that up.*

BelayingonofHands: *So what kind of movies do you like?*

Bellinghamster: *The old kind.*

BelayingonofHands: *Silent films. Interesting.*

Bellinghamster: *Not that old.*

BelayingonofHands: *Let me guess: black and white films with sharply dressed women and fast-talking men.*

Bellinghamster: *Yup. I'm very unoriginal.*

BelayingonofHands: *What's your favorite movie?*

Bellinghamster: *Probably* Casablanca.

BelayingonofHands: *I've actually never seen that movie before.*

Bellinghamster: *I think you just gave yourself your first task.*

BelayingonofHands: *Hey, I'm the one who's supposed to be assigning tasks.*

Bellinghamster: *And you haven't been. So it's my turn. I want you to watch* Casablanca *and tell me why it's considered one of the best films ever made.*

BelayingonofHands: *Okay, but be prepared for a task of your own soon.*

Bellinghamster: *I look forward to it.*

Chapter 17

WHEN AMMON ARRIVED FOR HIS shift Thursday night, there were only three patients on the floor. It was either the calm before the storm or the beginnings of a long, slow night. He forgot to check the weather report before coming in. Thunderstorms always made for a crazy shift. So did full moons. With so many empty beds, he was likely to acquire a few induction patients during the early evening and again in the early morning since there would be space for them.

He met his attending physician for the shift at the nurses station. Dr. Callister was the opposite of Dr. Sandoval. Where Sandoval was polite and considerate, Callister was cocky and brash. Ammon had seen Callister bully patients until they became speechless shells, and the guy looked for any excuse to add an intervention, where Sandoval was much more likely to let nature run its course. While Ammon might gripe about Sandoval's approach, he disliked Callister's even more. Or maybe he just disliked Callister.

"Parker. Come with me," Callister said by way of greeting. "Let's see if we can clear the floor by midnight." He grinned big and winked. Ammon definitely got to perform more C-sections when he worked with Callister. But at what cost to the patient? *That's probably something Audrey would think. Ugh.* He hated how often he thought of her.

They entered the first patient's room, and Ammon came to a halt just inside the door. Speak of the redheaded devil. Audrey stood at the patient's bedside, rubbing her back. What was she doing here? If this was another home birth transfer, Callister would have mentioned it by now. He would have made sure the patient knew it was a mistake to attempt birth at home.

Callister went through the patient's chart with Ammon, not bothering to introduce himself to the patient or Audrey. The patient appeared to be asleep; maybe that was why he didn't announce himself. But he flat-out ignored Audrey, which Ammon found rude, even for Callister.

Audrey stepped away from the patient. "Are you her doctor?" she asked Callister.

He gave Audrey a cursory glance. "She sees my colleague Dr. Tyler. I'm the doctor on call tonight. But Dr. Parker here"—he gestured to Ammon—"will be managing her labor under my supervision."

Callister went back to discussing the patient but now kept looking at Audrey like he couldn't keep his eyes off her. Ammon couldn't either. He still didn't understand what she was doing with this patient.

"Wait," Callister said, his eyes narrowing. "You used to work here. You were one of the nurse midwives."

Ammon noticed her jaw clench. "Yes, Dr. Callister, I was," she replied.

"What are you doing here? Last I heard you went off to Africa."

"I'm one of the volunteer doulas."

Oh. That made sense. But that didn't mean Ammon was looking forward to working with her.

"This patient doesn't need a doula," Callister replied. "She's already had her epidural placed, and she's asleep right now. You can go somewhere else, preferably home."

Ammon found himself sending Audrey an apologetic frown. She stood a little taller and leveled her chin. Ammon recognized it as her fighting stance. *Uh-oh.*

"Her name is Susan, and she requested a doula. Her husband is in Montana on a construction job and might not make it to the birth. She has no family nearby and doesn't want to be alone. She might be asleep now, but she will eventually wake up and need me."

"Fine. Stay," Callister mumbled and gave Ammon a look, one that said, "She's the worst." He glanced at Audrey once more, then continued his instructions to Ammon in Spanish. It was something Callister did when he didn't want the patient to know what he was ordering. "Check her cervix, break her water, and start Pitocin," he said. "Don't bother waking her up for any of it."

Ammon felt a little queasy but nodded. The subtext of the instructions made Ammon's skin crawl: patient consent didn't matter. Callister left the room, and Ammon approached the patient. Susan. He could feel Audrey's eyes on him.

"What did he ask you to do?" she asked in a low voice.

"The usual," Ammon replied. "Check dilation."

"*No la despiertes*," Audrey said. "Don't wake her up."

"You speak Spanish?" Ammon asked.

"I speak enough to get by during a birth." She shook her head. "Are you really going to leave her asleep? Don't you think she deserves to know what's happening to her body?"

Ammon felt his blood pressure rise. He would never check a patient's cervix while they were asleep. How dare Audrey lump him in with the likes of Callister!

Granted, he hadn't decided yet if he was going to wake Susan now or wait and see if she woke up on her own in the next hour. The latter would involve Ammon trying to avoid Callister for the next hour, which would be easier if it were a busier night. Callister did not like being disobeyed.

"How long has she been asleep?" Ammon asked, trying to remain professional and not let Audrey see how much she irritated him.

"Maybe fifteen minutes."

Ammon sighed. "I'm going to have to wake her up."

"I'd like you to come back later. She's had prodromal labor for the last three days and is exhausted."

"I'd like to, but I need to check her progress."

"And break her water and start Pitocin," Audrey added. "All without her permission." Her voice was rising. Ammon pulled her away from the patient. "You can come back later," she whispered through her teeth.

"I can't disobey my attending," he said.

"I'm not going to let you touch her."

Ammon stared her down. She had such passion in her eyes. It was both moving and irritating how deeply she cared about someone she'd just met. Her body was as tense as his, every sinew and ligament a taut line. Her breath came out in little puffs. There was an energy between them, like two magnets of the same charge, repelling off each other. But if one of them moved just the right way, they'd slam together.

"Audrey, please, let me wake her up." His voice came out gentler than he expected, a sincere plea. "Callister will come and check her himself, and he won't wake her up."

She sighed and took a step back. "You have to talk to her about breaking her water and starting Pitocin before you do any of that."

"I was going to," Ammon said. "What kind of doctor do you think I am?"

Audrey appraised him for a moment. "I'm not sure."

Ammon went to Susan's bedside and gently shook her. Her eyes fluttered opened. He gave her a moment to wake up and orient herself before he introduced himself. Then, with her permission, he checked her dilation and found she was six centimeters along. They discussed breaking her water and the use of Pitocin. She didn't want either. She wanted to delay as long as possible in hopes her husband made it in time. He was still four hours away. Audrey had remained quiet while Ammon and the patient spoke, leaving every decision up to Susan. He hated to admit Audrey behaved exactly as a good doula should: providing the patient with support and not injecting her personal biases and preferences into the birth.

Ammon left the room, a tightness in his chest. He'd have to tell Callister the patient didn't consent to the interventions. Most of the attendings were like Dr. Sandoval, eager to engage the resident in decision-making, willing to teach and demonstrate. Callister just liked having someone to boss around, and he found it amusing to humiliate and pick on residents.

Ammon felt someone grab his arm. He turned around to find Audrey. She pushed her curls out of her face, and Ammon wondered if they felt as soft as they looked. "You're not going to order Pitocin anyway, are you?" she asked.

Ammon held back an eye roll. When was she going to realize he wasn't a bad guy? "*I'm* not," he said. "But I can't stop what Callister decides to do. And I'm about to get chewed out, so maybe you'll want to stick around. It might make your night."

Audrey bit her bottom lip and looked away. "Throw me under the bus if it means you save face. Tell him I physically stood between you and the patient, and our fighting woke her up." She looked back at Ammon then. "I've gone head-to-head with Callister before. He might not remember, but I do. And since I don't really work here, I'm just a volunteer; I don't have much to lose."

Ammon eyed her suspiciously. "Why are you suddenly being nice to me?"

She sighed and bit her lip again. Was she trying to get him to notice her mouth? Because it was totally working. "Let's try to be professional and help each other out while we're here, okay?"

Ammon had to fight hard not to smile. Was he winning whatever unspoken competition they had going on? First her flirting with him and now this. "Okay."

"As long as you've got the patient's best interest in mind, I'll back you up," she continued. "But I won't hold back if you do something wrong."

"And here I was thinking you'd gone soft on me." He smiled now, and Audrey narrowed her eyes. He glanced at her neck, where her pulse fluttered under her smooth, pale skin. He really wanted to touch her.

"You'd better get back to work," she said. She turned and disappeared into the patient's room. Ammon shook his head and went to find Callister. Tonight was proving to be much more interesting than he'd expected.

+ + +

"Her husband's here. I want you out of my delivery room," Callister said to Audrey.

She acted like she hadn't heard and didn't move from Susan's side. "Would you like me to leave?" Audrey asked Susan.

The woman glanced at Dr. Callister and back to Audrey. Her eyes were round, and Audrey could feel the fear coming off her in waves. Susan's epidural was wearing off, and it was time to push. The anesthesiologist had been called, but he was still in surgery and it was likely he wouldn't make it before the baby came.

"Can you stay?" Susan asked. A contraction came on. Her face grew red as she panted and pushed. Audrey held her hand and spoke in a calm voice, reminding her to relax and breathe down. "Please stay," Susan said when the contraction ended.

"I'll stay." Audrey shot a glance over her shoulder at Callister. Ammon entered the room then and suited up to catch the baby. Callister switched to Spanish.

"What's he saying?" Susan asked. Audrey tried to listen, but Callister spoke fast and quiet, and her Spanish was really rudimentary. She caught words like *dilation* and *epidural*. Dr. Callister was the reason Audrey had started learning birth terms in Spanish. She needed to know what to warn her patients about.

"I think he's just catching Dr. Parker up on what's happening."

Another contraction came on, and Audrey talked Susan through it, reminding her she could push as much or as little as she wanted. "Would you like to know how close the baby is to coming out?"

Susan nodded. "I just want this to be over."

Audrey went to the end of the bed. Callister gave Audrey a look of disdain. "What are you still doing here?"

"My job," she replied. She then spoke to Ammon. "How is Susan's progress?"

"She's close to crowning," he said.

Audrey smiled. "Thank you." She returned to Susan's side just in time to support her next contraction.

Callister spoke to Ammon in Spanish again. She heard the word *episiotomy* as he passed the sterile package of surgical tools over to Ammon. Fury erupted in her chest, but she had to keep her outward appearance neutral. She didn't want to alarm Susan. Audrey kept her attention trained on Ammon to see what he would do.

Ammon glanced at Audrey before speaking to Callister in English. "We don't know if she'll really need one. Plus, her epidural has worn off. We'd need lidocaine."

Susan squeezed Audrey's hand. "What are they talking about?"

"Dr. Callister would like to perform an episiotomy," Audrey replied in a quiet voice.

"He wants to cut me . . . down there?" Susan asked, horror in her eyes. "Won't I feel it?"

"If you don't want one, you'd better say so now," Audrey replied, successfully sounding positive and not at all horrified. Callister often performed episiotomies without asking or even warning the patient first.

Another contraction was building. Audrey motioned to Susan's husband to hold her hand and moved to the end of the bed. Ammon held the unopened package but hadn't moved. "You need to do it now," Callister said. "Or she'll tear."

"Hi, me again," Audrey said cheerfully. She could see hatred in Callister's glare. This man had no business working with women. "Susan has some questions about what you're talking about."

"Oh, does she?" Callister replied sarcastically.

Ammon chimed in, "I'm happy to answer them." He kept the surgical tools and went to Susan's side. Audrey could have hugged him, but Callister fumed.

"I remember you perfectly now," Callister said to Audrey. "You assaulted me once."

Audrey held back a laugh. "Pushing you out of the way to stop you from breaking a patient's water without her consent is not assault."

"I tripped."

"Probably because your head is so big. It's hard to balance."

Ammon returned to the end of the bed. "She doesn't want an episiotomy."

"Big surprise," Audrey mumbled, and she rejoined Susan and her husband.

Callister kept an eye on Audrey for the rest of the birth.

When Ammon caught a healthy baby boy a few contractions later, Susan didn't tear. Not even a little.

✦ ✦ ✦

Saturday afternoon, Audrey pulled into her parking space at Windy Corner. She'd just returned from a hike by Parley's Creek and felt rejuvenated. The past week had been too busy and emotionally trying. Getting outdoors and enjoying some time alone in the spring sun was exactly what she needed.

She moved to open her car door when a car pulling in two spaces down from her caught her attention. The driver was Ammon. Her pulse jumped, and she slouched down in her seat. She didn't want to see him or, worse, walk into their building at the same time. Yeah, he'd worked well with her the other night at the hospital, but that didn't mean she wanted any extra interactions with him. She'd just stay in her car until she saw him go in.

She peeked out her car window to see if he'd left his car, but he sat in the driver's seat, typing on his phone. Ugh, what was he doing?

Her own phone chimed. She glanced at it and saw it was a message in the Mountain Collective. Forgetting she was trying to lie low, she snatched up her phone and opened the message. It was BelayingonofHands. *Okay. I watched* Casablanca.

Audrey smiled as her heart pitter-pattered. She felt excited and silly. *And?* she typed back.

BelayingonofHands: *I'll admit it's a *little* better than any Keanu Reeves film.*

Audrey: *Just a little?*

BelayingonofHands: *Maybe a lot better.*

Audrey: *And? What else did you think about it?*

BelayingonofHands: *I was surprised by how many of the lines are in our everyday lexicon.*

Audrey: *Lexicon. A ten-dollar word.*

BelayingonofHands: *The movie is iconic.*

He sent a quote from the movie to her, and she sent one back. They went back and forth a few times, and Audrey grew a little more smitten with each exchange.

What else did you think about the movie? she asked when she ran out of lines to quote.

BelayingonofHands: *Do you really want me to go into an essay on the film's use of lighting to convey its themes? Or how it's a moral tale about doing the hard thing for the greater good? How Rick is really just a romantic but hides it under his cynicism?*

Audrey: *No, you pass.*

BelayingonofHands: *Good. So anything new with you and the guy you don't like?*

Audrey hazarded a glance over to Ammon's car. He still sat there looking at his phone.

Audrey: *The last time we worked together wasn't so bad. Probably because I was also working with someone I dislike even more.*

BelayingonofHands: *You dislike a lot of people.*

Audrey: *I know. It's because of my hubris.*

BelayingonofHands: *A twenty-dollar word.*

Audrey: *My biological father was such a messed-up guy that I have an instant distrust of men.*

BelayingonofHands: *So you probably don't trust me.*

Audrey: *Not at first. But I think I could.*

BelayingonofHands: *High praise from the Bellinghamster. Speaking of which, are you from Bellingham, Washington?*

Audrey: *Born and raised. It's such a small town; I'm surprised you've heard of it.*

BelayingonofHands: *I lived in Seattle for a few years. You've got to drive through Bellingham to get to Vancouver.*

Audrey hesitated before typing the next question, but now she was curious. *Where do you live now?*

BelayingonofHands: *SLC. And you?*

Audrey: *SLC.*

BelayingonofHands: *We could have seen each other on a climb and not known it.*

Audrey: *I think we just breached our agreement about keeping this anonymous.*

BelayingonofHands: *And look how easily it happened. You must trust me after all.*

Audrey: *We've gotten off track. You said you'd have a task for me. What is it?*

BelayingonofHands: *I've decided to ask you a question instead.*

Audrey: *Should I be nervous?*

BelayingonofHands: *Why do you want to find Craggletooth Rock so bad?*

Audrey stared at his words on the screen and rested her head back against her seat. She closed her eyes for a moment and tried to breathe through the sudden ache before typing, *I had a friend who really, really wanted to climb it, but she died before she could. I want to make the climb as a tribute to her.*

His response was delayed. *Wow. That's not at all the reason I was expecting.*

Audrey: *It's the least I can do for her now.*

BelayingonofHands: *Can I ask how she died?*

Images from the day Shannon died flashed through Audrey's mind. *Complications from pregnancy.*

Audrey switched off her phone as emotion rolled through her. She couldn't talk about this anymore. She left her car and went inside her apartment. When her phone chimed, she didn't check to see what BelayingonofHands had to say.

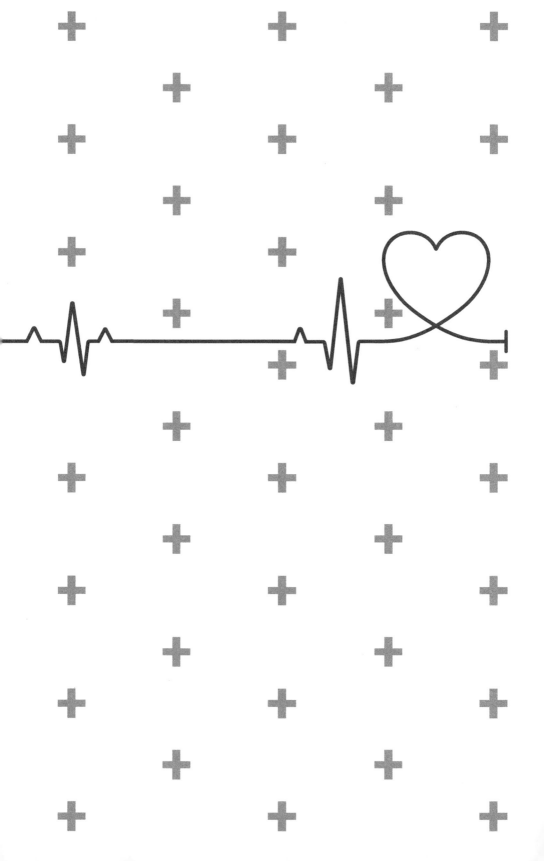

Chapter 18

SUNDAY AFTERNOON AMMON SAT AT one of the tables at his parents' house, surrounded by four of his five sisters, their spouses, and many of his nieces and nephews. The room was warm and filled with voices and laughter. But Ammon might as well have been on the moon. Two things occupied his thoughts: One, Bellinghamster actually lived in Utah and not Washington like he'd originally thought. This knowledge made him feel a little unsteady. He kind of liked her, but the crush had felt pointless when he'd thought she lived a few states away. If she lived in the same city as him, suddenly, this could become a whole lot more real. He wasn't sure how he felt about that yet. And two, he couldn't stop thinking about the friend she wanted to climb Craggletooth Rock for. What kind of pregnancy complication had she died from?

In the last twenty-four hours, it had become clear to Ammon that Bellinghamster was the type of person he could trust with the coordinates to the route. She was honest and cared about other people. But a part of him worried that if he gave them to her now, they'd stop talking. And he really liked talking to her.

He left the kitchen table, quickly put his plate in the dishwasher, and escaped to his old bedroom. His mom had turned it into a guest room while he'd been in Peru, but he still thought of it as his. He pulled out his phone as he settled on the bed, and opened the Mountain Collective app. *I can't stop thinking about your friend*, he wrote.

Her reply came a few seconds later. *I think about her a lot too. Not as much as I used to though.*

Ammon: *Do you want to talk about it?*

Bellinghamster: *Not really, if that's okay.*

Ammon wanted to press for details but worried that doing so might reveal what he did for a living. While they seemed to be moving in a direction of less anonymity, he wanted her to take the lead on that since it had been her rule. But he still wanted to know what happened to her friend. Death in childbirth or due to pregnancy-related complications was rare in the U.S., although he couldn't help but think Audrey would be quick to point out that that number was rising. The U.S. was the most dangerous industrialized nation to give birth in. In his two years at the hospital, one mother had died, and it hadn't been one of his patients, but it had shaken everyone in the Labor and Delivery unit.

He decided to change the subject. *How was your day?*

Bellinghamster: *Good. Just had church. Later, I'll go to my friend's house for dinner.*

Ammon: *I'm at my parents' house right now for an early family dinner. I love Sunday because it's the only day I don't have to feel guilty for doing nothing.*

Bellinghamster: *After getting baptized, the concept of a day of rest was really hard for me. I felt like a day of the week had actually been stolen from me. I used to go grocery shopping for the week on Sunday mornings and then go to the laundromat in the afternoon. It took a long time for me to adjust and start appreciating the Sabbath for what it is.*

Ammon: *How were you introduced to religion? Or is that too personal?*

Bellinghamster: *Is this another question to determine my character?*

Ammon: *No. I'm curious.*

Bellinghamster: *Okay. Well, it's not that interesting.*

Ammon: *If it happened to you, then it's interesting.*

Bellinghamster: *I wasn't raised with any religion but always inherently believed there was a God. I moved to Utah about six years ago to do my [censored because I'm not sharing any more identifying details with you] at the U. One of my mentors at school eventually became a good friend. He invited me along with his family on activities, like camping trips or climbing. He knew I loved the outdoors but also knew I was having trouble balancing the demands of my education program and life. He wanted to make sure I was enjoying both.*

Ammon could relate. He'd struggled with the same thing during med school, and now he struggled with his residency. But he was finding that talking to Bellinghamster every day was providing him with a little balance.

Bellinghamster's next message came in. *He has this really wonderful family: a lovely wife and three kids, one boy and two girls. The kids were teenagers at the time. And I just felt so cozy when I spent time with them. I finally asked him what made his family feel so special, and he shared his faith with me. I started to realize it was what had been missing from my own family growing up. And it was what I wanted for my future family.*

She continued. *I was hesitant to commit. I had a lot of questions and concerns and things I personally needed to work through before being ready to be baptized. And I had a lot of opposition from my mom, which added another layer of drama. Then my grandma died. Overnight, my family had shrunk by 50% since my dad has long been out of the picture. It was just me and my mom, and we have a horrible relationship. I'd never felt so alone in my life, and I realized I needed what religion could offer. That was three years ago.*

Ammon sat with her words for a moment, touched again by her honesty and openness. His family was the exact opposite of hers—big and loving—and he couldn't imagine what it would be like to have only a mom he didn't get along with and no siblings. He typed back, *Thank you for sharing that with me. It was kind of beautiful.*

Bellinghamster: *Thank you for asking.*

Ammon: *Anything you want to ask me?*

Bellinghamster: *Oh, so many things. But for now, just one. Do you consider us friends?*

Ammon almost didn't need to think about the answer. *Of course we're friends,* he typed back.

Bellinghamster: *Good. I'm glad to hear it.*

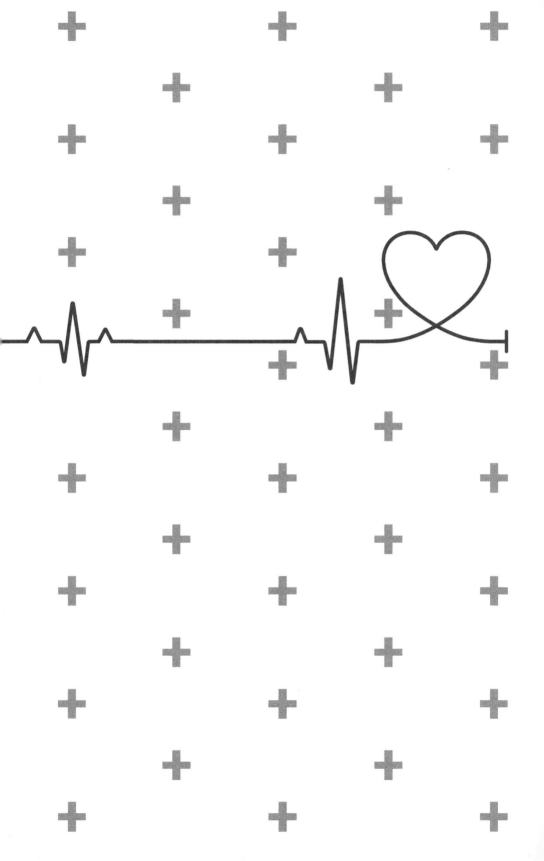

Chapter 19

CLAIRE SAT ON THE EXAM table in front of Audrey, her fingers combing over and over again through a lock of her long blonde hair. Audrey could feel the tension coming off the young woman like a blazing fire.

"You seem upset," she said, treading lightly. "Is there anything you want to talk about?"

Claire gave Audrey a stone-cold stare before rolling her eyes. "Prom is this weekend, and Hunter is taking Saydee Miller."

Audrey sucked in a breath and grimaced. *Ouch.*

Claire shook her head and stopped touching her hair. "I'm really angry, you know?"

Audrey nodded, prompting Claire to continue.

"My life is ruined." She gestured to her growing stomach. She took a deep breath and closed her eyes. She rested her hand on her bump and patted it. "I didn't mean ruined," she whispered more to the baby than to Audrey. "I prayed about it," Claire continued, looking up at Audrey. "Really hard. And everyone seems to think God should have told me to give her up for adoption. My mom certainly thinks that. And even if I were giving her up and I didn't get kicked out of my house and I stayed in high school, I would be a pariah at school and at church because I'd still be pregnant. But *he* gets to go to prom." She gave a humorless laugh.

"I'm so sorry, Claire," Audrey said softly. "It does seem like you have to bear the brunt of the consequences."

"It doesn't feel fair."

"I know. But he'll have to deal with a different set of consequences, one way or another."

Audrey wasn't sure how true that statement was. She liked to think her biological father was out there, feeling horrible for abandoning his daughter. But there was an equally good chance he never thought about her.

Claire nodded and gave Audrey a small smile. "Thanks for not judging me."

Audrey felt unworthy of the compliment because she had judged Claire, especially at first. But she knew what most people really needed was a listening ear and validation of their experiences. It didn't matter if Audrey disagreed; her patients just needed to know they were being heard.

"I'm here for you," Audrey said. "No matter what."

Chapter 20

AMMON: *HEY, BELL?*

Bellinghamster: *Yeah, Belay?*

Ammon: *What do you want most in the world?*

Bell: *I'm not sure I'm ready to tell you that.*

Ammon: *Okay. Is there something you do want to talk about?*

Bell: *Hmm. How about your favorite song?*

Ammon: *You'll just ridicule me.*

Bell: *So your taste in music is as bad as your taste in movies?*

Ammon: *Maybe you're just a snob.*

Bell: *Or sophisticated.*

Ammon: *Fine. When I was ten, I loved "American Pie" by Don McLean. My dad had it on vinyl, and I made him play it for me all the time. I thought I was pretty cool because I knew the words to all eight minutes of the song.*

Bell: *Aw, that's cute. Notice how I didn't ridicule?*

Ammon: *I'm sure you're just biting your tongue.*

Bell: *When I was in high school, I was obsessed with The Beatles.*

Ammon: *Hey, me too.*

Bell: *Which of their songs is your favorite?*

Ammon: *"Yellow Submarine."*

Bell: *Um . . .*

Ammon: *Oh no; here it comes.*

Bell: *You know what? I* will *hold my tongue.*

Ammon: *It's a jaunty tune.*

Bell: *It is.*

Ammon: *With a great story.*

Bell: *Let's agree to disagree.*

Ammon: *I think the kindness campaign is making you soft.*

Bell: *Only for you.*

Ammon: *Come on. You've got to have at least one guilty pleasure. Closet *NSYNC fan, perhaps?*

Bell: *Haha, no. But I guess Toto's "Africa" can get me going.*

Ammon: *Even your guilty pleasure ends up being an incredible song.*

Bell: *But here's the tacky part: when I was in Africa, I'd play that song whenever it rained.*

Ammon: *No!*

Bell: *Complete with dancing in the rain.*

Ammon: *Yup. Totally tacky. So maybe my "Yellow Submarine" isn't so bad anymore?*

Bell: *You're right. I am a snob.*

Ammon grinned. His chest felt all weird and fluttery. They talked some more before saying goodnight, and he went to the living room, where Freddy sat on the couch.

"What do you make of this?" Ammon asked and handed his phone over.

Freddy read the messages. "Is this the rock-climbing chick?"

Ammon nodded and sat down next to him. "She seems kind of cool, right?"

"She likes your sense of humor," he said, scrolling through their exchanges. "Which is a plus for you since you're not that funny."

"Hey," Ammon said and snatched back the phone.

Freddy laughed. "Yeah, she seems cool."

"I feel like she gets me."

"Aw." Freddy batted his eyelashes.

"I guess it's kind of weird," Ammon continued, ignoring Freddy. "I feel like I can't ask her out, because that's not why we started talking."

"Ask her out anyway. You know how many times a week I get shot down by Eleanor Lavish?"

"Dude, that girl is five seconds away from getting a restraining order," Ammon said.

"Okay, bad example. But, you know, seize the day and all."

"Yeah, maybe," Ammon said, standing. Just the thought of asking to meet Bell sent his nerves into a flurry. He felt like he was back in middle school: *Do you like me? Check yes or no* level of pathetic. Did Bell even think about him when they weren't talking? Ammon had found himself thinking about her more and more. If he met her in real life, would it feel like he already knew her? Would they hug or shake hands or stand there awkwardly?

His chest started to feel weird again. He wanted to know this woman better. He wanted to put a face to her words. He wanted a deeper connection. But what if everything changed after they met?

✦ ✦ ✦

Wednesday night, after prenatal appointments and meeting with two potential patients, Audrey checked her phone to find an email from her mom and another message from Belay. She smiled stupidly—about getting a message from Belay, not about the email from her mom. But the email did appear to be a business plan. It seemed Audrey would be out a hundred bucks.

She opened the message from Belay, her stomach full of butterflies.

Belay: *I've been thinking about you.*

She smiled and giggled and danced in place. She was sooooooo glad she was in the confines of her own room and no one could see her. Ellie would never have let her live that down.

Audrey was really starting to like Belay, which was weird because they hadn't known each other that long. But chatting with him in the evenings was becoming her favorite part of the day. She liked that he could make her smile. It had been years since she'd felt this way: bubbly and silly and young. The chip on her shoulder seemed to be shrinking. Maybe her tumultuous childhood wasn't going to ruin her love life after all. Not that she was seriously planning a future with this guy, but he made her feel like a future with *someone* was possible.

Belay: *What do you think about meeting in real life?*

Her breath stalled, and she placed her hand over her chest. He wanted to meet? She gulped, her mouth now dry. She'd thought this was a casual online flirtation. But if he wanted to meet, then maybe this was more serious for him. Her heart beat in double time. If they met in person, everything would change. It would become real. She could get hurt for real. Audrey took a deep breath, every instinct in her body telling her not to reply, that she should forget about this guy and using him to find Craggletooth Rock. She could get over this online crush as it was now, but the longer she talked to Belay, the more she liked him. And if they met . . . What if he was horrible?

But what if he's wonderful?

Audrey shook her head. She was being stupid. Pinning any hopes to some internet guy was a bad move. Flirting with some anonymous person was easy and fun. Meeting a stranger and then developing a relationship? That took courage and was a risk she didn't want to take.

What would Shannon want you to do?

An image of her friend popped into her head. Shannon had wanted to climb Craggletooth Rock so badly. "I've heard it has a secret crevice to stem through," she'd told Audrey at one of her prenatal appointments. "You can't see it from the bottom; it's hidden. But once you find it, you can see waterfalls on the other side."

Audrey let the ache wash through her. Shannon had been the kind of person who took risks even though her anxiety made her afraid of everything. For Shannon, Audrey could risk this tiny thing and meet a guy she had a little internet crush on.

After taking a few deep breaths, her fingers shook as she typed back a reply. *Yes! I would love to meet! Tell me when and where, and I'll be there!* She stared at the words. Too many exclamation points. Delete. She tried again. *Yeah, meeting would be cool.* Ugh, too aloof. She deleted that reply. She groaned and hit her phone against her forehead. She needed to sound interested but not like she was already planning a wedding. *Meet? I'd like that.* She hit Send and cringed. Anxiety grew inside her like an expanding balloon. She waited a few seconds, and when he didn't reply right away, she put her phone down on her bed. She paced around her room, waiting. This was just sad. Belay had a life. He didn't have to reply right away. His delay in replying didn't mean anything sinister.

Her phone chirped, and she nearly jumped out of her skin. She snatched it up and read his reply. *Since you might be a serial killer, I think we should meet in a public place.*

Audrey smiled and sighed in relief. Okay, this didn't have to be weird or serious. They were just two adults planning to meet. *I'm pretty sure I'm not a serial killer, but I'll let you pick the location since you're worried*, she typed back.

Belay: *Let's go climbing.*

Audrey: *Craggletooth Rock?*

Belay: *Nice try. Are you free this Saturday?*

Unless her last patient due this month went into labor, Audrey should be free. She'd have to let her patient know to call Charlotte if she needed anything while Audrey was out climbing, and Charlotte would call only if birth seemed imminent.

Audrey: *Saturday works. But I need to stay within cell range.*

Belay: *Have you climbed at the Red Rock in Draper? I think it has cell reception. Plus, it's a busy place, so if you kill me, there will be plenty of witnesses.*

Audrey: *I've climbed there. And if I kill you, I'll be sure it looks like an accident.*

Belay: *Does two o'clock work?*

Audrey: *Yes. How will I know you're you?*

Belay: *Mmmmm. Stop with the sexy grammar.*

Audrey blushed. Would he be like this in real life? Smart and funny? *Let's wear the same color bandanna*, she typed back.

Belay: *You pick the color.*

Audrey thought for a second. She didn't want to pick a color a lot of people would wear. *Neon Green?*

Belay: *Great. I'll be the tall guy wearing a neon-green bandanna.*

Audrey: *I'll look for you.*

Belay: *I can't wait.*

Despite her nerves, she felt like she could float right out the window. Maybe being brave wasn't so hard. And maybe he wouldn't break her heart.

+ + +

Working with Ammon again Thursday night did nothing to dampen Audrey's good mood. She was supporting another one of his patients, and luckily, Ric was his attending. She did her best to avoid interacting with Ammon, and he seemed fine ignoring her as well. The birth went smoothly, and when seven a.m. rolled around, she was pleased to realize she'd hardly spoken to him at all.

She went to the locker room and changed, then headed to the break room to get her leftovers. Ammon stood at the vending machine when she entered. He glanced at her, then made his selection. Audrey went to the fridge and grabbed her food, stuffing the plastic container into her bag. She felt Ammon before she saw him, his energy crowding behind her. She closed the refrigerator door and turned to find him standing near. She rolled her eyes, something that happened automatically in his presence. "Can I help you?" she asked curtly.

He held a bag of peanut M&M's in his hand and tossed a blue candy into his mouth. "Is it just me, or were you kind of pleasant to work with this time?"

"Are you trying to test my limits?" she asked.

He smiled, and Audrey realized she had played right into his hand. Why did she let him goad her?

"M&M?" he asked, holding the bag out to her.

"Sure." She took the bag from him, poured half the contents into her hand, and shoved them into her mouth. She chewed with her mouth open, imagining her teeth staining red and green. Not her most mature move. "Thanks."

Ammon took the bag back. "If you ever find yourself wondering why you can't get a guy, reflect back on this moment," he said.

Audrey swallowed and licked her teeth. "No need to. I have a guy," she replied. It was a little bit of an embellishment, as Belay was not her boyfriend or anything, but Ammon didn't need to know the details. "In fact, I have a date with him this weekend."

"And this guy's okay with the amount of time you spend thinking about me?"

Audrey walked past him toward the door. "I don't think about you, Ammon." She turned and looked at him before exiting. "So you can stop thinking about me."

Chapter 21

AMMON FELT CHRISTMAS-MORNING EXCITED AND first-day-of-medical-school nervous. Freddy pulled into the parking lot near the trailhead to the Red Rock. Ammon's nerves had made it impossible for him to focus enough to drive, and Freddy had offered to be his wingman.

Ammon tied the neon-green bandanna around his head like a sweatband and checked himself in the mirror. He breathed in and out. He was about to meet the woman of his dreams. At least, he hoped so. *You've got this.*

"You look fine, Fabio," Freddy said. "Let's go."

Ammon put on his sunglasses and got out of the car. The day was perfect for climbing: the April sun warm but the air cool and breezy. He hefted the climbing gear out of the trunk, and the two men started up the trail.

Freddy talked nonstop about something, but Ammon couldn't listen. He felt like his lunch was about to come up. What if she didn't live up to the image he'd created in his mind? Worse, what if she was perfect but *she* didn't like him?

Up ahead he saw the rock face dotted with climbers. It was a busy day. Hopefully, he and Bell could find a route to climb. Hopefully they had as much to talk about in person as they did online.

When Freddy and Ammon neared the end of the trail but before they found themselves at the base of the rock face, Ammon stopped. He turned and took a few steps into the foliage to hide behind a large bush.

"What are you doing?" Freddy asked.

"Can you scope her out for me?" Ammon mumbled, avoiding Freddy's eyes.

"What?"

Ammon rubbed the back of his neck. "Can you find her first and tell me . . . tell me what I can expect?"

Freddy put his hands on his hips and shook his head. "You want me to tell you if she's pretty."

"No . . . yes." Ammon groaned. This was pathetic.

"Dude, that's really shallow," Freddy said. "Haven't you already imagined a grand romance with her?"

"Just go, okay? This is what you're here for, right?"

Freddy shrugged and left the trail for the rock face. He returned about a minute later. Ammon had never seen a larger smile on his face. *Yes!* A smile like that had to mean she was gorgeous.

"So?"

Freddy laughed and Ammon's stomach lurched. Or a smile like that meant the opposite. Man, Freddy was twisted. "She's pretty, all right," he said.

"Then, why are you laughing?"

Freddy pulled him out of the bushes and pointed at a redhead with a neon-green headband. "She's also Audrey Novak."

Ammon felt all the blood in his body drain to his feet. This had to be a joke. He scanned the other climbers, searching for another neon-green bandanna. The amazing, funny, smart woman he'd been chatting with for the last three weeks could not be the bullheaded, prickly midwife.

But hers was the only neon-green bandanna. Unless the real Bellinghamster was late, Ammon had a real problem. He went back into the bushes. "In ten minutes," he told Freddy, handing him the climbing gear, "I want you to come over and say hi."

"You've already decided this isn't going to work?"

"I don't know what I've decided. Maybe her green bandanna is just a coincidence."

Freddy snorted.

Right. Ammon was being delusional. Audrey *was* Bellinghamster. He wanted to shake his fist at the universe. He stepped back out of the bushes and removed the bandanna from his head, then strung it around a branch. He'd get it later. "I'm just going to go talk to her."

Ammon headed in Audrey's direction. She stood, watching the climbers, not a trace of nerves in her body language. Ammon felt sick again. This couldn't be right. Audrey was nothing like Bell.

She turned just as he reached her. Her eyes flew to his face, and her mouth dropped open. "What are you doing here?"

Ammon arranged his face into a smile. "Freddy and I are climbing. Are you here with Ellie?"

Audrey crossed her arms over her chest. "I'm actually meeting my date here, and I'd appreciate it if you left."

This could still be a coincidence, right? Climbing wasn't the most original date idea. "Your date, huh? The guy who doesn't mind that you think about me?" He mustered a cocky grin.

Audrey scowled. "I don't know what I did to give you the impression I think about you, but I don't."

Ammon removed his sunglasses and placed them on his head. He moved closer to Audrey and could smell her rose-scented hair. "Maybe it's because your heart races at 120 beats per minute in my presence."

She took a step back. "I'd like you to leave," she repeated and glanced toward the trailhead. "When he shows up, I don't want you around to sabotage things."

"What's this guy's name?"

She looked back at him with a sharp glare. "I'm not telling you anything."

"His name is Clifford, isn't it? And you're embarrassed to be dating some-one with the same name as a big red dog." Why did he let Audrey bring out the worst in him?

She narrowed her eyes. "What will it take for you to leave?"

"How'd you meet this guy, anyway?" Ammon asked.

She put her hands on her hips. "If I tell you, will you go?"

Ammon nodded.

"The internet." She waved. "Bye. Have a nice day."

Drat. She really was Bellinghamster.

"Wait, you met this guy online and you're going to climb with him? How do you know he's not going to murder you in the bushes?" Ammon knew he was being obstinate. He should just admit he's BelayingonofHands, that they were both more interesting in cyberspace, and pretend this never happened. Because Audrey didn't like him. There was no point exploring this further.

"That's why we are meeting here," she replied. "There are plenty of people around."

"I don't know. Maybe me and Freddy should climb with you. Just to be safe." He was digging himself an early grave. Audrey would murder him for real when the truth came out.

"Ammon Parker." She poked him in the chest. "If you do not leave right now, I will start yelling for help."

Ammon stepped back and held his arms up in surrender. "Fine. Sheesh. I was trying to be helpful. But if you want to get killed by some psycho you met on the internet, by all means." He walked back to where Freddy waited near the bushes.

"What'd she say when you told her you're the guy from the internet?" Freddy asked.

"I didn't tell her."

"Dude, this is going to blow up in your face."

Ammon sighed. Yeah, it was. "Let's go."

As they walked down the trail, Ammon considered what to do next. He didn't want to totally crush Audrey, but he wasn't interested in her, despite the annoying stabs of physical attraction he felt toward her. When he got to the car, he pulled his phone from the glove box. He opened the Mountain Collective app and messaged Audrey. *Sorry, Bell, something came up and I can't make it today. I wish I could have let you know sooner since you're probably already there. Talk later?*

He felt like a terrible person as he hit Send, but at least she wouldn't keep waiting for him to show up. Freddy started the car, and they began to drive down the mountain.

Ammon stared out the car window. How could Audrey be Bell? They were nothing alike. Bell was caring and thoughtful and deep. Audrey was combative and mean. Ammon glanced back at his phone and read through their exchanges. Those first few messages she'd sent had been about him. He was the "insecure egomaniac" she sometimes had to work with. And he'd said the same thing about Audrey to Bell. Neither of them thought much of the other.

He kept scrolling through the messages. Audrey's random moments of kindness in real life had been prompted by her kindness campaign. She actually had been complimenting him, not trying to flirt with him, that day at the nurses station.

But who was the real Audrey? The one on the internet or the one he knew in real life? At this point, did it matter? A rock sat in the pit of his stomach.

"What are you thinking, man?" Freddy asked, using his therapist voice.

Ammon clicked off his phone. "I don't understand how I could have fallen for Audrey Novak."

"Maybe you don't really know her."

"Obviously." Ammon rolled his eyes.

"Ellie is going to love this when I tell her what's happened."

Ammon turned in his seat toward Freddy. "Freddy, you can't tell Ellie. She'll tell Audrey."

Freddy groaned. "You know I'm terrible at keeping secrets."

"You. Cannot. Tell. Anyone."

Freddy wiggled in his seat like he was going to explode. The car swerved a little into the other lane.

"You're a therapist. Isn't being able to keep secrets a part of your job?" Ammon asked.

"It's different when it's for work."

Ammon huffed. "How can I appropriately incentivize your secrecy?"

Freddy flashed him a grin. "Give me the coordinates to Craggletooth Rock."

Dang, he was good. "Fine. Whatever." Ammon looked out the window again. This was such a mess.

Over the next week, Ammon would have to slowly pull back on his chatting with Audrey. Maybe he'd just tell her the coordinates to Craggletooth and be done with her. She might be irritating, but Ammon figured she'd keep it secret. The woman did have integrity.

✦ ✦ ✦

Audrey kept waiting, trying to play it cool, but anxiety was creeping in. All her fears of being abandoned grew with every minute Belay was late. And stupid Ammon. Why'd he have to show up and taint what was supposed to be a great day? He was never going to let her live it down that the guy she claimed to be dating was actually a guy from the internet she hadn't actually met yet.

Her phone chirped.

Please don't let it be Charlotte. But it was worse: a message from Belay, canceling. The words felt like a cannonball to her chest. Audrey took deep breaths, trying to push down the disappointment. *He didn't really stand you up*, she told herself. If her patient had gone into labor, Audrey would have had to cancel. He probably had a good reason.

She headed for the trail, her legs feeling shaky and weak. *Keep breathing.* She didn't need to cry. If he hadn't messaged, then she would have been stood up. He said they'd talk later.

A swatch of neon-green in the bushes caught her eye. She ventured a few steps off the trail to see what it was. She plucked it off the branch. A bandanna. A slow coldness filled her veins. He'd been here. He'd seen her. And he'd left.

Chapter 22

AMMON COULDN'T PAY ATTENTION AT church. He knew he'd see Audrey today and wasn't sure how the interaction would go. He'd been unable to sleep, trying to reconcile the Audrey he'd fallen for online with the Audrey who annoyed him in real life. Which one was authentic? Why did he care so much? Why did he want Audrey to be both the passionate midwife and the funny, clever woman from the internet?

He found Ellie after the meeting, but Audrey wasn't with her. "Is Audrey at another birth?" he asked, trying to sound aloof. He didn't want Ellie reading too much into the question. Ammon wasn't even sure himself why he wanted to know where Audrey was, since he'd been so stressed about seeing her again.

Ellie gave him her usual cool smile. "She's sick. At least, that's what she told me."

Sick? Why did this make Ammon feel even worse?

He didn't stick around for Sunday School and instead made his way back to Windy Corner. When he reached the door of Audrey's apartment, he didn't knock right away. What was he doing here? He didn't actually care if Audrey was sick, did he? He ran his hands through his hair and groaned. He was standing outside her door. This probably meant he cared about her. Just a little. Because she was Bell, and he cared about Bell.

He knocked, and while he waited, that weird light, fluttery feeling returned to his chest. On the other side of the door, he heard movement and then, "Go away, Ammon." She must have seen him through the peephole.

He stepped closer to the door. "Ellie said you're sick. I just wanted to check on you."

The door flew open. Audrey's hair was an impressive mess of curls and knots. She wore a ratty T-shirt a size too big and sweatpants. Smeared mascara under puffy red eyes rounded out her pathetic appearance. She looked more like a girl who'd been dumped than someone who was sick. *Oh.*

"Can I come in?" Ammon asked, mustering up a smile he hoped looked charming.

She sighed and rolled her eyes and shuffled back to the couch but left the door open. He stepped in and shut the door behind him. Audrey grabbed an ice-cream carton off the coffee table and shoved a huge spoonful into her mouth. Piles of used tissues and an open package of Oreos also sat on the tabletop. *Wow.* He didn't think he'd hurt her this much. As Belay, he'd messaged to say he wasn't coming. It wasn't like he'd left her waiting for hours and never showed.

He slowly moved into the room, waiting for Audrey to change her mind about letting him stay or threaten his life if he took another step closer. When he made it to the couch without incident, he took a seat next to her.

"Since you dislike me so much," she said and seemed to roll her eyes at herself, "you're probably the best person to ask."

Ammon wasn't sure where she was headed but already dreaded this conversation. "Audrey, I don't dislike you."

"Well, you don't like me," she replied. She took another spoonful of ice cream. "Am I ugly? Like, if you saw me in a crowd of people, would you think, *Wow, that woman is a dog?*"

He felt literal pain in his chest to hear her say something like that.

"You can be honest," she continued. "There's not much left of my heart to break. I doubt anything can hurt me more at this point."

Ammon was surprised to see Audrey this upset. She'd always come off as so strong. If he'd known Audrey would react this way to Belay not showing, he would have come clean yesterday. He'd never wanted to hurt her. He didn't want to date her, but he didn't want her doubting herself. It made sense now why he didn't hear back from Bell after he'd sent his lame excuse message. She hadn't even sent back an *OK* or the deserved *You're dead to me.* Instead, he'd received nothing, and now he knew why: Audrey was shattered by his rejection.

"Where's this coming from?" he asked.

She unscrewed an Oreo and licked the frosting. "You'll love this," she said. "My internet guy stood me up."

Ammon swallowed the lump in his throat. He should probably go. Or tell her the truth. Instead, he stayed and asked, "Did he call or text to say why?"

"He sent a message with a flimsy excuse."

"So he didn't really stand you up," Ammon said. "He at least told you he wasn't coming."

Audrey laughed. It was more of a cackle. He could see her Oreo-stained molars. "Men are all the same. I should have known you'd be on his side."

"I was just trying to put a positive spin on what happened. I'm not on anyone's side."

"I was totally prepared to buy his excuse and give him a chance to explain himself, but then I found this." She dug around the cracks in the couch cushions until she pulled out his neon-green bandanna. Ammon felt sick at the sight of it. He'd forgotten he'd left it.

"See?" Audrey continued. "We were both supposed to wear neon-green bandannas so we'd be able to find each other. He didn't actually cancel on me, Ammon. He was there. He saw me, decided I didn't live up to whatever expectations he had for me, and left."

Ammon felt himself shrinking. He was a world-class dirtbag for ditching her. And a coward right now for not wanting to tell her the truth. But he hadn't left because of her looks.

"I'm sure it wasn't like that," he said quietly. "Audrey, you have to know you're beautiful."

"Don't." She put her hand up as if to push away the compliment, then wiped away a few stray tears. "It doesn't matter. Just another experience to confirm how disposable I am."

He grew even smaller. He needed to figure out how to make this right. Audrey wasn't disposable; she just wasn't for him. What could he do so she'd understand that?

The solution crashed over him like a bucket of ice water. But he couldn't do it—he couldn't tell her the truth. Not yet, at least. Maybe Belay could figure out a way to make this right.

"Have you heard anything else from this guy?" he asked.

"No."

"If he were to message you again, would you reply?"

Audrey ate another Oreo. "My self-preservation instincts say I should tell him where to shove it." She shook her head. "But I also have a weakness for giving people the benefit of the doubt." She glanced at him, and Ammon tried not to appear shocked. "Don't look so surprised. I'm nice to everyone but you."

He'd actually noticed that. She was nice to the patients she'd just met and all of the nurses and most of the doctors, except Callister. That he and Callister were the only exceptions to her niceness didn't sit well with him. How had they gotten off on such bad footing? And why did they keep misstepping?

"I'm sorry things didn't work out like you hoped," Ammon said, patting her awkwardly on the back. "Maybe this internet dream guy will figure out a way to make it up to you."

Audrey shrugged, and he removed his hand. He saw himself to the door and went down the hall to his apartment. In his dark bedroom, he opened the Mountain Collective app and started to compose a message.

Chapter 23

AUDREY KNEW WALLOWING IN SELF-PITY did nothing to change the past or improve the future, but for the life of her, she couldn't get off the couch. But now she was out of ice cream and needed to find her phone. Hopefully none of her patients had questions or had gone into labor. She'd silenced her phone (and now lost it) because she couldn't bear knowing Belay hadn't tried to contact her again. Or that he had and his apology was terrible. Every chirp of her phone had sent her spiraling further.

Heartbreak and humiliation aside, Audrey was also mad at herself. So what if she'd spent three weeks having interesting online conversations with some random guy? She didn't need to dive headfirst into a pint of Häagen-Dazs just because it hadn't worked out. It was her fault she'd let herself get emotionally involved to the point that Belay could hurt her. She was foolish for thinking cyberspace was safe.

And then there was stupid Ammon. He was probably in his apartment laughing at her. He seemed to catch her at her worst moments, and he was always the same cocky jerk. Although, he had been nice to her today.

She dug through the cushions of the couch until she found her phone. No missed calls or text messages from patients. That was good. She didn't have it in her today to attend a birth. Of course, she'd have to figure out a way to pull herself together if someone *did* go into labor. Good thing she had Charlotte working with her now. Charlotte could do almost everything but the actual baby catching.

In an act of self-torture, Audrey stared at the Mountain Collective app. She hadn't replied to Belay yesterday, so it was a little unreasonable to expect him to message her again. But he had said, *Talk to you later.* She tried to imagine what he could say that would make her still want to talk to him. He'd been there. And then he had left. But he wanted her to think from his message that he'd wanted to come but couldn't. Audrey was sick of games and being treated as disposable.

A memory she had been trying to ward off finally broke through. She was six, sitting at a table inside Dairy Queen. Her mom had dropped her off and left because she didn't want to see *him*. But Audrey was ecstatic, her little legs swinging like mad as they dangled off the hard metal chair. Her dad finally wanted to meet her. The last time he'd been around, according to her mom, Audrey had been three, but Audrey couldn't remember him.

He had called two days before, telling her mom he'd be passing through Bellingham and wanted to see Audrey. He could buy her an ice-cream cone, and they could catch up. Audrey had been nervous at first, because her mom never had anything nice to say about him when she asked. But when the day came for Audrey to meet him, her nerves had turned into bubbles of excitement. She'd finally get to hug him and ask all the questions she'd been saving.

Before Audrey's mom had left her at the restaurant, she'd given her a few dollars and told the manager, one of her mom's Amway friends, to keep an eye on her. "I'll be back in an hour," Audrey's mom had said, then planted a kiss on her forehead. Audrey had watched as her mom got back into the car and drove across the street to the nail salon.

Audrey waited the whole hour, her legs slowly losing their swing, the rapid beating in her chest turning into labored thumps. He never showed up. And when Audrey's mom returned an hour later, she pulled Audrey into a fierce hug and bought her an Oreo Blizzard, and they left. On the drive home, her mom remained silent, which was worse than the string of curse words or insults Audrey had expected.

That night, Audrey heard her mom arguing on the phone with her father. He showed up at the house the next day, gave Audrey a hug and a crisp $100 bill, and left after a few minutes. Audrey cried for two days straight, feeling like a piece of garbage.

It was hard not to feel the same way about Belay's rejection. Was he as awful a person as her father? Was she really that bad at judging someone's character? After all these years and all the hurt she'd experienced, had she learned nothing?

Audrey opened the app and took a deep breath. A message waited for her. A thickness developed at the back of her throat. She should delete her account and never speak to Belay again. But at the same time, she needed to know what he had to say for himself. And she needed the coordinates to Craggletooth Rock. That's what this was supposed to be about, anyway. She owed it to Shannon to find the route.

Dear Bell,

Was she actually dear to him?

We've always been honest with each other, the message continued, *so I need to be honest now.*

Audrey turned the phone over so she couldn't keep reading. It felt like an ice pick pierced right through the center of her heart. After a few slow breaths, she flipped her phone back over.

I was there yesterday.

Audrey tried to swallow away the emotion building in her throat. She felt like she was living in some alternate reality with fuzzy edges and unformed shapes.

I saw you standing there with a neon-green bandanna tied in your hair, and you became real in a way I wasn't ready for. I had imagined you a dozen times in my mind and realized you might have done the same for me. What if I wasn't what you expected or hoped for? What if in real life you actually hated me? I felt like I didn't have anything to offer you. So I left, angry at myself and confused.

I can only imagine how much I must have hurt you. I'm so sorry I was such a coward. But can I get another chance? Can you be patient with me? I think I need you in my life.

Audrey let out a long exhale. Oh, she wanted to believe him. Hadn't she had similar doubts and worries swirling around her head while she'd waited? She'd been terrified. He didn't know she'd found his bandanna, yet he was still being honest with her. But could she forgive him so quickly?

Her fingers clumsily typed back a reply—*I'm so angry at you*—and then deleted it. She tried again—*I found your bandanna, you idiot*—but deleted that one too. She closed her eyes and sat back on the couch. If she were in his situation, what type of response would she hope for?

Audrey really liked Belay, or at least, she had until he'd stood her up. She wanted to give him the benefit of the doubt because that was the generous thing to do. But she also didn't think she could take being rejected again. She needed to protect her heart. *I appreciate your honesty*, she finally wrote, *and I empathize with you because I had many of the same fears. I need time to figure out if and how I want our friendship to continue.*

She felt tears building up behind her eyes as she hit Send.

Of course, came his quick reply. *I'll be here if you need me.*

Chapter 24

AT NINE THIRTY MONDAY MORNING, Ammon found himself outside Audrey's door. He'd spent the last twenty-four hours worrying about her. He'd read her last message to Belay at least fifteen times, trying to figure out whether he'd be okay if she decided to end their friendship. He'd come to rely on her in a small way. When he talked to her, he felt like himself—not uptight, unsure Dr. Parker but Ammon—like he had been before med school and residency had sucked the life out of him. He felt more like the Ammon who had long hair and a beard, who climbed every weekend and lived for the next adrenaline rush.

Ammon had always wanted to be a doctor. His grandfather had been a trauma surgeon, and as a kid, Ammon would sit at his knee and listen to his stories. Ammon had known abstractly that med school and residency would be hard. What he hadn't been prepared for was how soul crushing it would be. Bell had added light back into his life. That she was actually Audrey Novak, one of the soul-crushers in his real life, confused him beyond belief. He needed to reconcile the two people he thought he knew.

Ellie answered the door after he knocked. She gave him an impatient look in place of a hello. Audrey had probably told her about his visit yesterday.

"Is Audrey home?" he asked.

She sighed and stepped back. "Have a seat. I'll see if she wants to talk to you."

Ammon sat on the very edge of the couch. A laptop with a Word document up sat open on the coffee table. He glanced over the words, trying not to violate the privacy of whomever the laptop belonged to, but it was hard when it was just sitting there. It was chapter five of a novel. A character was musing about her inability to find love. Before he could finish the first paragraph, the laptop screen snapped shut. Ammon looked up to be greeted by Ellie's glare. "Audrey's on her way out. You'll have to come back later."

Ammon stood. "It'll take just a minute."

Audrey walked into the room before Ellie could deter him further. He stepped around the couch and followed Audrey into the kitchen.

"I'm literally out the door right now," she said, grabbing a protein bar from the pantry. He smelled her rose shampoo as she moved past him.

"Where are you headed?" he asked. "A birth?"

"Prenatal appointments."

"I'll walk you to your car," he said. "Or bike," he added when he remembered she biked to a lot of places.

She let out a deep sigh but didn't stop him as he followed her out of the apartment. "So where's your office?" he asked, trying to keep pace with her quick footsteps.

"I do prenatals in my patients' homes. I don't have an office."

He didn't have anything to say to that. It made sense. She helped women birth at home, so doing their prenatal appointments at home meant she didn't have to spend extra money to rent office space.

"How many births do you attend a month?" he asked when they reached her car. So she was driving to her appointments. She opened the trunk and set her oversized bag inside. He tried not to roll his eyes at her bumper stickers: *Coexist, The future is female, Well-behaved women rarely make history.*

"Ammon, I doubt you came by just to ask me about my practice. Is there something I can help you with? Otherwise, I need to say goodbye." She slammed the trunk shut.

Ammon shrugged. "I just wanted to know if you were feeling better today."

Her face screwed up in confusion. "I'm fine," she replied.

"Oh. Good." Either Audrey was lying or she was tougher than he thought or Belay didn't have the same hold on her heart that Bell had on his. "Have you heard from the internet guy?"

She dug through her purse before noticing her keys were already in her hands. "Yes."

"And?"

"I'd rather not talk about this with you."

Ammon put up both his hands. "Okay. Sorry. I'll go," he said. "Nice to see you're back to your old self." He turned to leave.

"Hey, wait," she said.

He pivoted around, his heart suddenly pounding. Man, this was all confusing.

"Can I call you later? I need a consult."

"Like, you need to consult a medical doctor because you've encountered something a midwife can't handle?" He couldn't stop the wolfish grin from appearing on his face. He wanted to be nice to Audrey. He wanted to respect her. Because she was Bell, and he respected Bell. He was nice to Bell. But Audrey? Confusing.

She shook her head. "Never mind. I'll call Ric later today." She opened her car door.

"Wait. I'll help." He tried to wipe the smile off his face. "Consider it a part of our workplace truce. Why don't I come with you." He really should get some sleep, but he was curious about her work. And fine. He kind of wanted to spend time with her, too. He still wanted to understand how Audrey could be Bell.

She pursed her lips and nodded. They both got into her car. "Just so we're clear, you're doing this pro bono," she said, typing away on her cell phone.

"Yeah, sure." He kept his comment to himself about how he figured she didn't make enough money to pay him anyway. Audrey might be failing at the kindness campaign, but Ammon was killing it.

They drove in silence for a few minutes as Audrey headed to I-80. The silence held the same weird pressure that often grew between them: something between suffocation and repelling forces. He probably should have followed in his own car. She changed lanes without using her signal, and Ammon bit his tongue—literally—to stop himself from saying something. Once they were on the highway, he wanted to jump out of the car, as much from her scary driving as from the awkward tension. He glanced at her, wondering if she felt it too.

"So," he began, figuring talking was better than silence. "Why do you get to call Dr. Sandoval Ric and no one else does?"

She took her eyes off the road to glance at him. She swerved a little as she did so, and the car in the next lane honked. She jerked back over into her lane. Ammon grabbed the safety handle but still didn't comment on her driving. The kindness campaign was going to kill him.

"He's the one who first invited me to church four years ago," she said. "I met him while doing the midwifery program at the U. As the head of maternal-fetal medicine, he taught the seminars on high-risk pregnancies. I was interested in how midwives and maternal-fetal medicine doctors can work together to improve birth experiences." She stole a glance at Ammon before she continued. "Not all women can or should solely be under the care of a midwife." Ammon raised his eyebrows in surprise but chose not to goad her. So what if she was admitting advanced medical care was necessary for some pregnant women?

"But that doesn't mean," Audrey continued, "all pregnant women can't benefit from the care of a midwife. When I started my clinicals, I sought out Ric. He and I collaborated on a study looking at the birth outcomes of high-risk pregnancies under the care of a midwife and a maternal-fetal medicine team. Ric became my mentor and eventually my good friend. So when he invited me to attend church with his family one Sunday, I went, mostly out of a courtesy to him. A year later, I found myself getting baptized." She shrugged, and Ammon knew she was leaving out a lot of the story. As Bell, she had recounted the whole thing. Knowing Dr. Sandoval was the man who'd taken Audrey under his wing and given her a family to turn to raised Dr. Sandoval's esteem even higher in Ammon's mind. "So I get to call him Ric," she said, "because he's not just a coworker. He's family."

Ammon's stomach did a stupid little flutter. She sounded so much like Bell just then. He wasn't sure how to respond to her. Audrey had never been this open with him before. Maybe his seeing her so upset yesterday had broken down one of her walls with him.

"Tell me about the patient we're about to see," he said. The transition was inelegant, but so were his feelings right now.

"Her name is Elaine. She's thirty-five, pregnant with her fourth child. This is her first planned home birth though. She's forty weeks plus two days. Her blood pressure has been steadily climbing, but there hasn't been any protein in her urine."

"You test for protein?"

She scoffed. "Yeah. Why wouldn't I?"

"Because you're a home birth midwife."

She got into the exit lane, without signaling again. Should he say something? She could cause an accident or a deadly incident of road rage.

"That's right. You think I use magic crystals," she said sarcastically. "I follow best practices, Ammon. So that includes checking blood pressure at every appointment and checking for protein in the urine."

"But don't best practices also state babies should be born in hospitals, where emergency medical care is readily available?"

She let out a frustrated sigh. "Maybe you're not the best person to do this consult after all," she said. "You can wait in the car."

"No. Sorry. I want to help."

"I don't think you're capable." They came to a stop at a light, and Audrey gave him an exasperated look before returning her attention to the road.

"I'm a doctor. I know I'm capable."

"Ammon, what I need to know is if my patient is still a good candidate for a home birth, despite her rising blood pressure. Since you don't think home birth is safe in any circumstance, I don't think you can give a fair assessment."

Ammon opened and closed his mouth, but no words came out. She was right. He didn't think women should be birthing at home. The light turned green, and she drove on.

"I don't know why I asked you in the first place," she muttered and glanced at him out of the corners of her eyes.

"Probably because you have a crush on me." He gave her a cheeky grin. That earned him another eye roll, but a small smile played at the corner of her mouth. In the past when he'd teased her about this, it had been just that: teasing. He was sure Audrey hated him. But now that he knew how she felt about Belay, he couldn't help but wonder if in real life, she could have a little crush on him. Her pulse did race around him, and her cheeks often flushed pink.

They pulled up in front of a brick house in an older neighborhood. He thought they might be in Murray or Midvale, but he hadn't been paying very close attention.

"I'll leave the keys so if it gets hot, you can turn on the air conditioner." She unclicked her seat belt and opened her door.

He suddenly wanted to do this favor for her. And he wanted her to respect him as a doctor. "What's her blood pressure at?" he asked. "Where do you usually draw the line?"

She sat back in her seat. "One twenty-seven over eighty-three when she texted me her numbers last night."

"That's not too concerning," he said. "You say she's at forty weeks? How would you be managing this patient if you were still working at the hospital?"

Audrey shrugged. "I would be doing what I'm doing now: watching her numbers closely and praying she goes into labor soon on her own."

"So what you're looking for is some reassurance from me." He said it as a statement and not a question.

"I get nervous about blood-pressure issues. It's a long story I'm not going to tell you. But yes, what I really want is reassurance. Do you think you can give that to me?"

Ammon nodded, wondering what her personal issues could possibly be. "Just so I have a barometer, what would you consider unsafe for a home birth?" he asked instead.

"If you felt like she needed to be induced, like, today."

"Okay, I can do that," he said, determined to put his biases aside. He wanted to help her. Because one day, she'd find out he was Belay, and he wanted to not die an untimely death at her hands when that happened.

✦ ✦ ✦

Before heading into Elaine's house with Ammon in tow, Audrey checked her phone. She'd texted Elaine to make sure it was okay that Ammon came to her appointment. On the drive over, Audrey had held out hope that Elaine would say no and Ammon would have to stay in the car.

No such luck. *Yeah, that's fine* was Elaine's reply.

Why had Audrey agreed to let Ammon come?

She got her birth bag out of the trunk, and Ammon followed her up the front walk. Elaine let them in, and after introductions, they chatted for a few minutes before Audrey pulled out the fetal heart Doppler and went about her usual routine: fetal heart tones, fundal height measurement, blood pressure check. Ammon watched with polite interest. He was silent, thank goodness. Audrey handed Elaine a little paper cup to collect a urine sample, and her patient disappeared down the hall.

A little brunette girl wandered into the room. "Hi, Miss Audwey," she said.

"Hi, Chloe," Audrey replied. Chloe was Elaine's three-year-old. Elaine's two sons, eight and six, were at school, and her husband was at work. The little girl climbed up on Audrey's lap and, by the looks of her hair, had just woken up. She pointed a small finger at Ammon.

"Who's that?"

Audrey glanced at him. His face held a pleasant smile.

"This is Dr. Parker," Audrey said. "He's come with me today to learn all about home birth. He thinks it's the best place for mommies to have their babies."

Audrey shot Ammon a cheeky grin. His own smile didn't waver.

"I was born at home," Chloe told him. "On the potty. Isn't that silly?"

Ammon raised his eyebrows.

"Unplanned home birth," Audrey explained.

Elaine waddled back into the room. Audrey gave Chloe a little squeeze before the little girl hopped off her lap and went to her mom.

"I'll check your sample." Audrey stood and took her birth bag down the hall to the bathroom. Ammon followed. She glanced at him in the bathroom's mirror. "Yes?"

"Just watching the master at work."

Audrey shook her head and retrieved the test strips from her bag, dipping each one into the sample cup sitting on the counter. Everything looked good. Audrey cleaned up, washed her hands, and turned to leave the bathroom, but Ammon stood in her way.

"Would you like my professional opinion now or in front of the patient?"

"Now," she said.

He assessed her for a moment with his unnervingly blue eyes. "I think this patient is going to be fine."

"Me too," Audrey replied, successfully hiding her relief from him. She didn't want him to know his opinion mattered so much to her.

"What's your protocol for monitoring for postpartum preeclampsia?"

"I've already given her a blood-pressure cuff, so she'll continue to take her blood pressure regularly the first two days and text me the numbers. And I'll see her in person three days postpartum."

Ammon nodded. "Sounds reasonable."

She quirked an eyebrow but didn't ask him to explain what that meant. They went back to the living room. Audrey reported that Elaine still seemed healthy enough to proceed with the home birth. Then they listened to the baby's heartbeat again because Chloe wanted to hear it. The little girl moved the Doppler around on her mom's stomach until it picked up the whooshing heartbeat. Chloe giggled. Audrey stole a glance at Ammon, and even he seemed amused by the little girl.

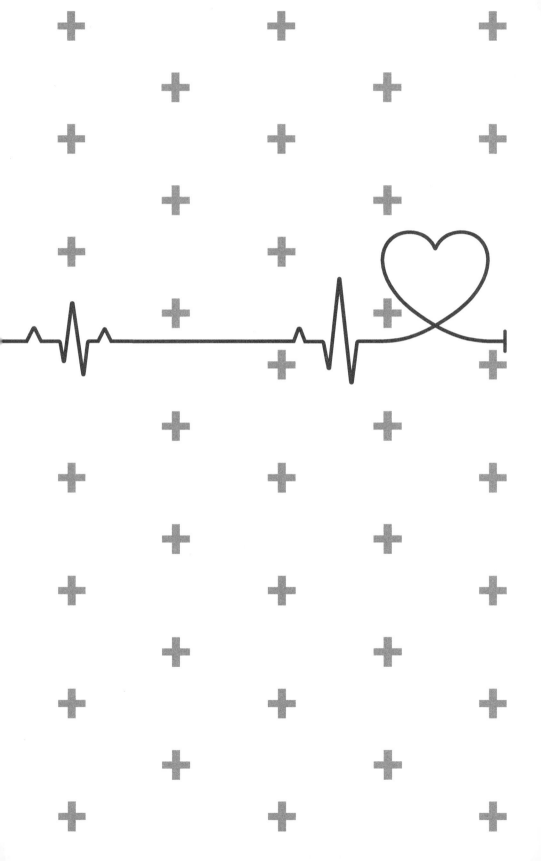

Chapter 25

AMMON LOOKED OUT THE WINDOW as they drove to see Audrey's next patient. He was surprised her appointment with Elaine had been so . . . medical. It irked him to think maybe he was wrong about this whole home birth thing. He would never be comfortable with the idea of a woman birthing at home. In his mind, an OR needed to be right down the hall for birth to be truly safe, but Audrey seemed competent. And there had been something cozy about the appointment: sitting on a sofa in a comfortable home, listening to the baby's heartbeat, which the three-year-old had found with the Doppler. Ammon could maybe, almost, see the appeal. But he still had doubts. And lots of questions.

"That was interesting," he finally said.

"Good interesting?" Audrey asked.

"It wasn't what I expected," he replied.

"What did you expect?" He could detect a laugh just underneath Audrey's question.

He shrugged. "You know. Herbs and energy work."

She laughed out loud this time. "Really?"

He shrugged again.

"It's in my and my patient's best interest that no one gets hurt," Audrey said. "So I provide the best care."

"Can I ask you a question without you biting my head off?" he said.

Audrey stopped at a red light and looked at him. She didn't look smug, like he expected, but rather interested in what he was thinking. "Sure," she said.

He hesitated. Did he really want to go back to the question that had started all of this? Especially since they were getting along so well? But he had to know. "What *do* you do if a patient has a post-birth hemorrhage?" he asked.

The light turned green, and Audrey drove forward, a smirk on her lips. "Would it make you feel better if you knew I carried Pitocin?"

"You do?" Ammon didn't want to sound so shocked, but he was.

"I'm a licensed midwife," she replied impatiently. "I can prescribe medication and administer injections and IVs."

"So if a patient is Group B Strep positive?"

"I can give her IV antibiotics if she wants them. But I'm also not opposed to doing a Hibiclens wash or retesting her closer to her due date or not testing her at all if that's her preference."

He had major problems with her not testing, but he let that go. "So do you give the newborn a vitamin K shot and erythromycin eye ointment?"

She shook her head, clearly annoyed with how confused he sounded. "If my patient wants them, yes."

"What do you do if they don't?" he shot back.

Audrey looked at him then, her gaze level. "What do *you* do if they don't?"

Ammon bristled. "I educate them and hope they make the right choice."

He saw a tiny trace of a smile flash on her lips as she returned her attention to the road. "You can't force people to do things. Medical care is supposed to be based on the concept of informed consent. My goal is to help women have the birth they want, as safely as possible. Sometimes my patients want less testing and checking, and that's okay."

"But sometimes people want stupid things."

"Yeah, but let me ask you something," she said.

"Okay." He crossed his arms over his chest, feeling defensive.

"Do you enjoy trying to control the uncontrollable?"

"I don't do that," he replied.

"Does arguing with your patients about their birth preferences ever actually change their minds?" He gave her a scathing look, but she kept her attention on the road and didn't see it. "I personally feel more comfortable if I can give a baby the vitamin K shot," she continued. "But if a patient doesn't want it, even after we've discussed the risks, I let it go. I can't control my patients; I can't control what happens to the baby. So what good does it do to act like I know better than her and treat her like garbage because she's made a decision I disagree with?"

"I don't treat my patients like garbage," he grumbled.

"I didn't say you did." Audrey pulled up in front of her next patient's house. Why wasn't she yelling at him? Angry Audrey was much more predictable than reasonable Audrey. "I guess I'm just trying to say you have options with how you interact with your patients. If you respect them and they come to trust you, then when it really matters, they'll be more likely to take your medical advice. Otherwise, you just feed into the narrative that doctors and hospitals are evil and you'll continue to get pushback, even if it means the patient or baby will die." She sighed. "And honestly, I'd love to have another doctor at the hospital I can trust if I need a consult or a transfer of care." He detected just a hint of uncertainty in her eyes. Ammon uncrossed his arms. Was she implying she wanted him to be that doctor? Could he? What would that even look like?

Maybe he'd never be okay with home birth, but Audrey seemed more than capable. And like Dr. Sandoval had said, if someone was going to help women birth babies at home, it should be her. Although, he knew better than to tell her that. "It was kind of cute having that little girl find the baby's heartbeat," he finally relented.

"Yes, it was," she said. "And it's something you can do when you have your own practice. There's nothing wrong with being less clinical." A smile tugged at the corners of her lips. She definitely thought she'd won this round. Maybe she had. "Are you ready to see my next patient?"

"Despite what you think, Audrey, I am teachable." Ammon opened his car door.

Audrey raised an eyebrow. "Then, come," she said. "Learn from the master."

+ + +

Later that night, when Ammon was at the hospital, he didn't roll his eyes when his patient handed him her five-page birth plan. When the nurses quipped, "The longer the birth plan, the higher the chance of a C-section," Ammon responded with, "At least this patient has done her homework." And when the baby was born ten hours later and the mother declined the vitamin K shot, the Hep B vaccine, and the erythromycin ointment, he bit his tongue and didn't insinuate she was a bad mother. He channeled his inner Audrey—if such a thing existed. Ammon took a seat at the patient's bedside to discuss the interventions. He explained the risks and benefits like he usually did but also took the time to hear her concerns, her understanding of the research, and to understand her values. He tried to allay her fears, but she still didn't want the medications. So he did what Audrey had suggested: let the patient make her own choice and let it go. And the strangest thing happened. Ammon felt like he had provided his patient with the best care.

Chapter 26

CLAIRE WASN'T AT THE FREE clinic first thing Tuesday morning like usual. Audrey tried not to worry, but as the morning progressed with still no Claire, Audrey wondered if something had happened. On her lunch break, she called the young woman. On the third ring, Claire picked up. Her voice sounded groggy and hollow when she said hello.

"Hey, it's Audrey."

Audrey heard the rustling of cloth. She pictured Claire sitting up in bed. "Oh, hi," Claire replied.

"I didn't see you at the clinic this morning," Audrey said. "I just wanted to check in."

"Oh yeah. I'm okay. Just beat is all. It's my day off, and I didn't set an alarm because I wanted to sleep in."

Audrey felt a little rush of relief. "Extra rest is good. You deserve it. How are you feeling otherwise?"

"As good as I can, I think," she replied. "Weighing a million pounds and peeing every five minutes is getting old though."

Audrey laughed. She'd heard those complaints many times. "Have you seen Dr. Ferguson recently?"

"I saw her again last Friday. Annie is still breech."

"You've picked a name?!" Audrey exclaimed.

Claire giggled. "Yeah. Annie Lee."

"That's adorable," Audrey gushed.

"Thanks."

"So she's still breech?"

"Yeah. Dr. Ferguson wants to see me this Friday for the external rotation thing if she doesn't flip on her own." Her voice sounded causal and detached, something Audrey knew she did when she wanted Audrey to think she didn't care.

"Would you like me to come?" Audrey asked, knowing Claire would never ask her.

"You wouldn't mind?" she replied, relief flooding her voice.

"Not at all," Audrey said. "What time is your appointment?"

"I'll check and text it to you."

"Is everything else going okay?" Audrey asked.

There was a sigh on the other end. "I reached out to my mom again."

Audrey closed her eyes and shook her head, already knowing where this was going.

"She still doesn't want anything to do with me or the baby," Claire said. "She feels like if she offers me any support, then she is in some way condoning my actions. I get that she's disappointed in me. I mean, I broke, like, the biggest rule. But"—her voice cracked—"I need her."

"I know," Audrey said. "There's still time for her to come around."

"Yeah, I guess so."

Audrey checked the clock on the wall. Her lunch break was almost over. "Sorry, I have to go. But call or text me if you need anything, okay? I'll see you Friday."

"Thanks, Audrey."

After she disconnected the call, Audrey had a terrible urge to message Belay. Claire needed her mother's forgiveness and love. Maybe Belay needed Audrey's, too. Plus, she kind of missed him. She wanted to tell him all about her kindness campaign success with Ammon on Monday. She'd been nice to him for a whole three hours while he'd come with her to prenatal appointments. Instead of fighting with him, she'd taken the high road. And if she looked past his shellacked bro exterior, she could admit he was kind of cool. Belay would understand what an accomplishment that was. He understood the depth of her loathing.

Audrey packed up her unfinished lunch, her hurt from being stood up feeling a little less raw, and went back to work. She needed just a little more time.

Chapter 21

THE RINGING OF HER PHONE woke Audrey from a deep, dream-filled sleep. Glimpses of rock and rope and sky faded from her mind as she became conscious, but the distinct feeling of fear clung to her as she found her phone. In her dream, she'd been climbing or running or falling. Something intangible had been looming over her.

Audrey checked her phone, hoping it was Elaine in labor and the whole blood-pressure issue would soon no longer be a concern. Instead Audrey saw it was Claire. Calling in the middle of the night. *Oh no.*

"Hi, Claire," Audrey said, trying to sound cheerful and not like she was worried or had just been woken up. Audrey was greeted by sobbing on the other line. Her body turned cold. "What's going on, sweetie?" Audrey asked.

"There's . . . there's so much blood."

Audrey took a deep breath as her heart raced. She stood and turned on her bedroom light. She went to the top drawer of her dresser, where she always kept a clean pair of scrubs. "Claire, some blood can be normal if you're in labor. How long have you been bleeding?"

"I just woke up in a puddle of it."

"Okay," Audrey said, setting her phone on the dresser and turning it on speaker. She had Claire describe the color and consistency and amount as she changed into the scrubs. It sounded like much more blood than was normal in early labor. Audrey did her best to keep her voice calm when she spoke next, but her adrenaline was pumping. "Are you still bleeding?"

"I don't know."

"Are you contracting?"

"I don't know." Claire started crying again. "Is Annie dead? I didn't want to name her yet because I was so afraid this would happen."

Audrey went to the bathroom and grabbed her toothbrush. "Claire, I don't want you to worry about that right now. Stay where you are and call 911. I'll be there in ten minutes."

Audrey got off the phone reluctantly. She grabbed her go bag and headed for her car. Claire lived west of downtown, so she wasn't too far.

The streets were deserted, and Audrey glanced at the clock on her dashboard, realizing she hadn't checked the time yet: 3:07. She set up her Bluetooth and called Labor and Delivery. She told the nurse who answered to notify Dr. Ferguson that her patient Claire Shaffer would arrive soon in an emergency situation.

She pulled up right in front of Claire's building, ignoring the *No Parking* sign but leaving space for the ambulance she could hear in the distance. Her adrenaline was still pulsing, but Audrey took a moment to think. She closed her eyes and whispered a prayer for Claire and baby Annie, asking for peace and guidance. When she opened her eyes, she was overwhelmed with the impression to call Claire's mom. There were about a million reasons why that might not be a good idea. Claire might not appreciate it. Her mom had made it clear she wanted nothing to do with her. But Claire needed her mom now.

Audrey rummaged through her go bag, where she kept copies of her patients' information. Claire had listed her mom as an emergency contact. If anything, Audrey could use that to justify the phone call.

A groggy voice greeted her after the third ring. "Hello?"

"Hi, Ms. Shaffer?"

"Yes? Who is this?"

Audrey got out of her car and entered the apartment building. "My name is Audrey Novak. I'm a midwife at the clinic your daughter, Claire, visits for her prenatal care."

"I don't have a daughter named Claire," the voice said. Wow. Audrey had not expected that. She pushed the sting away as she made her way down the hall, looking for apartment 121.

"Ms. Shaffer, Claire's probably going to have her baby today, four weeks premature," Audrey continued. "And there are likely to be life-threatening complications for her and her baby." She arrived at Claire's apartment. "We will be at the university hospital. She's going to need you." Audrey hung up the phone as two EMTs rushed down the hall with a stretcher. "Are you here for Claire Shaffer?"

The taller of the two men eyed her while the other knocked on the door.

"I'm Audrey Novak, Claire's midwife," Audrey said, her mouth dry. "She's eighteen years old; it's her first pregnancy—thirty-six weeks. She called me at about three a.m. and said she woke up in a pool of blood. I've already called the U of U Hospital, and her doctor is expecting her."

"Thanks," one of the EMTs said and knocked again.

She tried the knob to discover the door was locked. "Claire? It's Audrey," she called. What if Claire had passed out from blood loss? They'd have to get the police to kick down the door. Just before she knocked again, the door slowly opened, revealing Claire in bloodied pajamas. Audrey couldn't stop the gasp that escaped her lips. Claire began sobbing.

"She's dead, isn't she?" Claire cried. "My baby's dead!"

Audrey pulled Claire into a quick hug. "We're going straight to the hospital."

The EMTs asked Audrey to move, and they helped Claire onto the gurney. A wave of déjà vu overwhelmed her, and Audrey had to fight the panic that threatened to overtake her. This wasn't going to be like Shannon's case. Claire wasn't going to die.

Audrey held on to her hand and tried to keep up with the gurney as the EMTs moved down the hall. Claire was white as a sheet and shaking, probably from both blood loss and fear. "The ambulance will take you to the hospital," Audrey told her. "I've already called, and Dr. Ferguson will be there. I'll be right behind you in my car." She tried to reassure her as Claire shook her head and continued to sob, but Audrey couldn't tell Claire her worst fear might be true. Annie could be dead. And Claire could die too.

"Claire, we're going to do everything we can for you and your baby." The EMTs lifted up the gurney, and Audrey let go of her patient's hand as they pushed Claire into the back of the ambulance. "I'll meet you at OB emergency," Audrey told the EMT who was starting Claire's IV line. She then rushed to her own car so she could follow the ambulance.

Audrey's body shook as she drove, her lips moving in a silent prayer. *Please let Claire and Annie live. Please help me be strong for them. Please help me survive whatever the outcome of this may be. I can't fall apart again like I did after Shannon died.*

At the hospital, Audrey left her car keys at the valet desk and ran for the elevators on the main floor. Claire and the EMTs rushed through the corridor and boarded the elevator with her to go up to Labor and Delivery. Adrenaline continued to course through Audrey's body, and she took slow breaths through her nose. The elevator doors opened, and a triage nurse met them. One look at Claire's blood-soaked pajama bottoms and the nurse hit the emergency button. Everything then happened very quickly.

Claire was moved to a bed, and fetal monitors were placed on her stomach. The EMTs prepared to leave as Audrey gave one of the nurses Claire's medical history. "She has a possible placental abruption." A wave of nausea overcame Audrey as she gave the diagnosis out loud. "Is Dr. Ferguson here?" Her voice cracked, and tears stung behind her eyes.

"She's prepping for the surgery," a familiar voice said. Audrey spun around to find Ammon standing in the doorway. She could have sunk into his arms in relief at that moment but instead stayed rooted in place. He went to Claire's bedside and watched the monitors. Audrey realized she hadn't checked them yet.

"Let's wheel her back," Ammon said. The nurses adjusted the bed and began to push it. Ammon rushed ahead toward the OR.

"What's going on?" Claire asked as her bed moved down the hall. "Where am I going?"

Audrey glanced at the monitors. Annie's heart rate was extremely low. "You're being taken back for an emergency C-section," Audrey explained, knowing in situations like this, rarely did anyone take the time to tell the patient what was happening. She increased her pace to keep up with the bed as it sped down the hall.

Claire paled, and she grabbed Audrey's hand. "Is Annie . . . ?"

"Annie is alive, but she needs to come out right now." Audrey squeezed Claire's hand. "I can't come back with you into surgery, but I'll be waiting right out here." She knew only essential personnel were allowed in the OR during an emergency. "They will put you under general anesthesia, so you won't even know I'm not there."

"But I need you!" Claire said. A nurse pushed Audrey out of the way and placed an oxygen mask over Claire's face, but Claire tried to pull it off. "You promised you'd be with me!"

Audrey felt helpless, like a tree caught in a windstorm. Everything around her rushed and moved, but she couldn't do anything to help Claire.

"You need to keep the mask on," the nurse said to Claire, then turned to Audrey. "Please step back, ma'am."

They reached the OR doors, and Audrey stopped at the red line as they pushed Claire through. She watched through the window. Claire became frantic, trying to leave the bed while a nurse tried to tie down her arms. "But I need her!" Claire screamed. "I'm all alone, and I need her!"

The tears Audrey had been holding back leaked from her eyes. She needed to be strong right now for Claire, but she felt heavy and weak. This was not the outcome either had anticipated. The nurse pulled Audrey away from the OR door.

Audrey felt Ammon before she saw him, a warm, strong presence. "Let her in to the surgery," he said to the nurse.

The nurse shook her head. "Dr. Parker, we don't—"

"Audrey is this patient's midwife," he said. His gaze flicked to Audrey's for just a moment. "I'm running this crash. Let her in."

Audrey almost crumpled with relief when the nurse nodded. Ammon disappeared inside the OR before she could thank him. She knew it wasn't over yet, but a feeling of peace washed over her, and she said another silent prayer of gratitude.

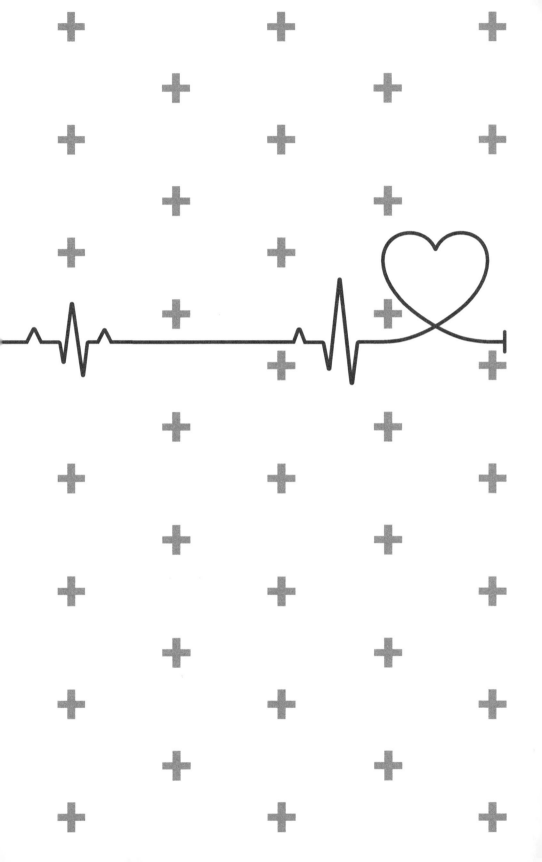

Chapter 28

When his shift was over at nine a.m., Ammon went to Claire's postpartum room, hoping to find Audrey. The emergency C-section for her young patient had gone as well as possible given the circumstance. Claire's placenta had almost completely detached, and the baby had been born nearly blue. Luckily, the NICU had been there to resuscitate the premature infant. The last Ammon had heard, the baby was doing well but would be on oxygen for the next few weeks while her lungs continued to develop. Claire had needed a blood transfusion but was expected to make a full recovery.

Ammon found Claire sleeping, a middle-aged woman at her bedside, but no Audrey. He took a quick visual assessment of the girl. She looked pale but not alarmingly so. Her breath came in the slow, deep rhythm of sleep. The heart monitor peeped in steady time.

The older woman stood when she saw Ammon and brought a finger to her lips. She motioned for him to follow her into the hall. When the door clicked shut behind them, she spoke. "She just fell asleep," the woman said. "I'm Claire's mother, Brenda."

"It's nice to meet you, Brenda. I'm Dr. Parker." They shook hands. "I wanted to check on her before I head home," he said, which was a half-truth.

"That's kind of you."

Ammon noticed the weary slump of her shoulders and the redness of her eyes. "Claire is young and strong. There shouldn't be any further complications," he reassured her. "And the outlook for your granddaughter is equally optimistic."

"I've met so many doctors," Brenda said. "What role do you play in her care?"

"I performed the C-section, alongside Dr. Ferguson."

Tears welled up in Brenda's eyes, and her bottom lip began to quiver. "Thank you for saving my daughter's life." She let out a giant sob.

Ammon wanted to pull back. He found strong emotions like this from strangers extremely uncomfortable. He'd done nothing special for Claire—just what he would have done for any other patient. That he would be considered a lifesaver was absurd to him. He was just a doctor doing his job. But Brenda continued, seemingly unaware of his discomfort. "I thought I wanted her out of my life after what she did," Brenda said. "But when Audrey called me . . ." Tears stopped her words. Ammon put a hand on the crying woman's back and offered a reassuring pat. She took this as an invitation to collapse against him, wetting his white coat at the shoulder. So he held her and, for a moment, thought of how much this woman could have lost.

+ + +

When Ammon arrived home and plugged in his long-dead cell phone, his heart boomeranged around his chest when he saw he had a message from Audrey in the Mountain Collective app. He was prepared to never hear from her as Bell again. Had she figured out she wanted to continue their friendship, or was this going to be a *never talk to me again* message? Everything that had happened with Claire and her mother had put Ammon in a vulnerable place. He didn't think he could handle rejection right now. But then again, it was what he deserved.

He tapped open the message.

I had a bad day, she'd written. *Like, a really, really bad day. And you're the person I'd usually turn to on days like this. Of course, originally, I wouldn't share any specifics about how or why my day was bad because that would violate our agreement about staying anonymous. Instead, I'd say, "I had a bad day; tell me something that will cheer me up." And then you'd make some ridiculous defense of a terrible pop song or tell me all about how the taste of Hot Pockets has really gone downhill over the last ten years. You'd make me smile, and I would forget about my bad day for a little while.*

Ammon's chest grew achy, and he read on.

I'm a midwife. (I figure since we were supposed to meet, you would have learned this about me.) And this morning, one of my patients almost died. She's a teenager, disowned by her mother for having sex before she got married, and she almost bled to death.

When I'm faced with a crisis like that, everything both speeds up and slows down. I can see what's happening right in front of me while simultaneously predicting and reacting to a hundred possible complications or outcomes. I'm living in both the present and the future. But regardless of what I do, how much focus I put into the situation, it inevitably becomes all about me. After worrying about my patient's life and the baby's life, I think about my life. Will I be able to live with myself if this patient doesn't make it? How will this loss affect me? What trauma or regret or inescapable burden will I have to live with? So while I might have helped save a life today, I can't help but wonder: did I do it for her or for myself?

Ammon swallowed the lump in his throat and let out a deep exhale. *Wow.* She'd put into words the ideas and feelings he'd never been able to fully articulate: this weird internal dance he played when it came to life and death and his desire to distance himself from both so he couldn't be culpable for either. Just like with Claire. He'd been doing his job—no reason to celebrate if things went well or get hurt if things went wrong.

He tapped on the icon to reply, but his mind froze. What could he say to her that didn't make it obvious Belay was actually him? He didn't think today was the best day for her to find out. He'd have to be understanding but not specific.

I'm sorry you had a bad day. It sounds like your work is demanding and takes a lot from you emotionally. I think it's only natural to develop ways to protect yourself so you don't get hurt. For some people that might look like pulling back completely, thinking of the patient as only a body so they don't have to deal with all the complex emotions and implications of healing a whole person. You go the other way: it becomes extremely personal to you. You know you can't actually control the final outcome, but you can control how you respond and what you do, and that makes you feel like you can control what will happen. That's how you cope with crisis, and I don't think there's anything wrong with that. I think that makes you brave.

Bell, I want to be here for you. I'm sorry I was such a coward and that I hurt you. I hope we can still be friends.

Ammon stared at the words before sending it, wondering what else he could add. Did he sound sincere enough? Did he sound too lighthearted, like he wasn't taking her pain seriously? Was he being honest?

He scrubbed a hand through his hair. Only now was he beginning to realize what he'd ruined and what he could still lose. Audrey, despite all her abrasiveness, was a remarkable woman who thought and felt deeply. He'd fallen for Bellinghamster almost effortlessly. If he let himself, would he also fall for Audrey? Could they ever stop fighting long enough to realize their potential? Would she ever forgive him for being Belay when she inevitably found out?

Ammon hit send on his message and tossed the phone onto his bed. He didn't want to be confused about this anymore.

Chapter 29

Audrey's patient Elaine went into labor Thursday afternoon. Before heading over to Elaine's house, Audrey texted Mel at the hospital to let her know she'd miss her volunteer doula shift that night. She would have to find another time to thank Ammon for letting her into the OR for Claire's emergency C-section.

As Audrey stepped over the threshold of Elaine's house, an almost sacred feeling rushed over her, pushing away the lingering anxiety she'd held on to since Claire's surgery. The house felt deeply quiet, the kind that moved beyond the absence of noise and permeated into the restless chambers of her heart. Audrey took a deep breath, the scent of lavender filling her lungs. Peace. Audrey finally felt peace.

Charlotte appeared from down the hallway. "Elaine is in her room," she whispered.

Audrey nodded. "Why don't you get the birth tub set up. I'll see how she's doing."

"I think this is going to be a special birth," Charlotte said and smiled. "Can you feel it too?"

Audrey felt tears prick at the corners of her eyes. "Yes. I can feel it."

+ + +

Elaine floated on her back in the warm water of the birth tub, her eyes closed. The room was dark except for two candles glowing nearby. Audrey poured water over Elaine's round belly. A contraction came, and Elaine took long, slow breaths; she seemed to surrender herself to the sensation. Her mouth opened in a low guttural moan as the contraction peaked. Her husband whispered encouragement into her ear and kissed her brow again and again. Audrey moved around the tub and sensed that it was almost time.

"Charlotte," Audrey whispered.

Charlotte's eyes widened, and she quickly but quietly handed Audrey the needed supplies: a headlamp, plastic smock, and gloves that went up to her shoulders. Charlotte stood by with towels.

"Elaine," Audrey said softly. Her patient opened her eyes. "Your baby will be here in the next contraction or two."

Elaine looked at her husband, a huge smile on her face. The labor had been relatively short, five hours or so, and Elaine had labored with the beautiful confidence of a woman who trusted her body. And soon it would be over.

Audrey slipped on her smock and gloves. Charlotte clicked on the headlamp for her and adjusted the direction of the light.

Audrey watched two more contractions. A flash of light seemed to fill the room as Elaine reached down and caught her own baby. She placed the infant on her chest, and Charlotte draped a towel over the tiny baby. Audrey quickly assessed the baby on Elaine's chest. She was pink and crying and perfect.

Elaine's husband woke up Chloe, who had fallen asleep on the couch. The little girl approached the edge of the birth tub, rubbing sleep from her eyes.

"You have a sister," Elaine said to Chloe.

The little girl burst into tears, then came closer to examine the new baby and tentatively touched the little tuft of hair on her sister's head. "Wow," she whispered.

Audrey helped Elaine out of the tub and settled her in her bedroom. Soon, Grandma brought Elaine's two sons up from the basement to meet their new sister. The boys cuddled around their mom and the new baby, grinning despite themselves.

Audrey sat back for a moment and watched the scene, her heart expanding with love. Tears touched her own eyes. She looked from Elaine to Elaine's husband to her children and saw their radiant happiness glowing in their smiles. Every time she witnessed a birth like this, Audrey couldn't ignore the small ache that bloomed in her chest. She wanted this badly—a family of her own.

+ + +

Friday, Audrey slept in until noon and stayed in bed another hour. Too much had happened over the last few days, and she finally had some time to decompress. She spoke to Claire, who would be released from the hospital Saturday. Annie would be in the NICU at least another week. Then she scrolled mindlessly through her various social media accounts.

Audrey read Belay's last message about a dozen more times, wondering if he would be worth the risk to resume their electronic friendship. She needed to decide whether to reply to him. And she needed to thank Ammon in person for letting her into the OR. Both tasks seemed too hard. She sort of wanted to stay in bed forever, but hunger finally pulled her from her room.

Ellie sat on the couch, her feet propped on the coffee table, her fingers flying over her laptop keyboard. Either she was making some serious progress on her latest novel, or she was in a very intense political debate on Facebook. Audrey moved around the kitchen as quietly as possible, trying not to distract her.

Even though it was May, Audrey fixed herself a cup of hot chocolate and arranged some cinnamon rolls on a baking pan. Next week, she'd get back on the whole-foods bandwagon. In the meantime, carbs were her best friend.

As the smell of baking cinnamon rolls filled their apartment, Ellie stopped typing and closed her laptop. She joined Audrey at the kitchen table. "Can I have one when they're done?" she asked, reaching for Audrey's cup of hot chocolate. She took a sip and pushed the cup back over to her.

"You can have two. And the rest of my hot chocolate." Audrey stood when the timer beeped. She took the cinnamon rolls from the oven and left them to cool on the stovetop. After fixing herself a fresh cup of cocoa, she joined Ellie at the table again.

"I haven't seen you much lately. You been busy with work?" Ellie asked.

Audrey stared at the liquid in her mug. "I almost lost a patient."

Ellie's eyes went wide, and she leaned back in her chair. "Don't tell me the details," she said, her voice almost a whisper.

"I won't," Audrey replied. She was curious about Ellie's visceral reaction but decided against saying anything. Audrey's grandma had been the kind of person who got woozy just hearing about blood, so she understood not to get specific with some people. Audrey sighed and took a sip of her cocoa. "Then, Thursday, my last patient from April finally had her baby."

"So things will settle down for you?" Ellie's voice had returned to normal, her expression falsely bright. Audrey debated calling Ellie out on her sudden mood change but didn't have the emotional energy for it.

"Well, I still have prenatals," Audrey replied. "And if my two patients due later this month go early . . ." She shrugged. "But yeah, I'm less on call than usual."

Audrey went to the cinnamon rolls and spread the icing on them. She didn't even bother getting plates and instead brought the whole pan and two forks over to the table. "Tell me about your latest book," Audrey said.

Cinnamon rolls with her best friend was exactly what Audrey needed. As the two women ate and talked, she slowly felt herself recharging.

Chapter 30

A KNOCK AT HIS BEDROOM door pulled Ammon from sleep. "Yo. You up?" Freddy called through the closed door.

Ammon mumbled some choice words under his breath, and he searched for his glasses. "Go away," he shouted back. He placed his glasses on his face and read the time on his phone: five thirty p.m.

Freddy opened the door and peeked his head in. Bright light sliced into the dark room, causing Ammon to squint. "You've got a lady visitor," Freddy said. "And so you don't have to spend the next five minutes of your life wondering who it is, it's Audrey."

Audrey? Ammon shot out of bed like a rocket, and Freddy shut the door, chuckling. Ammon fumbled through the darkness for the light switch. What could she want? He blinked as his eyes adjusted. He knew he didn't have any clean clothes because who had time for laundry? But he couldn't waltz out to meet her in his pajamas. His options were an old holey T-shirt and some basketball shorts that didn't smell too bad or his Sunday best. Ammon felt paralyzed by the decision, both options bad in different ways. Was this how his sisters had felt getting ready for dates? Because this feeling was totally valid, and he needed to make some phone calls later to apologize for all his teasing.

The holey T-shirt and shorts won out. He slipped from his room and hurried to the bathroom, hoping she hadn't seen him. His hair was a mess. While he brushed his teeth, he smoothed his free hand through his hair but stopped midcomb. What was he doing? Why was he freaking out about his clothes and hair? It was Audrey who'd come to see him. Audrey Novak, the woman who couldn't stand him. He spit and rinsed his toothbrush. Why did his stomach have to feel fluttery? Ammon cupped his hand and filled it with water. He took a sip and shook his head. Nope. Nope. Nope. He shouldn't waste his energy on her. She was never going to like him.

Ammon left the bathroom to find Audrey sitting on the couch in his living room. Something deep in his chest clenched. The image of her pale, frightened face the night Claire was brought into the hospital popped into his head. And then the words she'd later written him as Bellinghamster. Both had been Audrey in the raw. And he'd never felt more protective of a person in his life.

He realized his usual self-assured swagger didn't work on her, so he didn't know how to act now. Now that he wanted her to like him.

The realization almost sent him back to his room. He wanted this woman to like him. Not tolerate or put up with him but like him. Hold him in regard. Respect him. Because he felt all of those things for Audrey.

"Hey," he said, feeling uncomfortable in his own skin.

She stood from the couch. "Hi." Her smile wavered.

Ammon felt dizzy at the realization of his feelings for her but moved toward her.

"Let's sit," he said, not sure how much longer his legs were going to work. She nodded and returned to her place on the couch. He sat beside her, the scent of roses in the air around her. It took an embarrassing amount of effort not to lean toward her and bury his face in her hair. "What can I do for you, Audrey?" his voice sounded too soft and breathy. Gosh, this was awkward.

"I, um . . ."

He watched her swallow, his gaze drawn to her lovely neck.

"I want to thank you."

He felt a stab of surprise. "For what?"

"For letting me into the OR on Wednesday," she said.

"It was nothing," Ammon replied. His eyes caught hers. "Claire needed you." Her eyes were wet with vulnerability, and the urge to touch her tingled in his fingers. He thought again of her message to Belay. "Do you want to talk about it?"

She glanced away and pursed her lips. "I get too emotionally involved with some of my patients. My mom would say it's part of my hero complex."

"I don't think either of those are bad things," he said and angled himself toward her.

Audrey shrugged. "But it makes this job harder. I take on so much sometimes that I worry it affects my ability to be a really great midwife, like what I want or need to happen clouds my judgment so I don't actually end up providing the best care."

"But the alternative has its own set of problems," he replied. "Thinking of the patient as just a body can cause someone to act without empathy."

Audrey cocked her head to the side and studied him. "My internet guy said something similar."

Ammon stilled. What if she figured out he was Belay? It was too soon. "He sounds like a smart guy, then," he said, giving her a cocky smirk.

She chuckled but shook her head. "There has to be a way to practice medicine that's in the middle," she said. "I know there is. It's how Ric practices."

Ammon nodded in agreement. Dr. Sandoval was the perfect balance of empathetic and clinical. Sometimes during labor, he was only the patient's doctor. And other times he seemed almost like a friend. He seemed to know his patients well and care a lot about them as a whole person, but at the same time, he was always Dr. Sandoval to them, never Ric. Ammon knew that was the kind of doctor he should strive to be.

Audrey continued. "I don't think I have it in my emotional makeup to pull myself back though," she said. "I either care too much or not at all."

He wanted to ask where he fell in that dichotomy. Did she care for him? And if she didn't, could she one day?

"I think that makes you a great midwife," he said.

She shrugged her shoulders and shook her head. "Anyway, thank you again." She stood, and so did he, but he wanted to ask her to stay. She touched his arm but quickly let go. "See you around?"

"Yeah."

He saw her to the door, and she turned back to him as she stepped out. "Oh, Elaine, the patient with the high blood pressure, had her baby late last night."

He leaned against the doorjamb. He had wondered why she hadn't been at her volunteer shift. "You didn't end up at the hospital, so I assume everything went well."

"Textbook and beautiful." Her face took on a look of contentment, and his heart warmed. She looked so lovely and serene.

He smiled. "I'm happy to hear that."

She smiled back. "Okay, I'm gonna go now. If we keep being nice to each other like this, it might send me into an existential crisis."

Would that be so bad? he wanted to ask. *Being nice to each other?* "I'll be sure to say something snarky next time I see you," he replied.

"That would be much appreciated."

She walked down the hall, and Ammon watched her disappear into her apartment. He wasn't sure what would happen next, but he knew he wanted it to happen with Audrey Novak.

Chapter 31

TUESDAY MORNING, AS AMMON WALKED through the main lobby of the hospital on the way out to his car, he spotted a vaguely familiar-looking young woman. She stood in front of the hospital's floor directory, crying. No one seemed to notice her, or if they did, they didn't stop to help her. She wiped her nose and looked around. Then Ammon recognized her as Claire, Audrey's patient.

Ammon approached her slowly. He wasn't sure if she'd even remember him. When she'd arrived at the hospital, everything had happened so fast.

"Claire?" he said.

The young woman blinked at him. "Yes?"

"I'm Dr. Parker. I don't know if you remember me."

A smile broke through her distress. "I remember you." She quickly wiped her eyes. "You saved me and my baby's life."

Ammon let out a breath and shook his head. He really didn't want to take credit for that. A whole team of people had worked together to save Claire and her baby. He gestured to the piece of paper she held. "Do you need help finding something?"

She looked at him with big brown eyes, and he worried she was going to start crying again. "I'm supposed to get some blood work done, but I don't know where the lab is."

"Are you here alone?" he asked. She really shouldn't be driving so soon postsurgery, especially if she was still on painkillers.

"Not really," she replied. "My mom is up in the NICU with Annie."

Ammon nodded. "Let me see your lab orders. Maybe I can tell you where you should be." He held out his hand for her paperwork. She handed them over, and Ammon read the address at the top. "You'll want to go to clinic 4, which is right back there." Ammon gestured to a corridor behind them.

"Thanks." She took back the papers.

"You're welcome."

Claire looked frail, pale; her eyes were shallow, her brow uncertain.

"Let me walk you there," he said. They took slow steps across the lobby. "How are you feeling?"

"Like death," she replied.

"You're up and walking, so that's something."

"I guess," she mumbled.

"How's your baby doing?"

"Good." Claire stopped suddenly. Ammon heard a sob and turned to her. She pressed a palm into her face. "Sorry. I don't know what's wrong with me," she said. "I can't stop crying."

Ammon stooped to looked in her eyes. "Hey, it's okay. It's probably just the baby blues. You're what, six days postpartum? It's totally normal to feel like this."

She sucked in a snotty breath through her nose. "Yeah?"

He felt extremely uncomfortable, but he couldn't help but think about what Audrey would do in this situation. "You've been through a lot," he said. He wished he had a tissue he could offer her.

"I didn't think it would be this hard," Claire said.

"I get that," Ammon replied. "But you've got to give yourself more credit. You just had major surgery, and your baby is in the NICU. That's hard stuff. And you're killing it." He then made air guns with his fingers and popped off a few rounds.

Claire gave him a look like he was the biggest dork. Which he was. But she smiled a little, and that overrode any embarrassment he would have otherwise felt.

"I'm told it gets easier," Ammon said. He placed his hand lightly on her shoulder and guided Claire toward the clinic.

"That's what my mom said," she said.

"You've had a rougher introduction to motherhood than most," he added.

"And that's what Audrey said."

Ammon's heart jolted at the mention of Audrey's name. He resisted the urge to say anything more about her. He and Claire reached the entrance to clinic 4. "Well, here you are," he said. "Is there anything else I can help you with?"

Claire's eyes flooded with tears again. Poor girl.

Ammon gripped her arms. "Hey, Claire? It's going to be okay."

She nodded.

"I've heard there's a support group for new moms at the city library. Maybe you should go. Meet some other women who are going through the same things as you."

She blinked. "I didn't know there was something like that."

"Yeah. There's a lot of support out there."

She wiped her face. Ammon understood how Audrey got sucked into her patients' lives. It was hard to turn away when someone was in obvious need of help. "Why don't I give you my phone number," Ammon said. He'd never in his life imagined giving a patient his personal number. But he just felt so sympathetic with Claire. "That way you can call me directly if you need something," he added.

"I really don't think I'd ever call you," Claire said.

"Something might come up. And you'll have it if you need it."

Claire pulled out her cell phone and handed it over to him. He punched in his number and sent a text to himself. She took her phone back and bit her lip. "Can you text me more info about the mother's group?"

"Sure. I'd love to."

"Okay. Well, thank you, Dr. Parker."

"You're welcome, Claire." He patted her on the arm. She disappeared into the clinic. Ammon headed home, for the first time in a long time feeling like a real doctor.

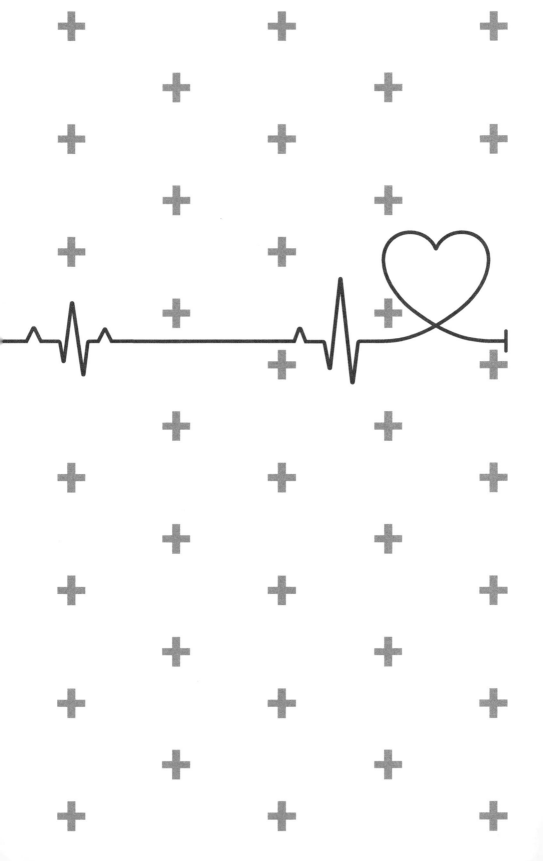

Chapter 32

WEDNESDAY AFTERNOON AUDREY PULLED INTO her parking spot at Windy Corner but didn't get out of the car. It was a beautiful spring day, everything green and blue. From her car, she gazed around the perfectly manicured grounds of the apartment complex, her survey stopping on the pool. Ellie sat on one side, with her legs dangling in the pool, and Freddy stood chest deep in the water near her. Just as Audrey was about to get out of the car, her phone rang. It was her mother. She answered the call, staying in the car.

The conversation went as usual: *Hi. How are you? Fine. Are you still into Jesus? Yes. Can I have money? No.*

Okay, this time, she wasn't asking for money.

"Business is booming," her mother gushed. "The farmers market season started two weekends ago, and so far I've made two thousand dollars."

"Wow," Audrey replied. That was a lot of money. And this was the first time her mom had actually given her a solid figure. Usually when "business was booming," her mom could only vaguely report on her sales. "Barney, the guy at the peach stand, has lots of great ideas."

"Ah," Audrey said. Why was she not surprised a man was involved?

"Don't say 'ah' like that."

"Like what?" Audrey smirked.

"Barney is an eighty-year-old man with an equally old wife. I know you don't want to believe it, but I'm evolving, Audrey."

"Two thousand dollars. That's impressive," Audrey said, changing the subject. She didn't want to discuss the details of her mother's "evolution," because only time would tell how true that statement was. And if Audrey disagreed, they'd fight.

"Yeah. I can barely keep the oils in stock. You know how hippie Belling-hamsters can be." That was a little like a pot calling the kettle black, but

Audrey held her tongue—again. The art of a successful conversation with her mother was to not say what she was thinking. Perhaps Audrey should have pictured Ammon as her mother when they'd first met and couldn't stand each other. The kindness campaign would have been much more successful. But now she and Ammon seemed to be getting along, which was super weird.

"So tell me about your life," her mom said.

Audrey sighed, resting her head on the steering wheel. "Just busy as usual."

"Hmm. You always say that, but I never really know what you're busy with."

"I'm working a lot and volunteering a lot."

"Are you making time to socialize? Life is only as good as the people in it," she said, sounding like a Pinterest quote.

"I talk to Ellie almost every day," Audrey said.

"Roommates don't count."

Audrey wasn't sure where her mom got that idea, seeing as how she'd never had a roommate herself other than Audrey or Grandma.

"Then, no, I'm not socializing." She rolled her eyes at herself just as much as at her mom. She looked up at the pool again. Ellie and Freddy were now splashing each other. "I was talking to some guy I met online for a while." She bit her lip. Why did she mention that? She hadn't talked to Belay since their exchange a week ago. She hadn't known what to say after being far too honest with him about Claire.

"Why'd you stop?"

Audrey shrugged. "It got complicated."

"And you probably made sure that would happen."

"What's that supposed to mean?"

"You're like me," her mother said. "You sabotage all your relationships."

Audrey sat agape. There was so much to unpack in that statement that she didn't know where to start. First, Audrey was nothing like her mother, aside from the red hair. In every way, Audrey made sure to be the opposite of her. And second, Audrey had had no idea her mother was that self-aware. All these years, she'd thought her mother was clueless about the consequences of her actions. She played the victim often enough that Audrey had figured her mom never thought she was responsible for anything.

Audrey found her voice. "I don't sabotage my relationships."

Her mother scoffed on the other line. "Let's see, there was your high-school boyfriend, who you dumped right after graduation because he admitted to eating pepperoni pizza."

Oh yes, Audrey's zealot vegan phase.

"And then there was Billy from your first year of college, who you said cleared his throat too much."

Audrey cleared her throat before answering. "It was excessive. Like, before every sentence."

Her mother continued. "And we can't forget Aaron. He was my favorite, by the way."

Aaron had been Audrey's favorite, too. She'd dated him from her junior year of college until she left Washington to attend her midwifery program in Utah. And her mother was right; she'd ruined that relationship. Having him come to Utah with her was a step she hadn't been ready for. And instead of admitting that and talking about it, she'd ended the relationship over something stupid. "I guess, looking back," Audrey said, "breaking up with him because he didn't buy a more fuel-efficient car was dumb."

"Those were just excuses," her mom said.

"But I'm not like that anymore," Audrey said. "I've grown up."

"Why did you end things with Internet Guy?"

Audrey had always wanted her mom to actually *mother* her, but now that she was, Audrey wasn't sure she liked it all that much.

"He . . . ," Audrey began, trying to figure out what Belay had actually done. In the end, he'd apologized over and over again and given her the space she'd needed. What had his actual crime been? Oh yes. Being human. Belay had turned out to be human, and that was too low a standard for Audrey. "He's done nothing I can't forgive him for," she said through clenched teeth.

She expected her mother to gloat. "I think you should give him another shot. But this time, don't be scared."

Audrey glanced out the car window to make sure a meteor or nuclear bomb wasn't headed straight toward her. The world had to be about to end if her mother had finally found wisdom to impart. Or maybe her mom was sick or dying.

"Mom, is everything okay?"

Her mom was quiet for a long moment. "Barney, the peach-stand guy, has given me a new perspective," she replied. Audrey heard some voices in the background. "Look, Audrey, I've got to go. Talk later?" And she hung up before Audrey could reply.

Audrey let out a breath that lifted the hair around her face. That was the strangest conversation she'd had with her mom. Had Barney from the peach stand really had such a profound impact on her mom's life, or was something else going on? If there were, Audrey wouldn't know until it reached maximum levels of dramatics.

She looked down at her phone's screen, and her mom's accusations overrode any worry. Audrey wanted to be good at relationships, and that probably meant forgiving Belay completely. Dropping him because he didn't meet all of her ridiculously high expectations was really just an excuse to protect her from dealing with her abandonment issues. Sheesh. When would this stop being a problem? She'd had more than twenty years—and hundreds of hours of therapy—to get over her dad leaving her. But he still seemed to color everything.

She tapped open the Mountain Collective app and started a message to Belay. *My mother has suddenly become a fountain of wisdom. She thinks I should forgive you. So should I listen to her, or should I keep being petty?*

Obviously, I'm with your mother on this one, came his immediate reply. *But I promise this is the only time I'll agree with her. The rest of the time, I'll be like, "Yeah, she's the worst. Mothers! So terrible."*

Audrey laughed. He could always make her laugh. *Fine. I forgive you for standing me up, and I want to be friends again.*

Belay: *Thank you. I really don't deserve it, so it means a lot to me. So how are you doing? Your last message was intense.*

Audrey: *Better. My patient is at home recovering, but her baby will be in the NICU for a while. Luckily, her mom came around, so things should be better.*

Belay: *Sometimes you forgive people simply because you still want them in your life.*

Audrey: *Oh, so now* you're *a fountain of wisdom?*

Belay: *I googled "quotes on forgiveness," and this is the first one that came up. But it felt fitting, for your patient and her mom. And for us.*

Audrey got goosebumps looking at the word *us*. She bit her lip. Could they really be an us? Before he'd stood her up, she'd been pretty smitten. But she couldn't help but feel more cautious now. She'd take it slow this time and make sure they were both ready before they chose to meet again.

+

Chapter 33

When Ammon clocked in at seven p.m. Thursday night, his eyes flitted around the nurses station for Audrey. Would she be here tonight? Or would she be at the birth of one of her patient's babies? He probably should have just asked her if she'd be volunteering, but he hadn't been able to think of a way to do it that seemed nonstalkerish. Especially since he didn't talk much to Audrey as himself. Belay and Bell had gone back to their nightly chats at five p.m., but Ammon had no reason to talk to Audrey in real life.

He saw her come through the doors of Labor and Delivery, and his heart went off at hummingbird speed. "Be cool," he whispered to himself as he headed in her direction. She stopped at the charge nurse's desk to get her assignment. He hoped she'd be working with him. Just as he was about to reach Audrey, he heard his last name called in a short, clipped voice. "Parker!"

Audrey glanced up at him just as he spun around to greet the voice. Of course it was Dr. Callister. "We're needed in surgery."

He followed Callister down the hall and stopped at the sinks to scrub in. "I'm keeping you in the OR as much as possible tonight," Callister said with a grin.

Ammon didn't know if that meant Callister planned to perform as many unnecessary C-sections on his patients as possible or if he planned to pass Ammon off to whichever attending happened to be in the OR. He hoped it was the latter. Ammon hated watching Callister crank up the Pitocin just to send a baby into distress so he could "save" it with surgery.

Once he was scrubbed in, Ammon entered the OR and tried to prepare himself for the long night ahead.

+ + +

Audrey's hopes for the evening were dashed the second she saw Ammon turn to Callister's voice and follow him down the hall, away from her. She'd been assigned one of Ric's patients for the evening and had hoped that meant she'd be working with Ammon. Their last few interactions had left her puzzled, and she wanted to see how long this niceness streak could last. Surely if they got together in a labor and delivery room in a nonemergent situation, their true colors would show and everything would go back as it should be. Because if Ammon wasn't the enemy, then who was he to her? The butterflies in her stomach whenever she was around him were getting annoying. Disliking him was so much easier than liking him.

Because she was finding there *were* things to like about him. He'd taken care of her when she'd needed it. He understood what she had gone through with Claire, and he'd listened and hadn't judged her and had been surprisingly kind and careful. There was clearly more to him than she'd first thought.

Audrey entered the labor room to find Ric showing a nurse how to do a double-hip squeeze on the patient. He looked up at Audrey and gestured for her to come over. "This is Gabby, one of our new nurses," he said. "Gabby, this is Audrey, one of our volunteer doulas."

Audrey nodded by way of greeting since the patient was in the middle of a contraction and she didn't want Gabby to stop the counterpressure just so they could shake hands. When the contraction ended, Audrey introduced herself to the patient and reviewed her birth plan.

For the next six hours, she focused on the birthing mother and (almost) didn't think about Ammon once.

✦ ✦ ✦

Audrey sat at the nurses station with Ric while he completed some charting. The birth had been textbook, and mother and baby had been moved to the postpartum wing. Ric was about to go home, and Audrey was waiting for another assignment. It was a relatively quiet night in Labor and Delivery, with a higher number of patients than usual ending up in the OR. Audrey hadn't seen Ammon once in the thirty minutes she'd been sitting at the nurses station.

"What kind of doctor is Ammon?" Audrey mused. She'd really not meant to ask out loud, but the words were now in the air.

Ric looked up from the computer screen. "Ammon? Oh, Dr. Parker. Yes. He's very teachable."

It was so like Ric to speak in code. He was such a nice guy that Audrey had never heard him speak ill of anyone, even Dr. Callister.

Audrey puzzled over Ric's response for a moment. Ammon had said the same thing about himself when he'd come with her on her prenatal visits.

"He's the highlight of a lot of women's birthing experiences," Ric continued.

Audrey furrowed her brow. "What do you mean?"

"Let's just say, compared to the old fogies like myself working here, Ammon can walk into a delivery room and brighten a woman's day with just a smile."

Audrey laughed, remembering the first time she'd worked with Ammon, when her friend Jessica had commented on his hotness. And now that Ric had mentioned it, Audrey had noticed that patients did tend to get a little gooey around Ammon at first.

"Why are you asking about him?" Ric asked.

"Just curious. He came with me to some prenatal appointments a few weeks ago, and I still haven't been able to get a read on his approach to birth."

"Ammon is still trying to figure that out," Ric answered. "Dr. Callister and I are both attempting to groom him in our philosophies, so to speak."

Audrey frowned. Callister was the worst kind of OB, and Audrey didn't want to think Ammon had anything in common with the way Callister practiced medicine.

"Ammon's a talented surgeon, and he has the potential to be a great doctor," Ric said.

Audrey felt her heart rate spike. Ah, man. If Ric thought Ammon had potential, that was almost all the endorsement she needed.

"What do you think is holding him back?" Audrey asked.

"Himself, mostly. Like most young doctors, he's still getting his sea legs. Something will happen, and he'll sink or swim. But when he swims, it will be with broad, confident strokes. I know it."

Audrey's insides felt warm. No wonder Ric's patients loved him. Audrey loved him too, like a father. It was nice to have someone in her life who saw the good in everyone and believed in them. When she was a young midwifery student, his kindness had changed her life.

Ric made a few more keystrokes, then shut down the charting program on the computer. "Well, that was my last patient for the night." He checked his watch. Audrey noted the time too. It was almost two a.m. "I'm going to head home."

Audrey nodded and Ric left. Soon she found herself supporting another birth. And hoping she'd see Ammon.

Chapter 34

AMMON WAS TWO HOURS AWAY from the end of his shift when he and Callister got word another patient was on her way to the OR. This would be Ammon's fourth C-section tonight.

"Ooh, this is an interesting case," Callister said, scrolling through the chart on the computer. "The patient is at thirty-three weeks and has been on hospital bed rest for the last four weeks for accreta. She's gone into preterm labor and needs an emergency C-hyst."

Ammon rolled his neck and blinked his eyes quickly, trying to wake himself up. His feet ached more than usual, and he felt a cramp in the palm of his right hand. He'd spent the last ten hours on his feet. He usually loved surgery, but tonight had been too much.

Callister kept talking. "You've done a C-hyst before?"

Ammon nodded. He'd done a few C-sections followed by a hysterectomy. All of them had been planned, and none had been emergent. The scrub nurse came over to Ammon and helped him into his gown and gloves.

"Ever done one with an accreta?" Callister asked as he tied a mask over his mouth.

Ammon's brain felt foggier than he would have liked going into emergency surgery. "No," he answered. Accreta, when the placenta grew too deeply into the uterine wall, wasn't something a second-year resident usually dealt with. The risk of hemorrhage was too high to trust to a newbie surgeon.

"Today's your lucky day," Callister said.

The OR filled with people—multiple nurses, an anesthesiologist, a doctor from urology, another doctor from OB oncology, and every resident on the floor—to observe the surgery. Ammon's head spun as the patient was wheeled into the OR.

Callister was giving him instructions, but Ammon couldn't focus above the commotion. ". . . just like any other C-hyst," Callister said.

The room felt stifling. Ammon gestured to a medical assistant to wipe the sweat off his forehead. "I'd rather just perform the C-section and let you do the hysterectomy," he said, surprised at his own words. Ammon was usually good about doing just as his attending advised.

Callister's eyes narrowed above his mask. "I'm giving you a great opportunity, second year. I suggest you take it, unless you want to be stuck only catching babies for the rest of your night rotation."

"No . . . okay, I'll do it. Thank you."

The surgical medical assistant made the final preparations, and Ammon reviewed images from the patient's most recent ultrasound. The placenta had grown through the outer wall of the uterus, but it didn't look like it had grown into the bladder or bowels. He checked the corner of the computer screen for the patient's name: Marisol. "This will be just like any other C-hyst," Callister said again over Ammon's shoulder.

The advice Sandoval had given Ammon during his first day of residency repeated in the back of his mind: "Never plan for a birth to go as planned." Ammon approached the patient, said a silent prayer for support, and took the scalpel.

"We've got to move fast," Callister said. "The longer we take the more blood the patient will lose."

After a quick, clean incision, Ammon pulled the baby from the uterus. He was tiny, probably only three or four pounds. Ammon clamped and cut the umbilical cord and handed the baby over to the NICU nurse. Marisol was under general anesthesia and likely wouldn't see her baby for hours, even after she was out of surgery. The NICU nurse walked the baby over to a window in the OR that connected to the NICU. A nurse on the other side took the baby and placed her in a plastic bassinet. The baby's father, his face pale, watched as the baby was intubated. An ache Ammon wasn't prepared for seeped through his chest. How scary and confusing this all must be.

Ammon returned his focus to the surgical site. Callister pointed out where the placenta had grown through the uterine wall. "Whatever you do, don't touch it," he said. "Even a tiny brush of a finger could break open blood vessels and cause the patient to hemorrhage."

Carefully, Ammon used the Harmonic scalpel to begin the hysterectomy. Callister walked him through step-by-step. Ammon took slow, even breaths and concentrated on the placement of his hands and scalpel.

"Now, lift the uterus to find the bladder flap," Callister said.

Ammon moved the uterus and instantly realized his grip was wrong, but he couldn't change his hold. His hand slipped, his fingers raking over the exposed placenta. Callister bit out a vicious curse as the surgical cavity flooded with blood.

"Start four units of blood," Callister shouted as he pushed Ammon out of the way. He swore again. Ammon watched in horror as blood dripped off the table. He stumbled back, his fingers losing sensation. The lights and colors in the room were too vivid, like someone had put a brightness filter over his eyes.

"She's crashing," he heard a nurse shout.

Ammon looked at his hands, and they looked liked they had been dipped in red paint. When he returned his gaze to the room, he saw a nurse performing chest compressions on Marisol's still body, another nurse administering bags of blood, and Callister appeared to be swimming in red. This couldn't be real. It looked like nothing Ammon had ever seen before; it couldn't be real.

He stood uselessly, to the side. The window between the OR and NICU slid shut, and Ammon locked eyes with the new father. Ammon read his lips: "What's happening?" he asked one of the nurses. The nurse tried to distract him from the scene unfolding on the other side of the window.

Time stretched ahead of Ammon, the seconds keeping time with the nurse's chest compressions. The blood on his gloves began to dry. Then flake. Ammon felt numb. Disconnected. Vacuous.

"I'm going to call it," Callister said. "Time of death 6:34 a.m."

Guilty.

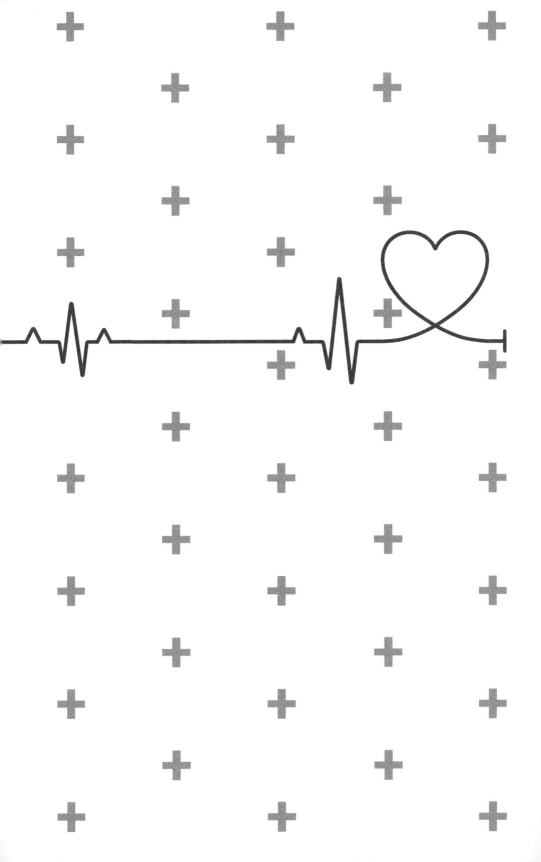

Chapter 35

Hours later, long after his shift had ended, Ammon escaped to the break room. He wanted to go back in time and insist Callister perform the surgery. He wanted to crawl into bed and sleep for the next forty hours. He wanted to be a different person with a different life when he woke up.

There had been piles of paperwork.

There had been a reprimanding by Callister.

There had been a phone call from Sandoval, reassuring Ammon he had done nothing wrong. It was an accident that could have happened to even a more experienced surgeon.

There had been a gut-wrenching post-op meeting where Ammon had had to break the news to the husband. Marisol was dead because of Ammon. Their baby would grow up without a mother because of him.

Ammon put his money into the break room's vending machine and made his selection for a Red Bull. Behind the plastic screen, he could hear the mechanical sound of the drink being released and falling, but the final clink of it being dispensed didn't come. Ammon checked the black opening for his beverage and found it empty. He gave the machine a little shake, but nothing fell out. He pressed the money-return button, but nothing happened.

He hit the machine, and when his drink still didn't come out, he snapped. He grabbed it with both hands and shook it, feeling overcome with rage. A string of curse words that would have offended even Freddy Kappal flew from his mouth. He pounded on the plastic front until he thought it would break. And as suddenly as the rage had come, it left him. His arms felt heavy. A shuddering sob broke through his chest, and he turned from the machine. His eyes landed on Audrey.

His legs lost all their strength, and he sank to the floor, his back against the vending machine. He felt so numb it took him a moment to realize the wetness on his face was from his own tears. Audrey came over, knelt in front of him, and set a tentative hand on his shoulder. "I heard there was a death. Was she your patient?"

Ammon could only nod. He took a few gulps of air, trying to swallow the sobs. He braced his hands on the floor to keep himself from shaking.

A soft hand brushed his cheek. "I'm really sorry," she said. He couldn't meet her eyes, feeling undeserving of her sympathy. "Why don't we move to the couch," she suggested.

Audrey helped him stand and led him to the sofa. She kept her hand in his as they sat down next to each other. He felt anchored by her touch. The ache and emptiness didn't go away, but he could almost breathe again. Ammon kept his gaze fixed on the blank TV screen. He wanted to tell her everything. But they sat quietly, hand in hand. Minutes passed. He wanted to float away.

"You know when you asked me why I went into obstetrics?" he finally said, his voice thick.

"Mm-hmm."

"The answer isn't as simple as I made it seem."

"Of course it isn't," she said, her voice gentle.

"I figured out early on in medical school I couldn't handle death," he admitted. "I wanted to be a trauma surgeon like my grandfather until I did my emergency department rotation. I realized the responsibility and pressure was too much. Every time I lost a patient, I felt my soul fracturing. So I switched to obstetrics. It had the same unpredictable nature of emergency medicine that I liked, and I would still get to do surgery. Less than a thousand women die during childbirth in the U.S., and half of those deaths are preventable. I thought if I was really careful, I could go my whole career without losing a patient."

He glanced at Audrey, her forehead furrowed and her eyes shining.

"We lose a lot more babies than mothers," Ammon said. "But those deaths feel different than this one."

She nodded. "Usually when a baby dies, there's nothing that could have been done," she said. "But when a mother dies, you can't help but wonder . . ."

"Have you ever killed a patient?" he asked.

"I've lost a few," she replied. "Most while I was in Africa."

He glanced at her. "But have you ever killed someone?"

Audrey closed her eyes for a second. Her nod was almost imperceptible. "My very first year after I graduated from the midwifery program, I was working here at the hospital. I'd become particularly close with one of my patients. Her name was Shannon. She and I had a lot in common: both from Washington, both redheads, both loved climbing. She crossed that line between patient and friend." She glanced at him before continuing. "It was her first pregnancy, and she was pretty overwhelmed by the experience. Looking back, I know she had severe prenatal anxiety. She always thought she was going into labor or that she was sick or that the baby had died. Because the midwives had on-call rotations, I wasn't always the one who got her after-hours calls, but I was the one she saw in clinic. Her pregnancy was healthy. She was healthy. I spent most of my time reassuring her that she was fine."

Audrey took a deep breath. "I was on call when she called the after-hours line complaining of right upper-quadrant abdominal pain. She was about thirty-six weeks along. I'd seen her earlier that week. Her blood pressure had been within normal range, and there hadn't been any protein in her urine. I told her it was probably just the baby squishing things as she got bigger and not to worry. If she had been any other patient, I probably would have worried more about the symptom. But Shannon called the after-hours line a few times a week with a complaint, and it was never anything. I figured she was being overanxious. I assured her over and over again she was fine and to go back to sleep. I told her if she was still uncomfortable when the office opened, to make an appointment and we'd talk then. I insisted she didn't need to go to Labor and Delivery."

Tears had built up in her eyes as she spoke and clung to her lashes like fragile raindrops. "The next morning when I went into clinic, I was immediately called away to the hospital. Shannon had just arrived at the hospital, unresponsive. Her liver had ruptured, and she had DIC. She was bleeding to death internally."

Audrey blinked, and the tears hit her cheeks. Ammon squeezed her hands. "Kathleen was able to perform a C-section to save the baby, but Shannon bled out on the table."

Ammon wanted to tell her it wasn't her fault, just like Sandoval had tried to reassure him the death today wasn't his fault. But it didn't matter if it objectively appeared to be just an accident or a misdiagnosis. Ammon felt like a murderer. He knew Audrey felt the same way, or she wouldn't be telling this story.

"She and I were supposed to go climbing after she had her baby," Audrey said in a quiet voice. "We always said we'd go after her six-week follow-up."

Realization fell heavy on his shoulders. As Bell, Audrey had told him she wanted to climb Craggletooth Rock in memory of a friend who'd died in childbirth. The patient Audrey felt she'd killed was that friend. She looked up at him, her eyes wet. He wanted to tell her everything: that he was BelayingonofHands. That he'd fallen in love with Bellinghamster and was now falling in love with her. That he was so sorry for lying to her. That if she'd let him, he'd make everything up to her.

She released his hands and wiped her eyes. "I ran off to Africa," she said. "I thought if I immersed myself in loss, I'd become numb to it. But it never got easier, and I think that's a good thing. If I ever find myself unaffected by the death of a mother or the loss of a baby, I think I'd have to walk away from this profession."

He understood. If he felt something, then that meant he still cared.

"But how will I live with the guilt?" he asked.

"Right now it probably feels like a millstone or a boulder pressing down on you," she said. "But with time, it won't feel so heavy. Not because the burden goes away but because you'll get stronger from carrying it around. And one day, it won't feel like baggage anymore because it will be a part of who you are." Audrey reached out and wove her delicate fingers between his. "Ammon, you're a doctor who has hurt people. But you've also saved a lot of lives. The scales are tipped in your favor."

His eyes captured hers, and the moment grew very quiet. A warmth seemed to encase him. He noticed flecks of gold in Audrey's eyes amid the deep forest green. Her beautiful mouth held in a soft smile, and he smelled roses on her hair. He felt content and safe with her hand in his, their legs touching as they sat side by side. The repellant force between them seemed to shift, and he felt himself instead being pulled toward her like gravity. He closed his eyes, and when his lips touched hers, he fell into the lush sweetness of their kiss.

Chapter 36

AMMON'S WARM, SMOOTH LIPS PRESSED into Audrey's with a gentleness that startled her. Why did it feel like she was getting something she'd always wanted? His hand brushed through her hair, and Audrey pulled away before the kiss could deepen, her heart pounding and her brain clouded. What was happening?

His finger wound around one of her curls, and the earnest look in his blue eyes sent her stomach into a free fall.

"Audrey, I'm—"

"It's okay," Audrey said, certain he was about to apologize. Because what else would he say right now? Certainly not that he liked her. Because they couldn't stand each other, right? She scooted back from him. "Wanting to connect with someone is a normal response after a death," she continued, touching her lips as if to wipe off the kiss. "We can pretend that never happened."

She glanced at him but couldn't read the expression on his face. Hurt? Regret?

"Yeah. Sorry." He sat up straighter. "I don't know what I was thinking." He let out a small laugh that sounded almost sad. "I'm pretty messed up right now."

Audrey patted his hand but didn't take it as before. "Why don't you go home and get some sleep."

He nodded but avoided her eyes.

"Are you okay to drive?" she asked.

"I'll be fine." He stood.

Audrey watch him leave the room, her insides feeling twisted. She felt like she'd failed him.

+ + +

At nine p.m., Audrey knocked on Ammon's door with one hand, balancing a pan of homemade mac and cheese and a Red Bull in the other. She'd tried to get some sleep to recover from the overnight shift, but she'd never fully settled. She couldn't stop worrying about Ammon. She didn't know him well enough to know exactly what he did to cope with tragedy. And she wanted to support him if she could. No one should have to deal with something like this alone.

Plus, that kiss had left her feeling . . . curious. Maybe it had just been a fluke, but she couldn't stop thinking about it. Reliving it. Trying to memorize the exact feel and taste of it. But what did that mean? She'd always been physically attracted to Ammon because who wouldn't be? But she thought she'd felt something more behind the kiss. Something tender and familiar. Something she wanted to feel again.

Freddy answered the door wearing a shirt and tie. Audrey could smell his cologne and noticed his hair appeared to be freshly pomaded. "Is Eleanor ready for me?"

"*You're* who she's going out with tonight?" Audrey asked.

Freddy blinked, surprised. "She didn't send you over to get me?"

"No. I'm here to see Ammon."

Freddy's face spread into a cheeky grin. He eyed the pan resting against her forearms. "Trying to find your way into his heart via his stomach?"

"Have you talked to him since he got home?"

"Nope. He's still asleep. Or at least still in his room."

Audrey sighed. "He lost a patient today. I've come by to check on him."

The smile on Freddy's face disappeared. "I didn't know. Should I cancel my date to hang with him?"

She shook her head. "I've got him," she said. "Ellie *is* ready. If you go over now, she'll probably only make you wait a few minutes just for show."

Freddy stepped into the hall. "Ammon's room is the one on the right."

Audrey entered the apartment, and Freddy closed the door behind her. She switched on the light in the kitchen and set the pan of mac and cheese and Red Bull on the counter. Then she went down the hall and knocked softly on Ammon's closed bedroom door. Her pulse jumped when she heard movement on the other side.

He said something in Spanish that was probably profane, judging by the tone.

"Ammon?" She placed her hand on the door. "It's Audrey."

There was more shuffling, and a moment later, the door opened a crack. She could see just a sliver of his face.

"I've brought food," she said.

She heard him sigh, the sound slicing her in half.

"Give me a minute," he said with a rough voice. He closed the door.

Audrey returned to the kitchen. When she heard the shower start to run in the bathroom, she turned on the oven and placed the mac and cheese inside to keep it warm. She sent a text to Ric to let him know she was checking on Ammon. Then she opened the Mountain Collective app to message Belay.

Audrey felt like she'd reached a tipping point. Her feelings for Belay were becoming less certain because of her recent interactions with Ammon. She liked Belay, but she'd never met him. Things were changing with Ammon, and she didn't understand why or know what it meant.

I'm feeling conflicted about so many things right now. About how I feel about someone in my real life. And about you, Audrey wrote. *I need to tell you something before this—whatever we have—goes any further. You once asked me what I want most in this world, and I was afraid to tell you. But recent events have made me realize I can't wait anymore for things to happen for me. I have to make them happen for myself.*

What I want most in this world is a family of my own. I want a husband and children. I want loved ones to share my life with. And I worry so much that it will never happen for me. That one day, I'll have to find a way to stop wanting this thing I desire so badly. But how do I give up on a dream like that?

I think I need to know how you feel about me. Because I like you, but I don't want to get hurt again.

Audrey pressed Send on her message, the words leaving her feeling fragile as a snow globe. She was so tired of feeling vulnerable. Lately, she felt inside out. But she needed things with Belay to progress or end, so she had to put it all out there. If her wanting a serious relationship scared him off, it was better to know now than in a few months.

The chime of a cell phone that wasn't hers sounded. Audrey looked up to see Ammon walking into the kitchen. He wore a plain gray T-shirt and a pair of worn jeans with a hole in the knee. His hair was wet and tousled. The word *yummy* flitted across her mind as she took him in. He glanced at his phone in his hands, looked at Audrey, and shoved the phone into his pocket.

"You can check that if you need to," she said, gesturing to where his phone had disappeared.

He shrugged. "It's just a message from someone I'm trying to date." He gave a wry smile. "I'll reply later. Best to play hard to get and all." His attempt at levity was almost as painful as the sudden ache that pierced her chest. Why did it bother her that he was trying to date someone? She'd done everything in her power to express no interest in him. He was free to date whomever he wanted.

"Does that actually work for you?" Audrey asked. "From my end, waiting for a reply can be torturous. You guys have no idea what you put women through."

"Is Internet Guy giving you a hard time?" he asked.

"No. Things are good between us again."

He pulled out the chair across from her and sat at the table. "I'm glad to hear that," he said softly. Now that he was closer, she saw how haggard he looked. His eyes were bloodshot. She wondered if he'd been crying all day. Or if his puffy red eyes and sallow cheeks were from a lack of sleep. After a loss, crying and not sleeping went hand in hand.

Emotion rose in her chest, and she reached out and covered one of his hands on the tabletop. "How are you doing?" she asked.

He studied her face for a moment, like he was trying to decide if he could trust her with the truth. "Not good," he replied.

Audrey nodded. There really was nothing to say. Time was the only thing that could heal a wound like this. She patted his hand and stood. "Let me feed you."

She went into the kitchen and took the pan of mac and cheese from the oven, then searched around the cabinets and drawers until she found a plate and fork. Ammon watched her from his chair, his eyes slowing tracing her every move. His expression was unreadable, and the scrutiny made Audrey shiver.

She returned to the table with the plate piled high with noodles. Ammon reached for the fork. "Is this vegan?" he asked as he loaded his fork.

Audrey smiled from the corner of her mouth. Nice to know he was still his snarky self. "Are you really going to bite the hand that's feeding you right now?"

He put the forkful into his mouth and slowly chewed. "I was just curious," he said after he swallowed.

"I'm not vegan," she said. "I'm a vegetarian. And this is my grandma's recipe, so there is plenty of real butter and cheese."

"It's good," he said after another bite. "Thank you."

"You're welcome."

He continued eating, and a heavy silence filled the space between them. Audrey chewed on her bottom lip, trying to decide if she should try to start a conversation or if he'd prefer the quiet. She surveyed the room. She noticed a stuffed-animal llama with colorful tassels tied around its head and neck sitting by the TV and a U of U throw draped over the back of the couch. What was the significance of the llama? And had Ammon gone to the U, or was he just a fan of their football team? She really didn't know anything about him.

When her gaze made its way back over to Ammon, she found him looking at her. His eyes darted away as soon he noticed he'd been caught. Heat moved over her face, and she bit her lip again. This was getting awkward. She needed to make her exit.

They both spoke at the same time.

"Audrey—"

"Is there—?"

She smiled, but Ammon looked miserable. His eyebrows formed a deep *v*, and his shoulders stooped like he was trying to protect himself from something hitting him. A lump grew in Audrey's throat as hurt expanded through her chest. She hated seeing people in pain.

"Is there anything else I can do for you?" she asked.

His eyes grew wet, and he suddenly stood, grabbing his plate. He took it to the sink, where he dropped it in with a clatter. He sniffed and cleared his throat, then leaned his hip against the counter, folding his arms over his chest. She could sense his fragility. He was a glass orb dangling on a worn string.

Audrey stood from her chair and approached him. He avoided her eyes until she stopped right in front of him. When their gazes met, Audrey felt something shift between them, the air between them growing charged. Ammon made a small movement toward her, and she turned her face to avoid a kiss.

"Chill out, Audrey," he said. "I know better than to kiss you without your consent."

"Oh."

"But can I have a hug?" His eyes looked so blue, and Audrey's stomach fluttered. She nodded, and he slipped a hand around her waist. With his gentle tug, she stepped into his arms.

She rested her hands tentatively against his chest. He felt warm and solid beneath her palms. She was the perfect height that her nose reached the hollow of his neck, where she could smell his soap and the masculine scent underneath that was just Ammon. Her breath quickened as he pulled her closer. She slid her hands up his shoulders and wrapped her arms around his neck. His hands moved up her back and into her hair.

It should have scared her, or at the very least confused her, how comfortable she felt in his arms. Instead, she breathed him in and pulled herself closer. A sigh escaped her. It'd been so long since she'd been held like this.

Chapter 31

WHAT AMMON HAD INTENDED TO be a brief thank-you hug grew into a long embrace. He was on the edge of both sobbing and soaring: still devastated and guilt-ridden over the loss of his patient but inexplicably happy to have Audrey in his arms. And she seemed to want to be there, pulling him closer and sighing in a way that sent his heart ricocheting.

After hugging her for an indecent amount of time because he couldn't make himself let go, Ammon did finally release Audrey. She looked at him with a woozy smile. He wondered if his own smile looked just as dazed. She held his hands, even through they'd stepped apart.

"Uh, thanks for coming over," he said, the words feeling inadequate.

She squeezed his hand. "It was nothing," she said. "What's your self-care plan for this weekend?"

He creased his brow. "Self-care plan?"

"Didn't they talk about this medical school?" She released his hands. "You need a self-care routine to help recover from really bad days. I like to watch old movies or take a hike or go climbing. I also journal."

"Don't you also eat ice cream and Oreos?" he asked.

She shot him a look but continued like he hadn't said anything, "It's also good to be around other people. It's a lot harder to spiral when someone is with you."

He thought for a moment what he could do. The ache in his chest was returning at full force now that he'd left the comfort of her embrace. He wanted to go back into his dark room and never leave again. Audrey watched him with careful attention.

"I guess I'll go visit my parents," he said slowly. He hadn't seen them much since he'd started his night rotation.

"Oh, they live nearby?" she asked.

"West Jordan," he replied, shoving his hands into his pockets.

She smiled. "That sounds like a really great idea."

He nodded, shifting his weight between his feet.

"Well, I'll go now," she said, stepping away from him. She replaced the foil cover on the mac and cheese and opened the refrigerator. "And I'll leave this in the fridge for later."

He wanted to reach out and pull her back into his arms. The memory of her lips on his during their brief kiss leaped into his mind. "Why are you taking care of me?" The question left his mouth before he'd thought it through.

She slowly shut the refrigerator door and turned toward him. He couldn't quite read the expression on her face. "You seemed so distraught earlier, and I wasn't sure what your support system looked like. I wanted to make sure you had someone to turn to, even if it was just me."

Ammon shook his head. It didn't make sense. She didn't even like him, so why would she care if he spiraled? Unless . . . Hope leaped in his chest. Did she like him? "Well, thank you," he said.

"I was happy to do it," she replied. He wanted to memorize the soft smile that appeared on her lovely mouth and the way her eyelashes cast a shadow on her cheekbones as she looked down. If he could decipher the emotion on her face in that moment, he would know how she really felt about him.

He led her to the door, his hand hovering over the small of her back. The door clicked shut behind her, and the space in his apartment suddenly felt like a vacuum. That raw feeling, like his heart was inside out, grew stronger. He went to the couch and collapsed, the phone in his front pocket digging into his thigh.

He remembered he had a message from Bell.

Ammon sat up and pulled the phone from his pants. He'd received the message just as he'd walked into the kitchen. Audrey must have written it while he'd been in the shower.

He pulled up the app and read her message as his aching heart tried to make room for all the conflicting emotions he felt. How could he both be so, so sad and so, so happy?

She felt conflicted about her feelings for someone in her real life. Did she mean him? She wanted a family. A husband. She liked Belay.

He took a deep breath, realization making his chest swell. He could give her the family she always wanted. But he had to figure out how to get her to love him enough so that when she found out he'd been Belay all along, she'd forgive him for deceiving her.

He didn't know how to reply without proposing marriage, so he left his apartment and drove to his parents' house across the valley. It was nearing ten thirty when he pulled up to the house, but he saw lights still on. His mom had always been the last to go to bed and the first up.

He ran up the familiar walkway, the smell of jasmine sweetening the air. He tried the door to find it unlocked. An unseen but palpable feeling lightened him as he walked through the door—the feeling of coming home. The air smelled of cooked meat and Pine-Sol. He walked into the kitchen to find his mom on her knees, scrubbing the old linoleum floor.

She looked up when his shadow fell across the space she was cleaning. Her eyes widened, and a huge smile that would have broken his heart if it weren't already shattered appeared on her face. "Ammon!" She left the brush on the floor when she stood. Her yellow-gloved hands reached for him, then stopped. Ammon felt a smile pull at his lips. She removed the gloves, set them on the counter, and pulled him into a tight hug. He hugged her back, emotion rising in the back of his throat.

"What are you doing home?" she asked as she pulled back to look at him. A crease appeared between her eyebrows, and she touched his cheek. "Oh, sweetie. What is it?"

He felt his smile waver and his chin tremble. He was sick of crying.

"Let's sit down." They went to the couch. "You know, I remember my dad coming home from the hospital some days with that exact look on his face." She wrapped an arm around him. "I'm so sorry, Ammon."

"What would Grandpa do on those days?" Ammon asked.

"He'd disappear into his office for the evening," his mom said. "And Mom would send us to bed early." She sighed. "I spied on him once. He was writing furiously in a journal. After he died, I found them."

"What was in them?" A little spark of hope lit in his chest. Maybe his grandfather had the secret to letting go of this guilt.

"Why don't I show it to you."

His mom shuffled upstairs, and Ammon slumped back on the couch. In his head appeared the devastated pale face of Marisol's husband as Ammon broke the news. The man had collapsed to his knees and sobbed. Ammon's heart felt like it had gone through a paper shredder.

When his mom returned, she held a blue-canvas-covered book. She handed it to him and returned to her spot next to him. Ammon flipped the journal open to its first page. His grandfather's almost illegible script filled the page. The entry was dated February 3, 1976. It described in clinical terms what had happened. The next three pages told of the same event but as a narrative from his grandpa's point of view: what his grandpa had done, how he'd felt, how he'd reacted. Ammon couldn't read it, the words triggering terrible images in his mind of his own tragedy, so he merely skimmed the pages. The final page of the entry broke down what had gone wrong and what his grandfather could do differently next time to change the outcome.

A tear dropped on the page. Ammon glanced at his mom. "How many journals are there like this?"

"Two others."

Ammon let out a long breath, his admiration for his grandfather growing. He wished he could talk to him now. Just knowing his grandpa had gone through what Ammon had, helped. When he was feeling less undone, he'd read his grandfather's entries.

"Grandpa would be proud of you," his mom said.

Ammon felt his eyes start to burn. His mom's touch on his cheek was all the permission he needed to cry again. Clenching the book against his chest, he sobbed in his mother's arms and told her everything.

+ + +

Ammon loaded the dishwasher while his mom finished scrubbing the floor. She then fed him chocolate-chip cookies with whole milk. Around midnight, his mom was ready to head to bed, and Ammon considered what to do next. His apartment would be quiet, if not empty, depending on how long Freddy stayed out with Ellie. Sleep wasn't in the cards for Ammon anyway. He'd slept all day. He'd probably turn on some Netflix.

"How much longer do you work the night shift?" his mom asked, putting the milk back in the refrigerator.

"One more week," he said. When he started the night rotation, he'd thought the ten weeks would never end. But now that the end was so near, he realized part of him would miss it. Or maybe he would miss seeing a certain midwife on Thursday nights.

"What will you be doing next?" she asked.

"Gynecologic surgery. No nights. No catching babies."

"That will be a nice change," his mom said. She finished putting her cleaning supplies away. "Are you still planning to come to the family reunion in two weeks?"

Ammon had forgotten about it. In two weeks, his life would be much more predictable. "Yeah. I'll head up after work on Friday."

"Some of Sarai's and Debbie's kids want you to take them rock climbing."

They were his two oldest sisters, and their kids were all young adults and teenagers. It would take hours to belay all of them. He'd probably need to drag Freddy along to help.

"I can do that," he said.

"Good. Everyone will be happy to see you." She kissed him on the temple. "Don't leave that table until the floor is dry."

Ammon nodded. "Goodnight, Mom."

"Goodnight, sweetie." She tiptoed out of the kitchen, leaving tiny crescent prints in the wet floor.

He pulled out his phone and reread Audrey's message to Belay. She was worried about having to give up on her dream of having a family.

Ammon had always assumed he would get married. It hadn't happened yet, but he figured it would eventually. He was confident he wouldn't be alone forever.

But it bothered him that Audrey thought one day she'd have to give up on getting what she wanted. What did that feel like? It had to hurt, reimagining a life you always thought you'd have. Ammon couldn't help but think of the widower and infant he'd left, how the father must have imagined his wife being with him as they returned home with their new baby, how he must have expected his wife would be there for the first steps and first words. Everything would be different now. For Ammon too.

Fire surged through his chest. But Audrey wouldn't have to give up on the life she imagined. If Ammon could manage to get her to fall for him in real life—because she had fallen for Belay—then he could give her everything.

He reread her words. She wanted a family. She'd told him before she'd always envied large families like his. He smiled, thinking of the family reunion he had coming up. He could make this all work.

His fingers typed back a reply. *Don't give up on your dreams, my Bell. I know you'll get the family you always wanted.*

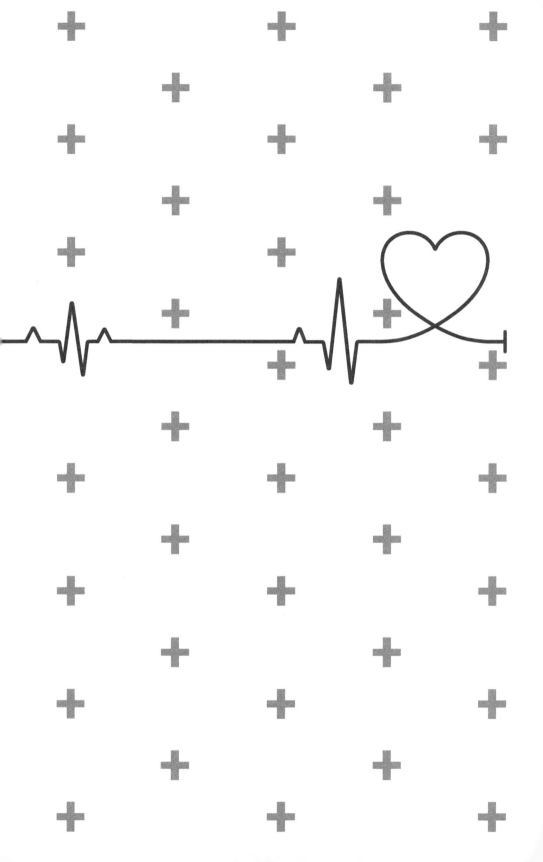

Chapter 38

NEAR THE END OF A busy shift at the free clinic Tuesday afternoon, Audrey was handed a chart with a familiar name. Surprise nearly lifted her off her feet, and she rushed to the waiting room. Her eyes landed on Claire, a tiny bundle in her arms, with her mom seated beside her. Audrey took a deep breath, love and hope swelling in her chest. These were the moments she lived for in her line of work—the beautiful ways a new baby could reaffirm life and love.

Audrey called out Claire's name, and a huge smile appeared on the young woman's face. They hadn't seen each other in person since Claire left the hospital three weeks ago. She'd texted Audrey almost daily, mostly with pictures of baby Annie. Audrey knew Annie had been able to go home from the NICU yesterday, but she hadn't expected to see either of them until Claire's six-week postpartum visit.

Claire put the baby in her car seat, and threw her arms around Audrey, the embrace filling her with healing. The last few weeks had been hard. Claire's mom was next, her hug awkward and short. "Thank you for calling me that night," she said, her eyes shining with tears. Audrey had met Claire's mom only briefly at the hospital after Claire had come out of surgery.

Mother and daughter, baby in tow, then followed Audrey down the narrow hall, back to an exam room. "I'm sorry for the long wait," Audrey said. "It's been a crazy day."

Once in the room, the baby fussed from her carrier, and Claire reached down to pick her up, her movements careful yet still clumsy in the way a first-time mom's were.

"Oh, she's precious," Audrey said, taking in the baby's tiny, squished face. Annie's fussing soon turned into cries. Claire bounced the little baby and tried to soothe her, but the wailing continued.

"I think I need to feed her again," Claire said, sitting down in a hard-plastic chair. Her mom took the chair beside her, and Audrey sat on the black-wheeled stool.

Claire fumbled with her shirt, clearly trying to be discreet as she positioned the fussing baby to nurse. Claire winced, adjusted Annie, who had grown quiet, and then seemed to relax herself.

"Anything particular bring you in today?" Audrey said

"I just wanted to see you," Claire said, uncertain. "Is that okay?"

A huge smile pulled at Audrey's lips. "Of course. I'm so glad you're here."

Claire sighed.

"So," Audrey said. "Tell me everything."

As Claire told Audrey about her recovery, struggles with breastfeeding, moving back home, and the miracles that occurred in the NICU, Audrey felt a cosmic shift, one that had been building up over the past few weeks and finally seemed to settle into place.

Seeing Claire and her mother together again, and thinking of the way Ammon had clung to Audrey in his kitchen, she knew she needed people to shore her up. It was what she'd told Ammon he needed. It was why she'd brought him food and made sure he wouldn't be alone in his grief. She needed her own mother; she needed to forgive her mother and accept and value the relationship they did have, regardless of how contentious it was.

And Audrey needed to let someone else in.

✚ ✚ ✚

When his phone chimed, Ammon didn't need to check to know it was Bell. It was five p.m. It could only be her. Ammon opened the message.

Bell: *Do you have much experience with babies?*

Ammon: *Is this an interview question for the job of future husband?*

Bell: *No. I'm not so pragmatic that I would conduct an interview.*

Ammon: *I have a lot of experience with babies. I have five older sisters. And about twenty nieces and nephews.*

Bell: *About? You don't know how many?*

Ammon: *Ten of each, give or take one or two. Let me check the family calendar, and I'll get back to you.*

Bell: *Family calendar? Is this another thing I'm missing out on because I only have a mom and a grandma?*

Ammon: *You could have a family calendar. It just wouldn't have as many birthdates or anniversaries on it. But really, why did you ask about my experience with babies (if not to interview me to be your future husband)?*

Bell: *Okay, fine, I was interviewing you. And the fact that you don't know how many nieces and nephews you have is concerning. How can I trust you to keep track of all twelve of our children?*

Ammon: *I just checked the calendar, and I have eleven nieces and eight nephews.*

Bell: *The seeds of doubt have already been sown.*

Ammon: *Ask me a different question.*

Bell: *Goodnight, Belay.*

Ammon: *Please, give me another chance!*

Bell: *Talk to you tomorrow?*

Ammon: *Yeah. Tomorrow.*

Ammon grinned as he left his room. Audrey was considering him—well, Belay—for a serious relationship. He had a plan to win her over as Ammon. His mom was even on board. He just had to play the next few moves perfectly. And hope she forgave him when all was revealed.

Freddy sat on the couch in their living room, game controller in hand. "Hey, man," he said. "Want me to add you in?"

Ammon shrugged and grabbed the second controller off the coffee table. Freddy was playing Minecraft, of all things. Ammon brought up his little avatar in the game and joined Freddy in building a roller coaster.

"How are you doing?" Freddy asked. He was using his therapist voice, so Ammon knew he was asking about the patient he'd killed. *Marisol. Her name was Marisol.*

Ammon took in a deep breath and held it for a moment before exhaling, long and slow. If he breathed deeply enough, sometimes he could stave off the ache. He'd almost forgotten while chatting with Bell how horrible he'd felt, but the pain was back now in full force.

"I've been better."

Freddy nodded. "I'm here for you," he said. "We can talk anytime. I won't even bill you."

That earned him a rueful smile. "Thanks," Ammon said. He cleared his throat. "I'd actually like to talk about it."

Freddy paused their game and turned toward him. Ammon took another deep breath and then told his story.

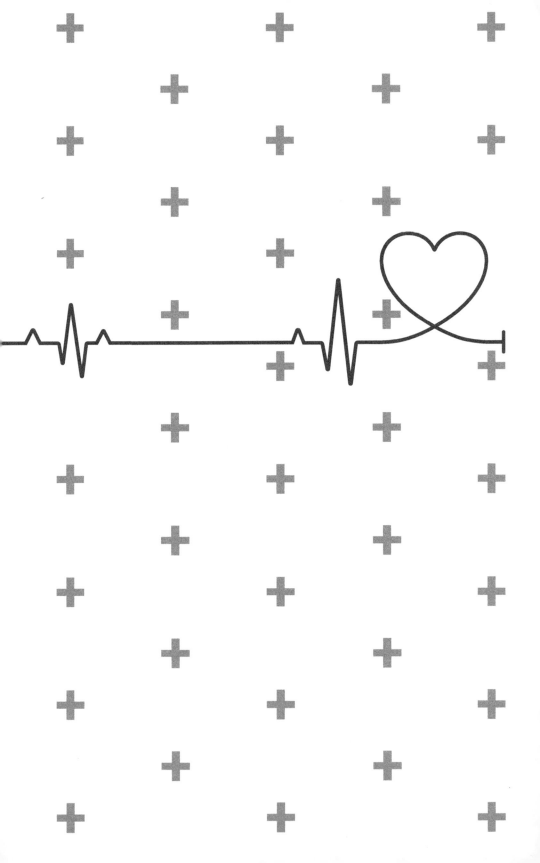

Chapter 39

"YOU'RE KIDDING ME," AUDREY SAID, her face both angry and adorable. She put her hands on her hips and stood between Ammon and the patient.

Ammon smirked. "I thought we were past all this," he said.

When he started his shift six hours ago and discovered Audrey would be the doula for one of his patients tonight, he'd been giddy. But that giddiness had worn off and was now replaced by annoyance.

"What does Dr. Sandoval think of this?" Audrey asked.

Ammon glanced at the patient, who watched the two of them argue, with interest. "Let's talk in the hall." He escorted her from the room. The hall was bustling with nurses and medical assistants. It was the busiest night Ammon had ever worked: every delivery room was filled, two of the triage rooms had been turned into delivery rooms, and a patient was even laboring in the hall, waiting for a room to clear out.

"Audrey," Ammon said carefully. "I know what the patient's birth plan says."

"Then, why are you suggesting Pitocin and breaking her water?"

"I was suggesting one or the other and was going to leave it up to the patient to decide. Had you not interrupted me, I would have happily had a thorough discussion with her about her options."

Audrey humphed and looked away.

"Sandoval said we've got to free up some rooms and to use my best judgment. This patient has been stuck at six centimeters for two hours. On any other night, I'd let you continue to do your doula voodoo to get things progressing, but we don't have that luxury right now."

She gave him a sharp look.

"Was it the voodoo comment?" he asked with a grin.

"You're so smug, you know that?" she shot back.

"The patient kind of agreed to this when she chose to give birth in a hospital," Ammon replied.

"Well then, maybe I'll give her my business card and we'll check out of here."

Audrey spun around to go, but he grabbed her hand. He gave a little tug, and she turned back toward him.

"We're okay, right?" he asked, his fingers playing against hers. He liked the way it felt when their hands were together. "Like, later you'll be nice to me again?"

A small, almost imperceptible smile appeared on her face before it disappeared. She pulled her hand from his. "Maybe."

He grinned again. "I think you meant yes."

"Get over yourself," she said and strode back into the patient's room.

✦ ✦ ✦

Ammon followed Dr. Sandoval out of the OR at the end of his shift, feeling curiously confident. The surgery had gone well.

Earlier in the week, Dr. Sandoval and Dr. Ferguson had staged an intervention and insisted Ammon jump right back into surgery. The longer he waited, the harder it would be to feel comfortable in the OR again. And they were right. His anxiety had lessened with each surgery. It also didn't hurt knowing Dr. Callister had been placed on an extended leave and would never work with residents again.

Once in the hall, Ammon removed his mask. This surgery had felt different. With Sandoval's calming presence beside him, Ammon felt confident again in his abilities. No wonder women loved having Sandoval in the delivery room. His vibe was so supportive. Feeling confident in the OR was a relief. Surgery was Ammon's favorite part of the job. It's what he'd always thought he was best at.

Sandoval removed his surgeon's cap and put it in the disposal bin. He offered Ammon a smile. "In case I don't see you next week, it's been a pleasure working with you, Dr. Parker," he said, holding out his hand. Ammon was surprised. It was the resident's job to thank the attending, not the other way around.

Ammon shook Sandoval's hand. "No, thank you for your mentorship, sir. I've learned a lot."

"You've come a long way these last ten weeks."

Ammon nodded, his mouth going a little dry. "Thank you, sir." Would Sandoval bring up what a punk Ammon had been at the start of his rotation?

But Sandoval's eyes shone with pride. "You have the potential to be a great obstetrician."

"I do?" Ammon choked out. He hadn't been expecting that. At all. He still had so much to learn.

"Do you know the difference between a good OB and a great OB?"

Ammon felt like this was a trick question. "C-section rate?"

Sandoval chuckled and shook his head. "What percentage of patients do you think show up to the hospital with a birth plan?"

Ammon shrugged. "Maybe ten percent?"

Sandoval nodded. "Yes, around that. Most women come into the delivery room with no idea they have a voice. They don't know they can decline interventions or have a say about who can check their cervix and how often. Most women don't even know those things matter."

"So a great OB encourages their patients to make a birth plan?" It was totally like Sandoval to lead Ammon around like this.

"That's part of it," Sandoval replied. "Here's the deeper principle: a good OB tells the patient what is going to happen to them, but a *great* OB empowers and asks permission."

Ammon gnawed on this for a moment. "So you mean a great OB practices like a midwife?"

Sandoval raised an eyebrow and chuckled. "It's not a doctor or a midwife thing," he said. "It's about providing women-centered care, regardless of birth setting."

Audrey would love this, Ammon thought.

"I'm going to keep my eye on you," Sandoval said. "And should you consider a fellowship in maternal-fetal medicine, I'd love to write you a strong recommendation."

Ammon's mind stopped reeling, and he felt like a million different puzzle pieces fell in front of him, landing in the perfect configuration. *Maternal-fetal medicine*. Why had he never considered that? He'd get to work with high-risk pregnant patients and solve complicated medical problems. He'd be able to perform more C-sections and surgeries. He'd get to use his strengths as a doctor and do what he loved. A big goofy smile tugged at his mouth. He stuck his hand out to Sandoval. "Thank you, sir," he repeated, shaking his hand again. "I'll consider it."

But Ammon had a sense he would do more than consider it. For the first time since starting his residency, he didn't wonder if he'd picked the wrong area of medicine to study.

Chapter 40

AUDREY LAY ON THE COUCH in the break room, her eyes squeezed shut beneath an extra T-shirt. Even with her eyes closed, everything seemed too bright. She could tell this migraine was going to be a bad one. And she needed to get it under control before she attempted to drive home, or she'd lose her vision. Then she'd be stuck at the hospital, lying on the old couch in the break room with a T-shirt over her face until the darn thing went away. Two Excedrin and a half hour of quiet in pitch-blackness usually did the trick.

She heard someone enter the break room, and she lay supremely still, hoping whoever it was assumed she was sleeping and would proceed quietly. The person dropped six coins into the vending machine, each making a sharp clink that seemed to hit her right between the eyes. Who still carried change these days anyway? The machine took credit cards, for goodness sake. She heard the person make a selection and held her breath, waiting for the drink to drop and split her head open.

The drink never came. So the horrible person gave the machine a hearty kick. Audrey flinched. He—she had to assign the unknown person a gender, and it seemed likely a man would kick the vending machine like that when a woman was clearly asleep on the couch—kicked the machine again. When his second kick still didn't yield the drink, he shook the machine, the sound of metal against metal leaving Audrey's aching head feeling like it would split in two. Too bad there hadn't been an empty delivery room for her to hide in.

After another solid smack to the machine, the drink rattled and clanked its way out. Audrey huffed a sigh of relief. Maybe now she'd get some quiet.

Except not.

The person tapped her on the shoes. "Audrey, you're hogging the whole couch." Of course the voice belonged to a certain blond doctor.

Audrey wanted to be furious, but she felt a smile on her lips. Ugh, how did he do that? She tried to school her face, but the smile stuck. Good thing she had a T-shirt covering her face. She could not go all gooey around him. So what if he'd kissed her and then later hugged her in a way that made her feel all safe and melty? Ammon was not who she wanted to spend time thinking about. She had a budding romance with Belay that she was trying to cultivate. Except now she wasn't so sure.

She removed the T-shirt from her face and sat up, hugging her legs to her chest.

"What are you still doing here?" he asked, sitting down a little too close to her. Her shift had technically ended two hours ago, but her last patient's labor had gone long and Audrey hadn't wanted to abandon her. And then the migraine had come on with a vengeance.

"Headache," she replied, her eyes hurting. She wanted to cover her face back up.

"You want me to write you a prescription for something?" His smile was a little crooked. She couldn't tell if he was being serious or just joking.

"No, I just need some quiet," she said pointedly.

"Oh, right. Sorry."

He stood like he was going to leave, and she felt a stab of disappointment. When he got to the door, he flipped the light switch off. The room fell into almost complete darkness, except for the red glow of the vending machine and the light leaking in through the cracks of the doorframe. Audrey's eyes fluttered shut in relief. Why hadn't she done that?

She felt Ammon return to the couch and sit right next to her. Her pulse increased, and when she took a deep breath to try to slow it, she could smell mint on his breath.

"Let me see your hands," he said. She put her hands out, trying to ignore the butterflies beating against her stomach. "My mom taught me this," he said, his fingers skimming along her palms. She rested her forehead on her knees, a tiny sigh escaping. His thumb and index finger settled on a familiar pressure point, and he massaged her hand in slow circular motions. The edges of her headache began to fray.

"No hard feelings about earlier?" Ammon asked, the delicious pressure on Audrey's hands not ceasing. "I was just trying to do my job."

"I know," Audrey said. She lifted her head and rested her chin on her knees. She could just make out his face in the darkness. His eyes stayed focused on her hands. "Sorry I gave you such a hard time. I was just trying to do my job."

"I know," he replied, his eyes flickering up to hers.

"Maybe next week we'll get it right," she said with a smile.

"Actually, this is my last night shift." He stopped massaging her hands, but he still held them.

"Oh?" Why did this disappoint her so much?

"My final week in L&D will be day shifts, and then I'll move to my gynecologic surgery rotation."

"I'm glad we got to work together." She squeezed his hands, liking their dry warmth.

He nodded but furrowed his brow, like he was disappointed. What was he hoping she'd say?

"How's your headache?" he asked.

Her fingers absentmindedly stroked his palms. "Better."

"Before you go, can I ask you a favor?" he said, his blue eyes meeting hers.

She didn't dare speak, afraid her voice would come out breathy. She nodded again.

"Are you free next weekend?" he asked.

Her stomach somersaulted with anticipation. That question shouldn't have excited her this much. After clearing her throat, she tried to sound nonchalant. "If my patient doesn't go into labor, I should be free."

His shoulders relaxed, and he let go of her hands. "I need someone to help me belay. Some of my older nieces and nephews want me to take them climbing."

She swallowed her disappointment. Wait. Had she actually been hoping he was asking her out? Her gaze drifted to his strong arms, and longing pinched her chest. Maybe she shouldn't have been so quick to dismiss their kiss.

Stop. You have Belay. "Yeah, I can help," she said. "Where are you taking them?"

"Creole Crag, in Park City," he said. "We're staying at a cabin. Do you want to carpool up Friday? I think we'll climb early Saturday morning, before it gets too crowded."

An overnight trip with Ammon and a bunch of teenagers? He definitely wasn't trying to romance her. "That sounds fine. Why don't you text me the details."

His signature smirk appeared. "Can I get your number?"

Her stomach flipped, and she pulled a pen from her purse. She reached down and grabbed his hand. He held his palm open for her, and in the dim light she could just barely make out his pulse fluttering beneath the skin of his wrist. She wrote her number on his hand. "Just like high school."

"I'll never wash this hand," Ammon said.

She closed his palm over the numbers. "Don't be weird."

Together, they left the break room and went to their cars. She couldn't help but wonder why being with Ammon suddenly felt so familiar.

✛ ✛ ✛

When Ammon got home from his last overnight shift, he tore off the foil on his bedroom windows and crumpled it into an orb the size of a basketball. Sunlight streamed into the once-dark space, illuminating the dust floating in the air like tiny dancers.

He'd survived. The doubts he'd had at the beginning of his night rotation had nearly faded. He no longer wondered if he'd picked the wrong field of medicine. And as impossible as it seemed, Ammon didn't find himself thinking every moment of every day about the patient he'd killed, like he'd feared he would. Reading his grandfather's journals had helped. Getting some free therapy from Freddy had made a huge difference. Knowing Audrey had survived the same thing made him feel less alone. He still thought about Marisol often, still wondered about her husband and baby, but that fresh ache he was so certain would always accompany him had lessened. Death was part of being a doctor, and he was learning how to cope with it.

In the midst of the long hours and the tragedy, he'd almost forgotten he was at the end of his second year. When he started his gynecologic surgery clinic in one week, he'd be a third year, which meant more responsibilities. Less hand-holding. And a first-year resident to usher around. All the hard work from the last six years finally seemed to be paying off. He caught a glimpse of Audrey's phone number written on his palm and pumped his fist. Everything seemed to be falling into place.

Ammon left his room, feeling too energized to sleep. He plopped down on the couch and pulled out his phone. Before he accidentally washed off

Audrey's number, he programmed it into his phone. He then opened the Mountain Collective app. If he wanted Audrey to turn her full attention to Ammon, he needed things with Belay to come to an organic end. He hoped once Belay was out of the picture, Audrey would fully fall for Ammon. And when he eventually revealed he'd been Belay the whole time, she'd forgive him because by then she'd be in love with him. Maybe. Hopefully. This was all very risky.

He typed and retyped his message to Bell before finally settling on the simplest one: *Here are the coordinates to Craggletooth Rock. I probably should have given them to you after you told me why you wanted to find the route so badly. I think I held back because I was worried if I gave you the coordinates, you wouldn't want to talk to me anymore. And then I messed up by not meeting you in person. I've known for a long time that you're pure in heart. In fact, you are one of the best people I know.*

Go climb the route for your friend. You deserve it.

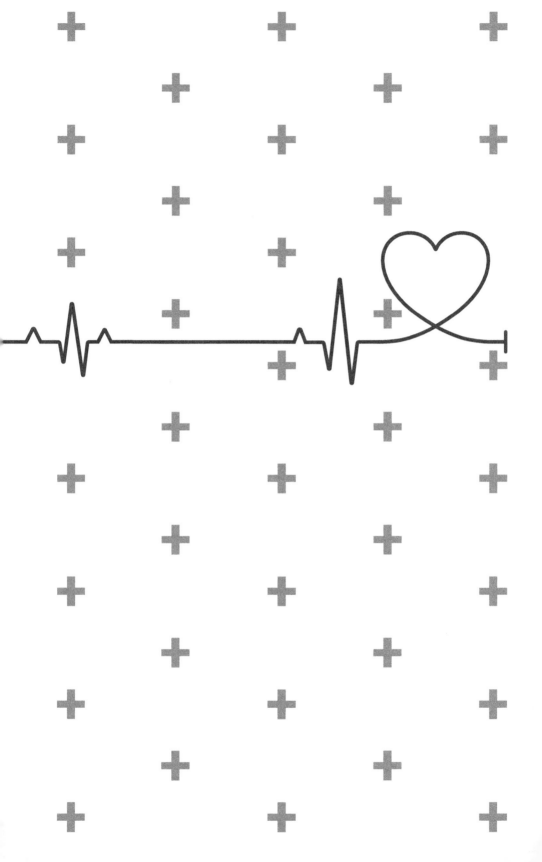

Chapter 41

AUDREY HELD THE COORDINATES TO Craggletooth Rock. If only she hadn't promised Ammon she'd belay for him, she'd climb the crag over the weekend. Instead, she had real life to attend to.

The week passed in its usual whirl, with prenatal appointments and her volunteer work. Her Tuesday shift at the free clinic didn't feel the same without Claire coming every week, and her shift as a doula at the hospital had felt empty without Ammon.

As she drove home from the hospital Friday morning, Audrey called her mom. The conversation started out with its usual tension, but Audrey didn't let it deter her. She kept talking and told her mom about Claire, and Elaine's home birth, and Ammon losing a patient. She'd never spoken this openly with her mom before, but Audrey was trying to have a meaningful relationship with her. Her mom just listened until she was finished.

"You've been through so much the last few weeks," her mom said. "Maybe this is a sign it's time to slow down. You've always done too much."

Her mother was right. Audrey had always been an overachiever and a people-pleaser. Maybe she should cut out one of her volunteer activities and put that time into growing her practice. She'd had only one patient with a May due date. If she wanted to stay in the black, she needed at least two per month and ideally three. When Charlotte graduated midwifery school next year, Audrey could hire her on to be her partner, and then she'd be able to take on even more clients. The idea of expanding excited her.

"Hey, Mom? Do you mind if we talk business sometime?" Audrey asked. "I think it might be time to grow mine."

The surprised catch in her mom's voice was tiny but there. "Yeah, Aud. I'd love to help."

Audrey pulled into her parking spot. "Okay, great. I'll call you later, then?"

They said goodbye, and she ended the call just as she got an incoming text message: *I'll be by at four if that works for you.*

She didn't recognize the number, but it was probably Ammon's. She was supposed to go to Park City with him today. She needed to pack and get some sleep before then.

She replied, *Do you need me to bring my climbing gear?*

The little dots flashed as he typed his response. *If you have extra shoes and gloves, those could be helpful. But I've got everything else.*

She felt an uncomfortable mix of anxiety and excitement competing in her chest. Things with Ammon were so unpredictable. Sometimes he was a cocky jerk, and other times he was genuine and vulnerable. And she didn't know which she'd get and who she wanted to be in return. If he was cocky, she could get away with being her bratty self, and that felt safe. It kept him at arm's length. But those moments when he was genuine? They left her wanting to pull in and never let go. She didn't want to feel like that with Ammon. If she were honest with herself, it had nothing to do with her feelings for Belay. Belay was still a fantasy. But Ammon . . . he was real, and any feelings she may or may not have for him were real too. If they were real, then she could also get hurt for real. The possibility of being abandoned again by someone she wanted was still too scary.

Audrey got out of her car and went into her apartment. The telltale sign of Ellie's clicking keyboard echoed down the hall from her bedroom. She'd been writing a lot more than usual, and the two hadn't had a conversation longer than five minutes in the last two weeks. Audrey couldn't decide whether Ellie was in crisis or just working hard. Maybe both. She'd check in on her before leaving and would cancel things with Ammon if needed.

Audrey grabbed a bag of carrots and a container of hummus from the fridge, then escaped to her own room. Her phone buzzed again just as she sat down. What did he want now?

It wasn't a message from Ammon though. It was from Belay. *Are you climbing Craggletooth Rock this weekend?*

No, she typed back. *I'm going with a friend to Park City. But I'm planning to climb it soon.*

Make sure you take a selfie at the top and send it to me.

Audrey sighed. This was too confusing.

Chapter 42

AUDREY YAWNED AND TRIED TO appear pleasant when Ammon showed up at her door at four p.m., but she was running on fumes. After packing for the weekend and touching base with her two June patients, she'd managed only four hours of sleep. Ammon's smile was annoyingly cheerful. "I should warn you," she said, "I'm not feeling very chatty."

His smile didn't falter. "No problem. I've got enough words for both of us." He took her duffel bag and hefted it over his shoulder. "You ready?"

"Yes." She shouted a goodbye over her shoulder to Ellie, who was not in crisis mode but just under a deadline, and followed Ammon out to his car. He drove a well-loved Toyota Corolla. While there wasn't trash on the floor, there was an abundance of crumbs and unopened ketchup packets stuffed into every available cupholder. She picked one up. "In case of the zombie apocalypse?"

"I'm hoping they'll go for at least a few cents on the black market."

She dropped the packet back into the cupholder. He put the car into gear, and she clipped her seat belt. "Mind if I put on some music?" he asked.

"Sure," she said as he clicked on the stereo.

The chorus to "Yellow Submarine" blared through the speakers. Ammon offered a sheepish grin before turning the volume down. "Sorry. Doubt you'd want to listen to that."

Audrey almost told him it was fine. It was Belay's favorite song, after all. Perhaps she could grow to like it too. Ammon pressed the skip button before she could stop him. The opening bars of The Beatles's "All You Need Is Love" played.

Ammon glanced at her out of the corner of his eye. "This okay?"

She smiled and settled back into her seat. "Yeah, this is fine."

+ + +

An hour later, they pulled up in front of the biggest, most beautiful cabin Audrey had ever seen. It was all dark-red wood and brick columns, huge windows, and rustic awnings. The mansion was surrounded by pine trees and perched on top of a hill. Audrey itched to see the view on the other side of the house.

Ammon shifted the car into park but kept his hands on the steering wheel. "There's something I probably should have mentioned before we left," he said.

As usual, when she was with Ammon, she became apprehensive. "Okay," she said slowly.

"It's not just my older nieces and nephews who will be here this weekend," he said.

Audrey glanced back at the huge house. Of course not.

"My whole family is here," he said.

Audrey snapped her head away from the house and looked at him. "What?"

"This is actually a kind of family reunion," he continued.

"A family reunion," Audrey repeated.

"Yeah. We get together at the start of the summer. It's not a big deal that you're here though. Freddy's come before. And my mom said I could bring someone to help me belay."

Anger swelled like a balloon in her chest. "Any particular reason you left out this detail?"

Ammon peeked at her. "Because I thought you'd say no if you knew."

"Yeah, I would have said no! At least to the staying overnight part. Ammon, this is really weird."

He let out a deep breath and turned to her. "Look, I'm sorry. I thought I was being considerate by inviting you to stay the night so you wouldn't have to drive up here at five in the morning. And my family is going to love you. It won't be weird at all; I promise."

Audrey started laughing because she didn't know what else to do. This was absurd. She was about to meet the whole family of a guy she was barely friends with, and they were "going to love her."

"So does the laughing mean you're no longer going to kill me?" he asked.

She wanted to slug him in his annoyingly firm bicep. "You owe me," she said. "And the moment it gets weird, and it will get weird, I'm going to disappear into one of this mansion's fifty bedrooms and not come out until tomorrow morning."

"Fine. Fair enough. Should we go in?"

Her anger subsided only to be replaced by anxiety. "Tell me what I'm walking into," she said.

"My parents, my sisters and their husbands, and my nieces and nephews. Some of my nieces and nephews are married and have kids. So, like, forty people. And two dogs. My sister Eve can't go anywhere without them."

"Okay." Audrey felt jittery. She wasn't a shy person, so why was she so nervous to meet these people? And would they actually like her? Ugh! Why did she care if they liked her? "And you're sure it's totally fine that I'm here?"

"Totally fine," Ammon assured her. He reached over and squeezed her hand. "You ready to get Parkered?"

This was so not cool.

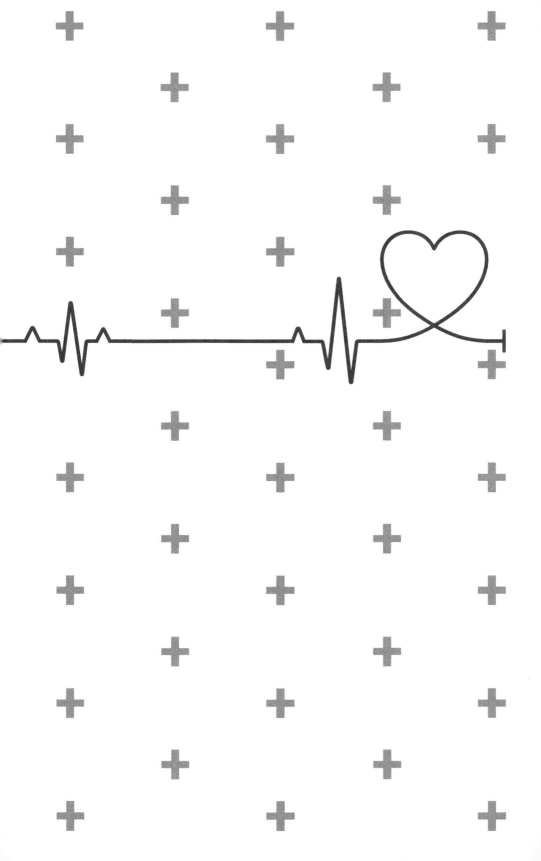

Chapter 43

EVEN THOUGH THE CABIN WASN'T actually his home, Ammon felt like he was coming home as he walked through the front door. Being anywhere with his family felt that way. And that Audrey was beside him, even though it was under false pretenses, made this even better. He'd been sure she'd demand to be driven home when he told her about the family reunion, and he would have done it. But for some reason, she was staying, and it was exactly what he'd hoped for.

Ammon's six-year-old niece, Katelynn, was the first to spot them. She jumped off the last two steps of the grand staircase. He caught her and spun her around in a dramatic hug. She smelled like gummy worms and dirty hair. He kissed her on the cheek, and she squealed. "Uncle Ammon! Your whiskers are tickling me!"

"Ammon's here?" his sister Naomi said as she came into the entryway. Her eyes bounced to Audrey, who stood beside him. She cocked an eyebrow but didn't say anything else.

Ammon set Katelynn down and gave Naomi a hug. "This is Audrey," he said, gesturing to her. "Audrey, this is my fourth oldest sister, Naomi."

Audrey smiled and shook Naomi's hand. "It's nice to meet you. I'm just here to help with the rock climbing tomorrow."

"Nice to meet you too," Naomi replied. "You're about to meet forty new people in the space of five seconds, so don't feel bad if you don't remember anyone's name."

And she was right. When they stepped into the main living room, it became an onslaught. Ammon's sisters and mom made loud exclamations and took turns hugging him. He introduced Audrey, leaving out any mention of what their relationship might be, because he wasn't sure how to characterize it. Were they friends? Coworkers? Neighbors? All of the above? He worried that whatever he labeled their relationship would get him in trouble. So she was just "Audrey, who is helping with rock climbing tomorrow."

If Audrey was intimidated or uncomfortable, she didn't let on. Her smile seemed genuine enough as she met his sisters, their husbands, his nieces and nephews, and the oldest two's spouses and their kids. After all the introductions, Ammon's dad announced it was time to eat dinner and called on Ammon's sister Eve to offer the blessing.

"You doing okay?" Ammon asked after the prayer as everyone lined up for food.

Audrey gave him a tight smile, but her eyes sparkled. "I'm fine. But you probably shouldn't have me belay you tomorrow."

"I don't think you're actually capable of murder," he said, a smile pulling up one corner of his mouth.

She patted him on the back. "You keep thinking that."

"Audrey!" his mother exclaimed as she approached them. "Guests go to the front of the line." She took Audrey by the hand and tugged her away.

Ammon let out a deep breath. He really needed his family to work in his favor, or Audrey would kill him for sure when she found out he was Belay.

+ + +

Ammon's mom, Diane, a round woman with gray-blonde hair, escorted Audrey through the packed kitchen. Audrey was always struck by how old other people's parents were. Her own mom wasn't even fifty yet. Ammon's parents looked to be in their late sixties.

The fixings for hamburgers and hotdogs had been set out on the granite countertop of the island. The space bustled with parents helping their children prepare plates of food. The smell of grilled meat wafted through the open door from the back porch, where Ammon's dad stood at the grill.

"Now, Ammon told me you're vegetarian," Diane said. "So we cooked you up a few veggie burgers." She went to the oven and pulled out a tinfoil-covered plate and set it on the stovetop. "We cooked them first so there wouldn't be any meat contamination on the grill," she continued.

"Wow, thank you," Audrey said. She was touched by the consideration. Most people just slapped the veggie burger next to the hamburger patty and cooked everything at the same time. Audrey never complained and still ate it, but this was above and beyond.

"It's a little chaotic in here, but once the kids get their food, things will settle down," Diane said, placing a bun and veggie burger on a paper plate.

Audrey watched all the people. "I've never been around a family this big," she said.

"Oh? Well, there are a lot of us. I have six children, and all five of my girls are married and have kids of their own. Ammon's my one holdout," Diane said with a chuckle. Audrey's skin prickled. Belay had five sisters.

"How many grandchildren do you have?" Audrey asked. She wanted more details about Ammon but didn't want to be totally obvious she was fishing for information.

"Nineteen total with one more on the way. Evie is due in October. My two oldest grandchildren are married, and I have four great-grandchildren." Ammon had nineteen nieces and nephews like Belay too?

"So did you name all your children after people in the scriptures?"

Diane laughed again. She and Ammon had the same blue eyes. "Most people don't notice because Deborah throws them off. So we have Sarai, Deborah, Mary, Naomi, and Eve. And then Ammon, of course." Diane passed the paper plate with the burger over to Audrey. "But enough about us," Diane said. "Tell me about yourself."

Audrey accepted the plate and glanced at Ammon near the back of the line. It was a coincidence that he had five older sisters, right? "Oh, well, I'm from Washington, and I moved to Utah about six years ago."

Ammon saw her and waved from across the room. He smiled big, and happiness seemed to drip off him in sheets. She could tell just by his body language how glad he was to be with his family. Audrey gave a little wave back, feeling warm and a little unsteady. This is what she wanted so badly: to be surrounded by people who clearly loved each other and for her to be one of those people.

"Ammon did medical school in Seattle," Diane said. "Where did you live?"

Audrey returned her attention back to Diane. Seattle too? She gulped. "I'm from Bellingham, a little town at the U.S.-Canadian border."

Ammon approached them, looking at ease while Audrey felt wound up. "My mom talking your ear off?" he asked Audrey.

"No, but it has been very educational," Audrey replied.

Ammon's grin widened. "I'm sure it has."

"Ammon," Diane said. "Why don't you help Audrey cut in line."

The woman nudged the two of them off.

Most of the children had gone through the line, and Audrey assembled a veggie burger with lots of tomatoes and got a sampling of each of the potato and pasta salads. She didn't know what to say to Ammon about his five sisters and his time in Seattle. The coincidences left her feeling . . . She wasn't sure how she felt. What if Ammon was Belay? Had he been playing her this whole time? Or was it really just a strange coincidence? And did she actually want Ammon to be Belay?

Chapter 44

AUDREY FOLLOWED AMMON OUT BACK, where everyone ate. His nieces and nephews sat on blankets on the lawn; his siblings and their spouses sat on chairs in a large circle on the wide porch. Ammon found them two seats together, and Audrey sat, balancing her plate on her knees. Everyone was talking and laughing, and she felt like she was on the outside of some marvelous inside joke. After a few minutes into her meal, she was ready to disappear into a bedroom.

"How's your residency going?" one of Ammon's sisters—maybe Debbie, though Audrey couldn't keep them all straight—asked.

"Good," he answered. "I just finished a night rotation in Labor and Delivery."

Audrey ate her veggie burger in tiny mouse bites. She didn't want to get caught with a mouthful of food if someone talked to her.

"Got any gross medical stories?" one of Ammon's teenage nephews asked. He looked to be about seventeen.

Ammon laughed. "Not now. But I'll tell you later." He winked. Gah. He even acted charming with his family. How irritating.

"Yes, save them for later," another one of his sisters—Sarai?—said.

"Enough about Ammon," his pregnant sister said. "I want to know what's going on with him and this girl."

Audrey stopped chewing and felt like she'd stepped into a spotlight. The other conversations stopped, and all eyes focused on her and Ammon. She swallowed her food and tried to smile. Ammon looked amused, but Audrey felt a betraying blush warm her face.

"Audrey and I are just friends," he said. He looked at her with a crooked smile. "Right, Audrey? We're friends?"

She cocked her head and gave him a narrow look. "More like frenemies."

The pregnant sister—Eve, Audrey remembered—laughed. "Ooh. This is much more interesting than I thought! You've got to explain."

Ammon lowered his voice so just Audrey could hear. "Sorry about her. Eve's a little tactless. I can shut her up."

Audrey's mouth curled into a wicked smile. "No need," she said to him, then turned her attention back to Eve, who sat a few people away. The whole family was paying rapt attention. "Ammon lives down the hall from me, and we met at church. But that's not the interesting part."

"Great," Ammon muttered.

"As you know, Ammon is an OB, but *I'm* a home birth midwife," Audrey said. She could feel the delight dancing in her eyes. "And the very first time we met, he accused me of being an unsafe provider without knowing anything about me." She nudged him with her elbow. "And it's been nonstop bickering ever since, right, Ammon?"

Eve looked beyond thrilled by this revelation. "I've always wanted a home birth," she said. "But Ammon scared me out of it. As you can imagine."

"Oh, I can," Audrey replied. Now Ammon's face was red with embarrassment. He shifted in his seat.

"Eve, if Audrey is your midwife, you can have a home birth," he said.

"Aww, Ammon, that's so sweet of you to give me permission," Eve said sarcastically. She looked at Audrey. "The patriarchy, am I right?"

"Preach, sister," Audrey replied, thrusting her fork into the air. Audrey liked Eve already.

Ammon sighed and shook his head.

"So if you don't even like each other, why'd he ask you to help him belay?" Eve asked her.

Their conversation no longer seemed to be interesting to the rest of the family, which was a relief to Audrey. Ammon eyed the two of them suspiciously.

"Great question," Audrey replied, now questioning his motives. "He also failed to mention the presence of his whole family this weekend."

Eve laughed. "And you two really aren't dating?"

Audrey and Ammon looked at each other, and while it was supposed to be a quick look of mutual disgust, the look lingered, and Audrey's heart went all fluttery.

"Audrey's got a boyfriend," Ammon replied, looking away from her. "Some guy she met online." He sounded almost disappointed. Maybe he wasn't Belay after all.

"I met my husband online," Eve said.

So Audrey and Eve talked about her husband, then her two kids, and her current pregnancy. Naomi soon came over and joined the conversation. Audrey learned they were the two sisters closest in age with Ammon and had the best relationship with him. They joked that he was an "oops baby," born seven years after Eve.

Everyone was friendly, and Audrey no longer wanted to hide away in some bedroom. The evening progressed how Audrey had always fantasized a large family gathering would: with lots of desserts, a game of charades, and laughter. Ammon's family's love wrapped her in a warm cocoon she never wanted to leave.

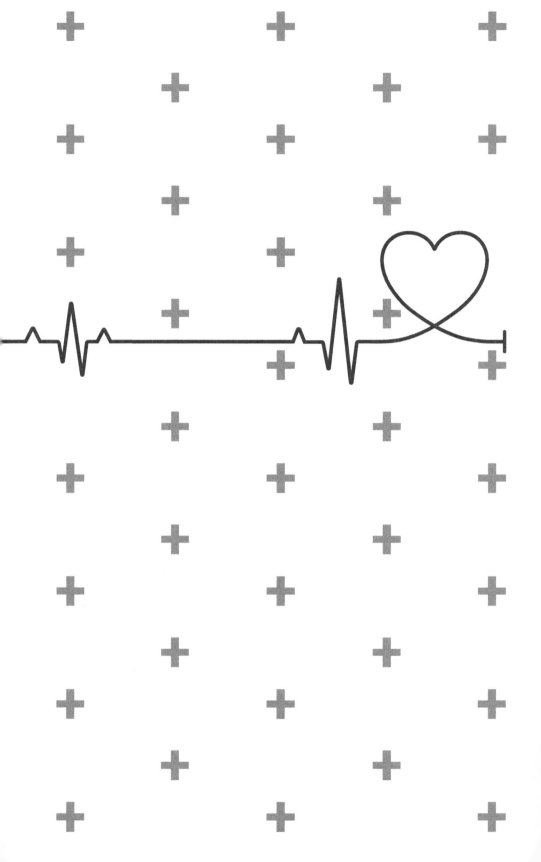

Chapter 45

AMMON TAPPED LIGHTLY ON AUDREY'S bedroom door the next morning. She'd been given a bed in the room with some of his teenage nieces. He hoped they hadn't kept Audrey up too late with whatever it was teenage girls did when they got together. Ammon had slept on the floor in the loft with his teenage nephews. They'd teased him endlessly about Audrey and asked for his grossest medical stories. He'd finally made them shut up at one a.m. because they were supposed to go climbing at six. It was now seven, and only the people with young children were up.

When he didn't hear a reply from Audrey, he turned the doorknob and peeked his head in. All four occupants of the room appeared to be in a deep sleep. Ammon crept in and approached Audrey's bed. Her red hair covered the pillow in a messy tangle. He took a moment to appreciate the delicate way her eyelashes rested on her cheekbones and the soft curve of her mouth. He spent an embarrassing amount of time thinking of their brief kiss, and his lips tingled at the memory.

Before she woke on her own and caught him creeping on her, he whispered her name. She didn't move, but one of his nieces turned over. He took two fingers and poked Audrey on the arm. "Wake up," he said.

Her eyes fluttered open, and she blocked the light coming from the open door with a hand. "Ammon?" She closed her eyes again. "What time is it?"

"Seven," he replied. His nieces began to stir.

"Weren't we supposed to be out climbing an hour ago?" She sat up, and Ammon noted the ratty Tori Amos T-shirt she wore.

"Yeah, but my nephews stayed up late. They didn't want to budge this morning."

She yawned, and her mouth settled into a small smile. "Your nieces kept me up with some great stories about you."

"I bet they did."

"I totally understand where you get your big ego." Audrey combed a hand through her hair until it got caught in a knot.

"My big ego?" He felt his lips move into a full smile.

"Yeah." She twisted her fingers around the knot until her hand was free. He didn't know why, but he liked that she hadn't said anything about her morning appearance or shooed him out of the room. Did that mean she felt comfortable with him? He thought she looked as pretty as ever, raccoon eyes and all. "Now that I've met your family, everything makes perfect sense."

He crossed his arms over his chest, trying to look put out. "I've got to hear this."

She pulled her knees up to her chest and patted the bed where her legs had been. "Have a seat; this may take a while."

Ammon eyed the spot for a moment before settling on the very edge of the bed.

"You're the family golden boy," she started. Her voice went singsongy. "The long-awaited son. The youngest child." She laughed, it seemed to herself. "So much younger than your sisters that you were almost an only child." She brought a hand to her heart. "And you're following in your grandfather's footsteps by being a doctor. Your sisters adore you, your mother couldn't be more proud. No wonder you think you're such hot stuff."

Ammon couldn't keep the grin off his face. "I know why my *family* loves me, but why do *you*?"

She swatted at him. It was pathetic, but he didn't try to dodge it, just so he could feel her touch. "There you go, projecting again."

"Is that it?" He grabbed her hand, smoothing his fingers over her palm. He met her eyes and felt the oxygen suck out of the room. "You think . . . I love you, Audrey?"

Saying the words out loud seemed to solidify them in his heart, even if he was teasing. Her eyes widened just a fraction, and he saw her pulse fluttering in her neck. If he put his hand there, how fast would her heart be beating? Like she'd read his mind, her fingers moved to his wrist, where his own pulse pounded.

She leaned forward and dropped her voice. "Ammon, is that why your heart is racing?"

One of his nieces sat up from her sleeping bag on the floor. "If you're going to keep flirting, can you leave? I'm trying to sleep." She dramatically flung the covers over her head when she lay back down.

"Aw, it was just starting to get good!" a different niece said.

Ammon glanced at Audrey, who'd turned scarlet red. He tried to laugh like that wasn't one of the most incredible moments of his life, witnessed by a roomful of pretending-to-sleep teenage girls. The tension between him and Audrey disappeared, and he pulled his hand from hers.

"We're still planning to climb," he said, standing up. "I'd hate for you to have endured my family for no reason."

"Stop it," she said. "You know your family's great." She smoothed a hand through her hair until it got stuck again.

Happiness surged through him. But just as quickly as the good feeling arrived, it went away. Man, he wanted this. Bad. Audrey with him in the morning, his family loving her as much as he did. He released an unsteady breath. But would Audrey forgive him when she discovered he was Belay?

"Yeah, I know," he replied and left the room before he gave any more of himself away.

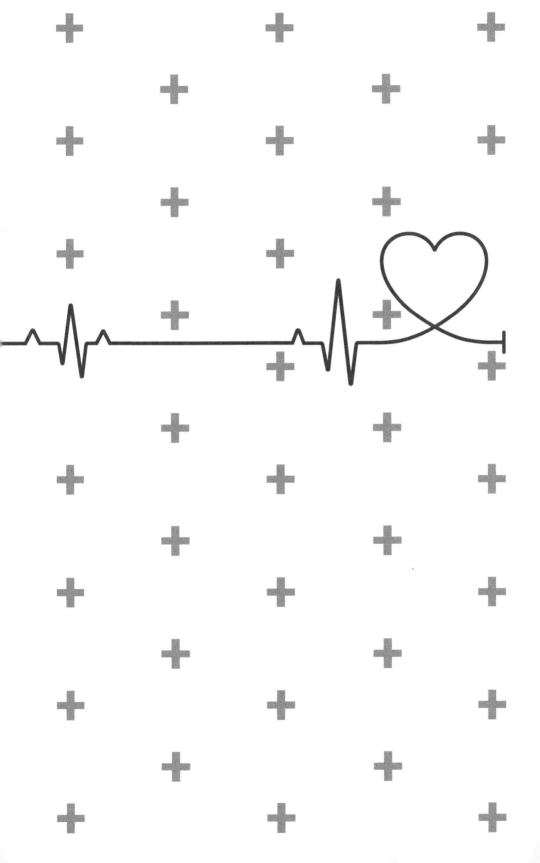

Chapter 46

HELP! Audrey texted Ellie. *AMMON is being really nice and charming, and his family is totally awesome. I cannot develop a crush on him.*

You've had a crush on him for weeks, came Ellie's reply. *Who do you think is inspiring my latest romance novel?*

Ugh. Writers had no sense of privacy. *I LIKE BELAY*, she texted back with furious finger strokes. *I do NOT like Ammon. And I don't want to.*

A shadow fell across Audrey's phone, and she quickly pulled it to her chest.

"Who are you talking to?"

It was Ammon. Naturally. The whole day he'd managed to always be within twenty feet of her. She'd snuck away while everyone played touch football and was now sitting behind the trunk of a big tree, hoping to not be found. She needed space to think.

"Just checking in with Ellie," she replied, turning the screen off. He stuck his hands into the pockets of his shorts and rocked back on his heels. He looked sexy and smug, and Audrey scowled. Her phone chirped with a reply.

"You gonna get that?" he asked.

Audrey stood and dusted the pine needles off her butt. "No."

"Okay."

She started back toward the cabin. Ammon walked right beside her. "I was coming to let you know my mom said anyone who'd like to help prepare dinner is wanted in the kitchen."

"All right."

"But if you need some time to yourself, that's fine," he said. "My mom just asked me to invite you. I think she wants to get to know you better."

Audrey stopped and turned toward him. He stood a few paces away. "Why would she want to do that?" she asked. She'd enjoyed her time with Ammon's family, a lot, but she couldn't help wonder why they were treating her like one of their own. Was this how all families were? Or was Ammon's special?

Ammon shrugged. "She likes to make new friends."

Audrey felt something tenuous building inside her. Was it hope? Fear? Love? She let out a deep breath, trying to knock the feeling over before it grew too big and became a part of her.

"Everything okay?" he asked, reaching out and touching her arm.

He'd been so nice all day. They'd had their usual banter and arguments, but underneath had been this regard for her she'd never noticed before. It was almost like he cared what she thought about him. His words from this morning flitted through her mind for the hundredth time: *You think . . . I love you, Audrey?* He'd said it almost like a statement. Had he been teasing her? Her stomach dipped when she thought of the alternative, that he did love her.

"Ammon, what am I doing here?"

There was that arrogant crooked smile of his. "Well, on the first day, God created—"

"Never mind," she muttered and stepped past him. He grabbed her wrist.

"I'm sorry," he said. She stood closer to him now, and when he let out a sigh, she felt it tickle her neck. He let go of her wrist. "You're here because I want you to be."

She looked into his eyes. Her stomach dipped lower, if that was possible. An intense heat grew in her body. She could feel it in the air around them. "And why would you want me here?"

A football flew above their heads and crashed into the nearby bushes, destroying their moment.

"Hey, Uncle Ammon, can you get that?" a nephew called from the back lawn.

"Yeah, sure," he yelled back. He looked at Audrey, his blue eyes uncertain. "Maybe we should talk later," he said.

Audrey nodded. Ammon went after the football, and Audrey headed for the kitchen.

+ + +

The firepit had burned down to coals, and Audrey enjoyed the warmth as everyone sat around it roasting marshmallows on sticks. Ammon held his niece's three-year-old daughter on his lap, helping her hold the skewer over the cinders. He said something that made her giggle. The sight was adorable, and the image of Ammon holding a little girl with Audrey's red hair and his blue eyes popped into her mind.

Audrey shoved another marshmallow into her mouth. She didn't even bother roasting it. Her body was filled with restless energy. After their moment earlier, Ammon had given her space, but they seemed to search each other out. Every glance from him sent her into flames. Her heart beat too fast, and she felt like there was too much air in her lungs. She didn't want to feel this way.

Eve plopped down next to her, breaking her reverie. "We're about to head out," she said to Audrey. "We have nine-o'clock church tomorrow, and I'm the organist."

"Oh? It was so great to meet you."

Eve pulled her into a hug, which surprised Audrey, but she quickly returned the embrace. She and Eve had become quick friends, almost like they already knew each other. *Is this what having a sister is like?* Audrey wondered.

"I'm seriously going to call you," Eve said. "Even if I can't get my husband on board for the home birth, we can still be friends."

Their hug ended, and Audrey felt emotion build in her chest and prickle behind her eyes. Why was she reacting like this? She had never cried before over making a new friend. She blinked a few times and took a deep breath to get it together.

"Just remind Dan that even Ammon has given me *his* stamp of approval," Audrey said.

"Well, Dan knows who's actually in charge." Eve winked. She gave Audrey another hug, then stood. She started the rounds to say goodbye to the rest of her family. Eve leaving seemed to signal the end of the evening, and everyone started to head indoors. Mary's family was also going home that night, and everyone else would leave early tomorrow.

Ammon looked at Audrey across the firepit as if to say, "Wait," so she didn't go in with everyone else. Soon they were alone.

The air had chilled, and Audrey shivered. Ammon added kindling to the hot coals and blew on the embers until a flame caught. She watched him add sticks and then logs as he coaxed the coals back into fire. The air in front of them grew hot. Before he sat back down next to her, he wrapped a blanket around her shoulders, his brief touch making her stomach flip.

"So you talked Eve into a home birth?" he asked.

"More like you talked her out of one first," Audrey replied.

He leaned forward and set his elbows on his knees, staring into the fire. "I still think a home birth is a terrible idea," he said. "But it's not my choice to make."

"Look how much you've evolved." Audrey bumped him with her shoulder.

His smile went limp, and he creased his brow. He didn't have his glasses on, and in the purple twilight, his eyes looked a deep blue.

"Do you think maybe we were wrong about each other?" he asked.

Audrey swallowed and wanted desperately to run away. "In what way?"

He angled his body toward hers, his knee touching hers. "I think back to the first time we met, and I wish I could do it all over."

"You do?" She felt too warm.

"I'd say, 'Hi, my name is Ammon. What's yours?'"

He held his hand out to her. She looked at it for a moment before slipping her hand into his. "I'm Audrey," she said, shaking his hand. "Nice to meet you."

"What are your hobbies, Audrey?"

She cleared her throat and decided to play along. "I like to rock climb," she replied.

"So do I," he said. His fingers brushed her palm, sending goosebumps up her arms. "Have you climbed Craggletooth Rock?"

Everything stilled around her, and she looked into Ammon's eyes. He looked so earnest, and her heart jumped toward the moon. Could he be? Her chin started to quiver, and tears flooded her eyes. She wanted to ask him but didn't know which answer would devastate her more: that he was Belay and had strung her along or that he wasn't and she'd fallen for the wrong guy.

"I was wrong about you, Audrey," he said, his voice just above a whisper. "You are smart and funny. I admire your passion and skill. I'm constantly impressed by your generosity."

Audrey blinked back her tears, the intensity in his gaze making her skin burn. "But you were absolutely right about me," he continued. "I am an insecure egomaniac. And it's taken knowing you to realize what kind of doctor I want to be and what kind of man I want to be."

She took in a deep, shaky breath. *An insecure egomaniac.* That was how she had described Ammon to Belay. How would Ammon know that? Unless . . . Her heart beat so fast she thought it would stop.

"I know I don't deserve you," he said. "So I can only hope one day you'll forgive me for everything."

She wanted to both move into his arms and stay far away. She didn't know what to say or even how to process his words. How could he be Belay? It couldn't be true. Why couldn't she find the courage to ask him?

Ammon had been trying to pull her in—she saw that now, looking back at the last few weeks. His kiss hadn't been a desperate attempt to connect with just anyone. He had kissed her because he'd wanted to. He wanted her. And she kept flinching and pushing him away. She'd kept telling herself she liked the random guy on the internet and that Ammon was too much her opposite to be anything more. But maybe she had been wrong about him, too.

Finally, after too long, when the silence between them had nearly turned them to stone, Audrey spoke. "I think I should go." Her eyes flitted over his face before her gaze returned to the dying flames. "I'll have Ellie come pick me up." She had no idea what time it was, but Ellie was the kind of friend who would bury a dead body with her, if only so she could garner material for her books. She'd come if Audrey called.

"Don't bother Ellie," he said, digging into his pocket. Audrey couldn't look at him. She didn't want to read any expression that might be on his face. She didn't want to confirm that he was Belay and that he'd lied to her. As long as a small part of her doubted it, she could press on. He pulled out his keys and held them out to her. "Drive my car back. I can get a ride home with my parents in the morning."

Without thinking too much about it, Audrey took the keys from him. Her heart felt like it had been twisted into a pretzel, and her hands wouldn't stop shaking. She sneaked through the house to get her bag and then drove away.

+ + +

Ammon couldn't bear to watch her leave and instead stared into the flames. Why hadn't she asked if he was Belay? He could tell by the way tears filled her eyes that she had figured it out. He should have just told her directly, but his courage had failed him. And then she had left.

He scrubbed his hand over his face, his stomach twisting into knots. He couldn't lose her, especially now that he suspected she liked him. He'd seen it in the way her eyes always seemed to find him, in the radiant way she smiled when Eve teased him and the way Audrey laughed. He didn't want to lose her when things had just started to be good between them.

Please help her forgive me, he prayed. *Help me know what to do next.*

✦ ✦ ✦

When Audrey got home, she saw the light on in Ellie's room. She tapped on the door, and Ellie soon answered. Without a word, Ellie pulled her into a hug. "What did he do?" she asked.

Audrey's shaky inhale turned into a sob. She didn't even understand why she was crying. Every time she went to open her mouth to give a reason, she stopped herself. *His family is amazing* and *He probably loves me* sounded like terrible reasons to cry.

Ellie smoothed her hands through Audrey's hair, then guided Audrey to sit beside her on the bed.

"I'm really confused," Audrey finally managed to say. "I think I like him. But I think he's the guy from the rock-climbing forum. And if he is, then I definitely don't like him. Because he's been deceiving me for weeks."

Ellie tapped a perfectly manicured finger against her lips. "What makes you think Ammon is the rock-climbing guy?"

"Too many similarities," Audrey said. "They both have five sisters. They've both lived in Seattle."

Ellie shook her head. "Those could be coincidences."

"Ammon asked about Craggletooth Rock."

Ellie's mouth formed a silent *o*. Audrey swallowed the bile rising to the back of her throat. If that detail was enough to convince Ellie, then it was true. Audrey wanted to crumble.

"How do I deal with the fact that he's been lying to me for weeks? He's had so many chances to tell me."

Ellie tucked one leg under the other. "Forget about the rock-climbing forum and the lying for a second. How do you feel about Ammon?"

How did she feel about Ammon? His smug smile popped into her head, and her stomach flipped.

Oh.

But wasn't it a problem that the smile she pictured was his smug one? That he was smug, and she was smug in return? That they liked to out-smug each other? That he challenged her and she challenged him back?

Oh.

Her heart jolted. Ellie sat perched on the edge of the bed, her eyebrows raised, waiting. And like a flood, Audrey felt a hundred warm feelings. She liked Ammon's face and his hair and his eyes. And who could forget his body? Geez. How much time did that man spend at the gym? But she also liked his confidence, his sense of humor, the way he thought about his work, his kindness beneath all the pomp. And she loved his family.

Oh no.

Somewhere between "Do you have any idea how dangerous home birth is?" and "I was wrong about you, Audrey," she'd fallen for him. Like, down-the-rabbit-hole fallen.

"You've found him," Ellie said.

Fresh tears sprang to Audrey's eyes. She didn't know if they were sad tears or if she was so, so angry that she was crying. Ugh, realizing she loved someone wasn't supposed to be this *horrible*. She should feel like she was walking on sunshine or dancing on rainbows; instead, she felt as fragile as porcelain.

Because Ammon was Belay. And he had lied.

She would shatter for sure.

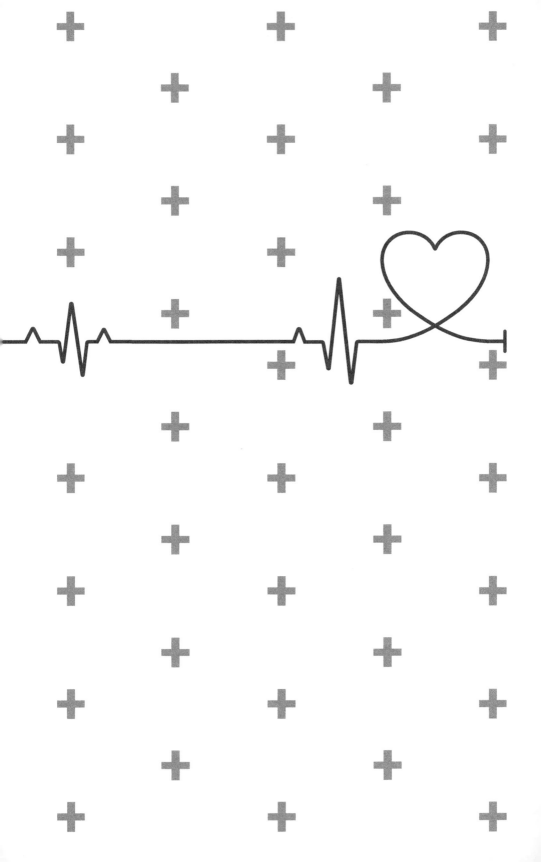

Chapter 41

A KNOCK AT AMMON'S DOOR Sunday afternoon sent his stomach into a nosedive. Was it Audrey? He scrambled from his room and sprinted down the hall to beat Freddy to the door. But the rush wasn't needed since Freddy sat unmovable on the couch, engrossed in some headset-required video game.

Before opening the door, Ammon ran a hand through his hair, then tugged on his T-shirt in a useless attempt to smooth the wrinkles. After Audrey left last night, he hadn't been able to sleep, so he'd taken a long nap after attending church with his parents. He'd messed things up with Audrey so badly. She was never going to trust him. He opened the door, but it wasn't her on the other side.

It was Ellie, his car keys dangling from her outstretched finger. She rose an eyebrow by way of greeting. "Audrey asked me to return these."

She tipped her finger forward, and the keys slid off into his open palm. "Thanks," he said, his stomach and his heart both competing for space in his throat. Ellie's gaze wandered to a spot behind Ammon's shoulder. He turned and saw she was looking at Freddy. "Do you want to come in?"

"I'd rather not," she replied. *Hmm.* They must be off again.

"Okay." He spun his keys on his finger. "Thanks again."

She made no movement to go, and Ammon didn't want to slam the door in her face. Her eyes narrowed. "So you're the guy from the internet?"

Ammon ran a hand through his hair. "Yeah."

"I can't believe you."

"I know." Shame crept up his neck.

He leaned against the doorframe, his legs feeling like sandbags. He should have just told Audrey weeks ago. Now he didn't know what to do next. Would she welcome a conversation about it? Or had she already decided never to speak to him again because he was a lying, horrible person?

"So is she pretty angry with me?" He tried to laugh to hide how much this hurt him, but it sounded more like a choke. Ellie rolled her eyes so deeply that Ammon was surprised when they didn't get stuck. She took a menacing step toward him and lowered her voice. Man, she was scary.

"You've got to do something huge to make this up to her."

Ammon's heart skittered to a stop. Did this mean he still had a chance?

Freddy yelled at the TV behind him. He must have lost or died or killed something important. Ammon stepped into the hall and closed the door behind him. Ellie looked very patient, which made him more nervous than when she looked annoyed. His arrogant facade cracked, and he felt heavy. "I love her," he said, the words making him warm and almost delirious. "Can you tell me what to do? Please?"

Ellie assessed him with her dark gaze for a moment too long, then shook her head like she felt bad for him. "You're going to have to wait for her to come around. When she does, then we'll talk."

"So I'm supposed to just hang back and wait?"

"Yeah. And try not to be such a tool."

"Gee, thanks."

She tipped her head. "You're welcome."

Ellie spun and sauntered down the hall.

Ammon went back to his room feeling tremulous. There was still a chance.

+ + +

Audrey didn't see Ammon for a few weeks after his confession at the cabin. Well, that wasn't entirely true. They saw each other at church but did a marvelous job of avoiding each other. Audrey wasn't sure what to say to him, and Ellie claimed he wasn't avoiding her, just giving her space to figure things out. She also hadn't heard from him as Belay during those same weeks. Not that she had messaged him either, so she couldn't entirely blame him for the lack of contact. Her love life had returned to its usual status: nonexistent.

Without the burden of potential boyfriends weighing her down, Audrey now had more time to focus on growing her business. She dropped her volunteer doula shift at the hospital and was learning how to market via social media and looking into renting an office space that could one day grow into her own birth center. She was too busy to wallow in the ache over the disappearances of Ammon and Belay from her life. So even if she thought of him in quiet moments, she didn't dwell too long on him. Because if she did, she'd find herself wondering if she loved Ammon enough to believe whatever explanation he could give her for the deception.

The Tuesday morning three weeks after the cabin, Audrey arrived at the free clinic for her usual shift. While she'd dropped a lot of extra things from her life, her volunteer work at the clinic stayed. The hours were predictable, and she could work during the day; plus, it was important to Audrey to give back to the community.

Claire was seated in the waiting room, a pink bundle in her arms. Was it her six-week follow-up already? So much had happened since then that Audrey felt like she was living a different life.

Audrey helped Claire carry the car seat and diaper bag back to the exam room. "If I put her down, she'll wake up and cry," Claire said as she took a seat. She had the telltale signs of a new mom: bags under her eyes, unwashed hair in a sloppy bun, clothes that didn't quite fit right, and an underlying glow of happiness.

"Tell me how you've been," Audrey said.

Claire sighed but smiled. "So tired. But good, I think."

Audrey smiled back. "And how are feedings going?"

"I'm still trying to figure out breastfeeding. I saw a lactation consultant, which helped, but I still end up giving Annie a bottle of formula at least once a day."

"Keep at it, okay? It will get easier," Audrey said. "Maybe seeing a lactation consultant again would help."

"There's one at the WIC office," she said.

"That's perfect."

Claire nodded but stared at her baby's face, a frown creasing her forehead. Audrey could sense the girl's fragility over this. Breastfeeding could be so hard for new mothers.

"Hey," Audrey said. "You'll figure out what feeding method is best for you and Annie. And if that means she needs a bottle, that's okay."

"Okay," Claire said softly.

"How are you doing otherwise?" Audrey asked. "Annie's birth was pretty traumatic. You are taking care of yourself, too?"

"Oh yeah," Claire said, brightening up. "I go to this new-mothers support group at the library. Ammon told me about it, and he sometimes gives me rides."

Audrey couldn't stop her jaw from dropping. "Ammon?"

"I mean, Dr. Parker." Claire cleared her throat, looking guilty. "I ran into him at the hospital right after Annie was born. I was there for some blood work, but I got lost and totally broke down. You know, postpartum hormones." Audrey nodded, prompting Claire to continue. Why was her heart beating so hard?

"Anyway," Claire said, "he gave me a pep talk and helped me get to the lab. He told me about the support group and then gave me his phone number and told me to call if I ever needed anything."

Audrey had no idea what expression was on her face, but something about it caused Claire's eyes to widen. "I'm not into him," she said quickly. "I mean, he's hot but, like, way too old for me. And I know you two have something going on, so I'd never interfere. You're like a friend to me, Audrey."

Something going on? Audrey felt an awkward laugh bubble out of her mouth. She schooled her face the best she could and decided not to continue that line of conversation. She didn't want to think about Ammon and how she might feel about him. And she didn't want to worry what the two of them had looked like to the outside world. If it *looked* like they had "something going on," then maybe they did, and what was Audrey supposed to do now? "You could have called me if you needed something," she said instead.

Claire looked down and adjusted the blankets around Annie's face. "I know," she said. "I just hate being the person who always needs something. I mean, *I am* that person. But I didn't want to pile it all on you if I could help it."

Audrey nodded. She understood that: spreading out the vulnerability and favors, not wanting to be a burden, making sure only certain people saw certain aspects of your disastrous life and never the whole picture.

And as she thought of Claire trusting a small part of that vulnerability to Ammon, Audrey couldn't avoid thinking about him anymore. Ammon had been helping Claire and never once said anything to Audrey about it. It was the exact type of thing she expected someone like him to drop casually into a conversation to demonstrate how awesome he thought he was. And maybe that was who Ammon used to be. Or maybe he was never like that.

Audrey felt like she'd been sucker punched in the stomach. She'd repeatedly jumped to conclusions about Ammon's integrity as a doctor because she'd thought he was arrogant, but he had consistently put his patients' needs before his own desire to be right. He had shown her over and over again in small ways that he was teachable. It was Audrey who was arrogant. *She'd* been wrong about him the whole time. Her body flamed, and she felt embarrassed and stupid. *Oh boy.* She *loved* Ammon. A lot.

"Are you okay?" Claire asked. "You look like a tomato."

Audrey giggled deliriously and touched her cheeks. "Yeah, I'm fine. It's just . . ."

And suddenly she knew what she needed to do, but was she brave enough to do it?

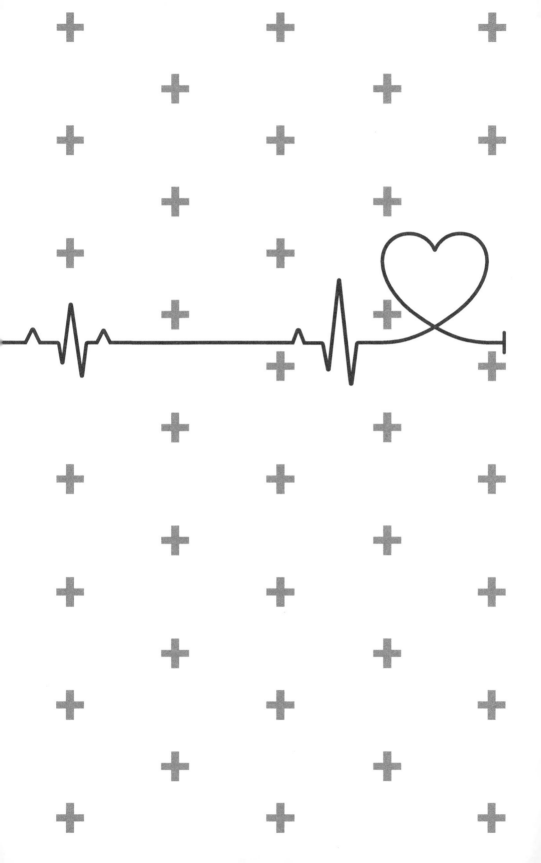

Chapter 48

WHEN AUDREY GOT HOME FROM her shift at the free clinic, she climbed into bed with a package of Oreos. Realizing she loved Ammon had left her feeling rattled. How could she fall for someone who had deceived her? And even if he had a good explanation about why he'd lied, did it make her weak to forgive him? Would he continue to lie to her in big and small ways? Was she setting herself up for more heartache?

Audrey lay under the covers and stared at her phone. She could feel the Oreo crumbs on her pillow pressing into her cheek. Was she ready to confront him? Should she message him or call him? Would a face-to-face conversation be best so she could read his face and see if he was contrite enough? She shoved another Oreo into her mouth. Why did Ammon do this to her?

Audrey grabbed her phone, hesitated, then made the call. The line rang once. Twice. Three times, until she heard a familiar "Hello?"

"Mom?" Audrey said, her voice cracking. "I need some advice."

There was a moment of stunned silence on the other end before her mother spoke. "Oh, bunny, what can I do?"

Tears leaked from the corners of Audrey's eyes as she told her mom everything. How she'd fallen for Belay but then for Ammon in real life but that she was ninety-nine percent sure they were the same person and now didn't know if she could trust or forgive Ammon for lying to her for weeks.

"Do you think Ammon is a good person?" her mom asked.

"Yes," Audrey replied without hesitation.

"Do you think he did this maliciously?"

"I don't know." Audrey chewed on the inside of her cheek. "I want to believe he has a good reason for not telling me when Belay and I were supposed to meet for the first time."

"How would you have reacted if Ammon had told you the truth then?"

Audrey shrugged. "I'd have been stunned and maybe even a little grossed out. I didn't really know Ammon then."

"And would you have given yourself a chance to get to know him?"

"No. I didn't think he was worth knowing."

"Audrey, you've always been good at picking men," her mom said. "All of your ex-boyfriends were good, kind people. They treated you well and never gave any indication they wanted to hurt you. It was always you who called things off or never let them get too close."

Tears pricked at the back of Audrey's eyes again.

"Don't let your experiences with your father or my bad judgment in men make you afraid to give your heart fully to someone."

"But is Ammon that guy?"

"Pretend the thing with the internet never happened. How do you feel about him?"

Warmth like Audrey had never felt before expanded through her chest. "I love him."

"Then, I think he's worth a chance."

"How do I forgive him?"

"You hear him out and then just decide to forgive him. Forgiveness might not come right away, but it will eventually if you really want it to."

She made it sound so easy. Audrey let out a deep breath. "I wish you were here, Mom. I could really use a hug."

"I wish I could be there too."

"Mom?"

"Yeah?"

"I love you."

"I love you too."

+ + +

As Ammon left the hospital and walked to his car, his phone buzzed. He pulled it from his pocket, expecting to see a text from his mom, one of his sisters, or Freddy. Instead, it was a notification from the Mountain Collective. His stomach did a weird twist. He hadn't heard from Audrey on the app in weeks and hadn't really seen her either. Well, they'd seen each other at church and would sometimes step out of their apartments at the same time, but they didn't make eye contact. It made sense to Ammon that Audrey didn't want to talk to him.

But she was messaging him now. He got into his car and opened the message. His heart ricocheted around his chest. *I still haven't climbed Craggletooth Rock*, she'd written. *Are you free this weekend to go with me?*

Ammon reread the words about fifty times. No mention of her silence for the last three weeks. No references to him not showing up the last time they were supposed to meet. Just an invitation. He blew out a deep breath. What was Audrey doing? Did this mean she'd forgiven him? Or was she planning to push him off the mountainside?

His fingers wobbled as he typed his response. *I'm free Saturday. What time were you thinking?*

Rather than wait for her reply, he started driving home. When his phone buzzed a few minutes later, he made extreme effort to keep his eyes on the road and not read the message until he was safely home. Texting and driving kills and all.

Freddy sat at the kitchen table, eating a huge sandwich, when Ammon entered their apartment. Ammon's stomach was so messed up with nerves and anticipation, the smell of the salami and mustard nearly made him gag. He joined Freddy anyway and slid his phone across the table to him. "Would you mind reading the message I just got?"

"Sure," Freddy said, putting his sandwich down and wiping mustard off his hands with a paper napkin. "Who's it from?"

Ammon didn't answer, and Freddy picked up the phone. He typed in Ammon's password without asking what it was. On any other day, Ammon would have asked Freddy how he knew the password and then maybe talked to him about boundaries. But today, with the possibility of Audrey reconciling with him (or cutting his climbing ropes), he couldn't bother. He needed Freddy to help him dissect her message, whatever it said.

Freddy cleared his throat and read, "*Yeah, Saturday's cool. One o'clock? Let's meet at the rock face.*"

Ammon waited for more. Maybe a *Don't stand me up this time* or *I know it's you, Ammon, and I love you anyway*. But Freddy shrugged his shoulders and slid the phone back over to him.

"So Audrey's still into your alter ego," he said.

Ammon let out a groan of frustration. "Ellie told me a few weeks ago Audrey figured out I'm the rock-climbing guy."

Freddy took a bite of his sandwich and chewed slowly. His gray eyes stared Ammon down. Ammon didn't need his judgment, too.

"What do I do for a living?" Freddy asked after swallowing.

Ammon pushed both his hands through his hair, frustration making him antsy. "You're a therapist," he said.

"Right. I spend all day giving people awesome life advice."

Ammon held his tongue. It was disturbing to him that people came to Freddy with their problems. But it was also probably disturbing to Freddy that Ammon caught babies and performed surgery. Work *was* different from life. What really should have disturbed Ammon was how often he *did* turn to Freddy for advice.

"Do you remember the awesome advice I gave you months ago?" Freddy asked.

Ammon was pretty sure the advice had been to tell Audrey the truth, but he couldn't actually recall such a conversation with Freddy. Because it was obvious that's what Ammon should have done as soon as he realized Bell was Audrey. He didn't actually need Freddy to give him "awesome life advice," because he'd known the right thing to do all along.

"Look," Ammon said. "You were right. Do you have any life advice for me now?"

Freddy chuckled. "You're going to have to think of a spectacular way to apologize."

"Obviously," Ammon grumbled.

"Give Ellie a call," he said. "She'll help you devise a romance-novel-worthy HEA."

"HEA?"

"Happily ever after." Freddy winked. "Go get her, tiger."

Chapter 49

AUDREY'S WEEK WENT BY SLOWLY, which was not at all what she'd hoped for. She'd wanted to be so busy she wouldn't have time to breathe or think about her upcoming climb with Belay-who-was-probably-Ammon. Instead, she had only three prenatal appointments, two meetings with potential clients, and no births. But she had seen Ammon's sister Eve, who was now thirty-one weeks pregnant and planning a home birth. Audrey had been professional and didn't pepper her with questions like, "Does Ammon have an unhealthy obsession with Keanu Reeves movies?" or, "Do you happen to know Ammon's favorite Beatles song?"

Part of Audrey still hoped the similarities between Ammon and Belay were just coincidences and the men weren't the same person. At the same time, she didn't know which would disappoint her more: that Ammon was Belay or that Belay was someone else. Whenever she thought about it, her stomach would flip and twist and drop to the floor. Because she *did* know in her heart which one would be worse. So she needed to woman up and stop torturing herself. She needed to meet Belay.

Saturday came, and Audrey spent an absurd amount of time taming her curly hair, getting her mascara just right, and pacing. Lots of pacing around her apartment, waiting for noon to arrive so she could leave. And also wondering where Ellie was. Ellie was supposed to come with Audrey, for moral support and to belay her. Hopefully, Belay was bringing a friend to help him so they could climb to the top of Craggletooth Rock together. Audrey was never supposed to climb it alone. Shannon was supposed to go with her.

Audrey forced herself to eat a bowl of pasta for lunch. She didn't want to pass out from low blood sugar. But she might still pass out from nerves.

She felt jittery, like she'd drunk too much caffeine. Her hands seemed to have minds of their own and shook and moved without her permission.

She thought Ammon was Belay. *But what if he's not?*

Audrey paced some more. She glanced at the clock. Fifteen till noon. Where was Ellie?

Audrey checked her backpack again and filled her water bottle at the sink, and just as she was sending Ellie a text, Ellie walked through the front door.

"Sorry," she said, looking flushed. Her clothes were dirty, like she'd been bushwhacking. "I was helping Freddy with something." She puffed out her cheeks and blew out a breath. "But I'm ready if you are."

Audrey stepped toward Ellie and pulled a twig from her ponytail. Ellie didn't go places looking like this. "You sure you don't need to change or shower first?" Audrey asked.

"No, it's fine. We've got to hike to the rock face, right? I'll just get dirty again."

"Okay."

The two women headed to Audrey's car. "Can you drive?" Audrey asked. "I'm too nervous."

"Sure."

Audrey tossed the keys to Ellie, and they got in. She pulled up the directions on her phone to Craggletooth Rock, and twenty minutes later, Ellie pulled off to the side of the road a few miles up Big Cottonwood Canyon.

Audrey stepped out of the car, her feet crunching on the rocks. The air felt cool and smelled green. The familiar caress of the breeze calmed her nerves just a little.

"How are you feeling?" Ellie asked.

Audrey tried to take a deep breath but couldn't. "Terrified. What if he doesn't show up again?" She shook her head. "What if he does?" She wanted to get back into the car. "I don't think I can do this."

What if Belay isn't Ammon?

Ellie came around the front of the car and put her hands on Audrey's shoulders. "Audrey, this is going to be fine." Audrey took a deep breath. "Let's start walking. What do the directions say?"

Audrey checked her phone and pointed to a trailhead. "We walk down this trail for about a quarter mile."

"Okay. Let's start with that."

Audrey got her backpack from the hatchback and locked the car. As the two women started down the trailhead, Audrey observed her surroundings. Cottonwood and aspen trees lined the trail, and white and yellow violets carpeted the ground. In the distance, she could see a rock face but knew it wasn't Craggletooth. She'd been on this trail at least a half dozen times since living in Utah and had climbed the rock face ahead of her at least twice. Craggletooth must not be visible from the trail. It must be hidden by the trees.

About three minutes into the hike, Ellie stopped. "I forgot my phone in the car."

Audrey pivoted around. "You don't need it, do you? I don't think there's signal out here anyway."

"I wanted to read while you and Lover Boy make out," she replied.

Audrey rolled her eyes even while her stomach did a backflip. "We aren't going to make out."

Ellie raised an eyebrow. "You keep walking. I'll run back to the car and meet you at the rock face."

"What if you get lost?"

"Let me peek at the directions."

Audrey held her phone out to Ellie. "Got it," she said. "I'll be fast."

Ellie jogged off, and Audrey turned and started down the trail again. She hiked a few more minutes when a swatch of neon green in a bush caught her eye. She stopped and stared, her heart beating hard. It was a bandanna, like the ones she and Belay were supposed to wear before he'd stood her up. Audrey looked around her and didn't see anyone. She untied the bandanna from the branch and wrung it between her nervous fingers.

A small trail cut through the forest by the bush. The bandanna was marking where she needed to turn off the main trail. Audrey looked behind her and didn't see Ellie. She tied the bandanna back on so Ellie would know where to go and headed down the thin path.

Her eyes flitted around. The bushes and grass and trees prevented her from seeing too much farther ahead. Branches scraped her bare arms as she walked. The sun burned in the bright-blue sky. Audrey was going to be a sweaty, dirty mess by the time she made it to the rock face.

She came upon a wild rose bush and saw a small yellow submarine toy nestled among the pink flowers. Audrey picked up the toy and smiled. Had

Belay marked the trail all along the way for her? She continued walking, searching the foliage for more items.

Hanging from the branch of a box elder tree was a DVD case for *The Lake House*. She touched it, and it spun like a mobile.

She found a copy of *The Chicago Manual of Style* nestled in the branches of a salt cedar. Of course. Because Belay was a grammar nerd.

Next, tied to the stem of a sunflower, she found a postcard for the University of Seattle. Audrey's breath caught, and her heart began to pound. Ammon went there for medical school. Belay had never mentioned he'd gone to school in Seattle—only that he lived there.

Audrey moved quickly down the trail, her throat tight from emotion. Sitting in the shade of a scrub oak was a llama stuffed animal. She picked it up and saw a picture beneath it. It was a group shot, a hundred young men and women in their Sunday best, their faces tiny. Audrey flipped over the photo. It was captioned, *Lima Peru Mission*. She flipped the picture back over and scanned the faces of the young men, looking for Ammon, but the faces in the photo were too small for her to pick anyone out. She replaced the picture under the llama's foot and continued walking. Her legs felt like jelly, and her heart had lodged itself in her throat. *Please be Ammon*, she thought. *Please be Ammon*. There was no use pretending anymore. That's who she wanted Belay to be.

There was a break in the forest's tree line, and up ahead she could see a rock face. It looked like it had in the pictures she'd seen online: like crooked teeth, white and smooth, two rock faces overlapping. It was the view from the top that she had wanted to see. That she had wanted to share with Shannon.

Audrey continued her journey down the small path, searching for more clues. Her heart pounded loudly in her ears, masking the sound of her steps on the ground and her body moving through the bushes. She realized Ellie hadn't caught up to her, which was strange since Audrey had stopped so many times. Hopefully, Ellie hadn't gotten lost. Should she go back and find her?

Something in the distance glinted from a low-hanging branch. It took extreme discipline for Audrey not to run to the object and rip it from the tree. She needed to keep her cool, even if this was the most exciting thing she'd done in a long time.

She froze when she recognized what it was. It was like she had stumbled upon quicksand and the ground held her prisoner. She reached up, and her fingers gripped the cool metal of a stethoscope. She pulled it down, and her gaze drifted to the rock face. Foliage still blocked her view of the bottom, so she couldn't see him yet.

Audrey looped the stethoscope around her neck, took a deep breath, and forced her legs to move despite her nerves. The sound of her footsteps hit the same rhythm of her internal chant: *Please be Ammon. Please be Ammon.*

She broke through the forest, and her stomach simultaneously dropped to the ground and shot to the moon. She felt how she always did when she was around him: the urge to both run to him and run away from him.

Ammon stood with his hands in the pockets of his shorts. He hunched a little and appeared unsure, the opposite of how he stood in the delivery room or when he was with his family. His eyes matched the color of the clear sky above. Audrey walked toward him, trying to appear calm, although her legs wobbled.

"I don't know if I should kiss you or kill you," she said.

A smile broke across his face, and he chuckled. "Freddy said you'd say that."

She reached him and took a long moment to assess him. He met her gaze but only held it for a second before starting to fidget. Aside from looking totally gorgeous and golden in the sunlight, he also appeared contrite. He wasn't standing like someone who felt entitled to her but someone willing to accept whatever she would or would not give him. He pursed his lips. "So which is it going to be?" he asked.

Audrey closed the spaced between them, grabbed the front of his T-shirt, and pulled him in for a kiss. She should at least make sure his explanation for his deception was decent. But she'd spent too long overthinking this.

He pulled her closer and kissed her back, slow and deep. She felt dizzy and happy and relieved. Ammon broke the kiss and threaded his fingers through her hair. "I don't deserve this," he whispered.

"I know." She kissed him again, a stupid smile breaking across her face. She felt breathless. "But I want you to deserve this."

He cupped her face and looked into her eyes. "I'm sorry for everything."

Audrey nodded. "I want you to explain it to me." Because it had to be said. Because before she could be with him, she needed the whole story.

He pulled back and dropped his hands. She felt cold and incomplete without his touch. "I fell for Bellinghamster because she was smart and funny but also willing to be vulnerable and honest with me, a complete stranger. But in real life, I couldn't see past your professional persona, so when Bell turned out to be you, I couldn't reconcile the two of you."

Audrey understood. Until a few weeks ago, she never would have believed Belay and Ammon were the same person.

"But I got to know you in real life. And you were kind to me even though I was still an arrogant jerk. I realized how you behave in the delivery room is only a small part of who you are. You're passionate and generous, and I would be an idiot not to fall in love with you." Her breath caught in her throat.

"Then, why did you lie to me for so long?" She took an involuntary step back, trying to protect her fragile heart.

He looked away. "When I realized I had feelings for you, I knew you still hated me. Before I told you the truth, I wanted you to like me, too, so there'd be at least a slim chance you'd forgive me."

"So you're a coward." She bit her lip, hating that she'd said the word.

He flinched, but his eyes went to hers. "Yes," he said. "But I love you, and I want to make this right." He reached for her and took her hands. Audrey felt an incredible warmth move through her. If he could let go of his pride, so could she. She could forgive him. "I'll do anything," he said.

"Ammon Parker, I'm going to make you suffer." She felt him start to pull away, and she gripped his hands tighter. She waited until his eyes met hers. "And that will be much easier to do if we're together."

He smiled. "So you want to be my girlfriend?"

"I love you, Ammon," she said, slipping her arms around his neck. "And I want to be your girlfriend."

She found his lips again. "Wait," she said, pulling back. "If we end up getting married, are we going to fight about where our babies will be born?"

"I sure hope so," he replied with a grin.

"Just to be clear, I'm having my babies at home," she said.

"Or you could have them in a hospital," he replied.

"No, we're having them—"

He covered her mouth with his lips to quiet her. Then he broke away just enough to say, "Why don't we go for a climb first. It's what your friend would want."

"Okay, let's climb," she said. Ammon released her and held out a harness for her. Ellie and Freddy stepped out of the bushes. "But we aren't done talking about this."

He smiled. "I would expect nothing less."

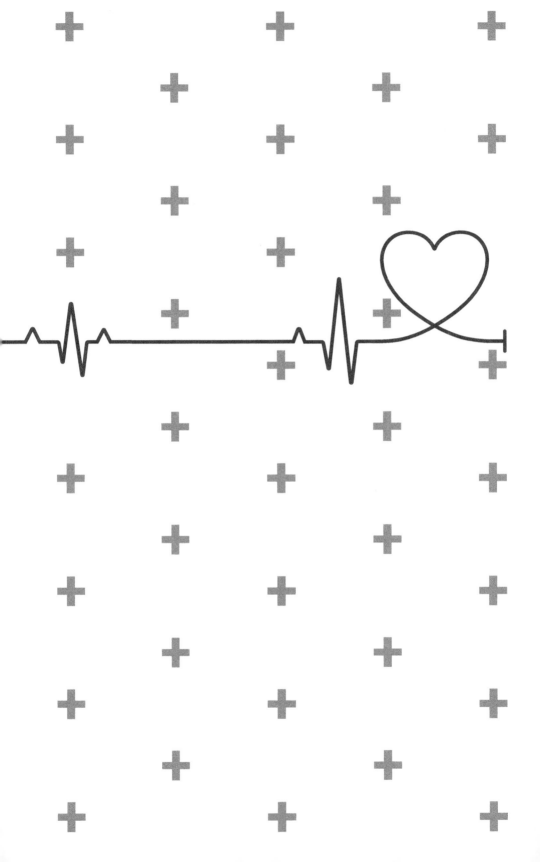

Author's Note

AFTER I HAD MY FIRST child, I became obsessed with childbirth. For me, it was an empowering experience, and I wanted to hear other women's stories. I quickly discovered *empowering* was the last word many women would use to describe their experiences with childbirth. Eventually, I trained to be a doula. In my interactions with the birth community, I learned of many difficulties that can prevent women from having positive experiences with birth.

After I completed my first book, *Everything She Wants*, I knew I wanted to tell a story in which I could incorporate the knowledge I had acquired and explore some of the issues that are important to me. What better way to do that than in a romance between a doctor and a midwife?

If you are interested in learning more about maternity care in the United States, *ProPublica's* article "The Last Person You'd Expect to Die in Childbirth" is a good place to start. If you want to learn more about how you can have a better birth experience, find the Positive Birth Movement at positivebirthmovement.org. To learn more about how you can become an advocate for improving health outcomes for birthing women, visit Improving Birth at improvingbirth.org or on Facebook. Lastly, if you or a loved one has experienced a difficult or traumatic birth, know you are not alone and help is available. Improving Birth has a "Pathways to Healing" guide available for free on their website, along with many other resources.

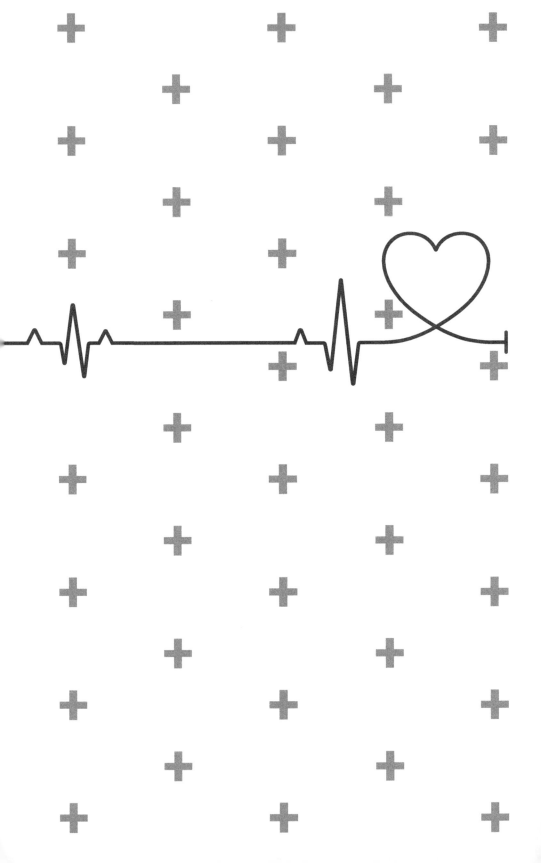

About the Author

Sᴀʀᴀʜ Aʟᴠᴀ ɢʀᴀᴅᴜᴀᴛᴇᴅ ꜰʀᴏᴍ ᴛʜᴇ University of Arizona with degrees in creative writing and political science. She once told a creative writing workshop she wanted to be a stay-in-bed mom when she grew up. She's almost living that dream, but her two little boys don't like naps as much as she does. When Sarah's not busy with her kids or husband, she enjoys reading romance novels in excess, grocery shopping, and listening to National Public Radio. She currently lives in Salt Lake City with her husband, two children, and a bunny named Audrey Hopburn.

Find her online at facebook.com/writerlysarah/ and sarahalva.com.